THE *Gentle* KIDNAPPER

KEN MOORE

ISBN: 978-1-4834-4028-6 (sc)
ISBN: 978-1-4834-4027-9 (e)

Library of Congress Control Number: 2015917296

Lulu Publishing Services rev. date: 10/21/2015

DEDICATION

For Doe, my dear wife forever loyal and true
And for the family we both love.

EPIGRAPH

Eve had the apple. Adam lusted for it.

ACKNOWLEDGEMENT

With warmest thanks to Pip and Dale Rye,
my daughter and her husband, who made
The Gentle Kidnapper possible.

INTRODUCTION

Elizabeth Bradley wakens to find herself stripped naked, bound hand and foot, in the dark, not in but on a strange bed with, sitting beside her, also naked, the senior psychiatrist from the hospital in which she works as a mental health nurse. Although he has kidnapped her he treats her most kindly. All he wants is that she join with him in a weird experiment. There follows a battle of wills in which her honour is at stake. Can she survive and retain her innocence?

PROLOGUE

I was as near to being petrified as I had ever been in my whole life. I nearly passed out. I knew from my training what was happening. My brain was suffering from over load to the point where it couldn't cope. It wanted to shut down and thus protect me from further trauma. With an effort I hung on. This was not the time to collapse. What I had seen hanging was a skeleton.

CHAPTER ONE

It was dark. Very dark. Pitch black, in fact. It reminded me of that time I was in Kalgoorlie, the goldmining town about five hundred kilometres to the east of Perth and decided to go down the tourist gold mine, just to see what it was like. It was deep underground. The guide had switched off the lights and said, 'This is what it is like for the miners when the lights fail. Anyone here like to be a goldminer, or a coalminer for that matter, when the lights fail?' There were no takers. He went on to tell the five of us who had taken the ride down in the lift just how soothing to the eye was the dark, once the eye became adapted to it. 'Very restful it is,' he said. 'The trouble for the miners came at the surface when they stepped into the glare of the unrelenting Aussie sun. That could be painful until the eye again adapted to the glare. Those of them who had sunshades then were glad of them.'

Now I knew how trapped miners felt when there was a cave-in and the lights were extinguished. I have always been afraid of the dark. Always. Wherever I have been, in whichever house I have lived, I kept at least one light burning all night. I don't know why it was. Maybe it is something in my innermost being that goes back to the beginning of time; some primeval thing that brings with it an uneasiness I have never understood. Whatever the reason, darkness makes me cringe. Now, there wasn't a chink of light anywhere and, in spite of what the guide down that Kalgoorlie goldmine had said, it was not soothing. My mouth was dry, my skin clammy, my whole nervous system stretched to screaming point. Yet I was so paralysed with fright I couldn't scream or move. To move or make a noise would be to die. This didn't seem to me to be the darkness of night; more like an artificial darkness where all the light had been shut out, like a deliberately darkened room. Could it be that I was down a mine? I couldn't be down a mine, could I? Don't be silly - they don't have beds down goldmines or coalmines or any other mines. And I was in a bed. It wasn't my bed. This was a double bed. I hadn't slept in a double bed for years. Not since when, as a little girl, I had stopped sleeping with my mother. I had always had my own single bed since then. My heart was pounding. Each beat like a hammer blow inside my head. I never get headaches so why had I a headache now? Why was my mouth dry? I felt as if I had been drugged. Anyway, if this was not my bed, and it wasn't, just where was I? I usually slept in pyjamas. Now, I was lying on top of the bedclothes and I was completely naked. Oh, my God! I had no clothes on. Never in my whole life had I gone to bed without my pyjamas. So, how was it that I was naked now? Someone must have taken my clothes off. Why? Where was I? I felt ashamed. I could feel myself blushing. So how could this be? Why? It wasn't as if I had come home drunk, discarded my clothes and flopped into bed. I didn't drink. Was never a drinker. So where was I? How did I get here? What time was it? A million questions were hurtling through my mind. I went to raise my hand to look at my watch, which had a reflective dial, but was pulled up short with a stinging jar to my wrist. Why was that? Only then did I realise that my left wrist was tied to the side of the bed, so was my right. Oh, God! What had happened to me? I immediately tried to move my legs and found that they, too, were bound. Why? Why! Why! Steady! Steady! Don't panic. Panic will get you nowhere; only lead to disaster. Hadn't your training been all about keeping calm no matter what the situation? The last thing you do except in an emergency, and emergency means a matter of life and death, is run. Don't run, they said. Walk. So think, girl, think. Relax. Take a deep breath. I took a deep breath, held it and counted to ten. I let it go. Then another. I let that one go more slowly. Then my mind began to clear and I remembered with a shudder what had happened to me.

I had been in my bedroom when there was a knock at the door. I took a quick look in the mirror, straightened my hair and went to see who it was. I saw, through the opaque glass panels at the side of the front door, the headlights of a car in the driveway. It couldn't be a taxi, I hadn't rung for one. I preferred to drive my own car to the airport and park it in the long-term car park. That way I didn't have to sit on tenterhooks wondering if the taxi was going to come or not and then, when I got back, I could collect the key at the airport and didn't have to wait in a long queue for maybe an hour until a taxi was available. I could just walk to the car park, pick up the car and be home whilst some people were still queuing. I didn't rush. There was no hurry. I had plenty of time to get to the airport. The Red Eye Special didn't leave until ten minutes after midnight and it was now just after 8 pm. So I had time for a guest, as long as they weren't too long-winded. I hadn't arranged for anyone to come and see me off, so who could it be? Maybe one of my friends from the hospital coming to wish me bon voyage before I set off for Tassie on my annual pilgrimage to Wineglass Bay? I laughed to myself as I thought it could be a burglar. Burglars don't drive up to the front door and knock. Anyway, I would only open the door a peek, just to be on the safe side. I turned the key and was in the act of opening the door when it was smashed fiercely against me and I was sent reeling. As I tried to recover my balance I saw the silhouette of a man as he threw himself through the door, grabbed me by the throat and squeezed. I knew enough about physiology and the cardiovascular system to know, in that fraction of a second, that the blood supply to my brain had been cut off. If I didn't do something now I was done. Against all my training, I grabbed desperately at the gloved hands holding my throat but I had no chance. The person holding me knew what he was doing. Within ten seconds all had gone black. Who was this person? With his back to the light of the car I couldn't see his face. I was so disorientated that I could take nothing in. I was too busy trying to release those hands which were squeezing the life out of me.

I shook with fear now. I had been kidnapped. But why? I had no money. My parents had no money. I didn't feel as if I had been ravaged. So why? What was going on?

What a fool I was. I should have put on the door security chain. Why hadn't I? I told myself it was just that in the euphoria of the moment I had forgotten all about it. I would be off to Tassie shortly and was so caught up in the excitement of it all that it completely slipped my mind. Not that a security chain would have helped in the least. The onslaught through the door was so fierce, so violent, that I don't think my security chain would have stood against it. It would just have been ripped off. I knew I was making excuses for myself. The simple fact was that I had been slack and was now paying the price. Had the security chain been in place it might have given me time to put up some form of that defence Byron Osborne had so patiently taught us once a week in the hospital gym in London. Had I had time to react I might have had a fighting chance. Too late now.

My mind went into over-drive racing through all the possibilities leading to finding myself in a strange bed, bound and naked. I didn't sleep naked in strange beds or even in my own bed. I always slept alone. No sleeping around for me. That was not my style. At twenty nine I was still in one piece and I intended to stay that way until I found Mr Right. There were not a lot of Mr Rights around. I had had several boyfriends but, generally, they didn't last long; just didn't measure up. Most of them just couldn't keep their hands to themselves, in the fish world they would have been classified as gropers; wanted sex the first night. No thanks. Some of them were a little more refined. They thought, I suppose, that they were much more subtle. Would court me, like gentlemen, for two or three outings, then suggest that because they were so deeply in love with me and wanted to see as much of me as they could, it would be more convenient if we just moved in together. They really did want to see more of me, without clothes. Again, no thanks. The remainder were mostly dead-beats who were either rude or crude or simply had just no idea how to relate to another person, male or female. It's not that I am a prude or one of those stuck-up little madams who think that they are somehow better than everybody else and want nothing less than a Prince Charming, millionaire class, of course, to come by on his trusty steed, sweep them off their feet and ride with them into that Fairyland at the end of the rainbow to live happily ever after. That would be nice, I don't disagree, but all I want is an ordinary Joe who loves me for what I am and has just a little bit of the gentleman about him. Up until now, no such person has crossed my path and, anyway, I have been too busy becoming qualified and trying to be better at my job than anyone else.

But why would anyone want to kidnap me if they weren't after that money I hadn't got? Unless they wanted to make money out of me, another way? Was I going to become another of those desirable white girls who are grabbed and shipped off to some of those countries where a white girl is considered a rare delicacy? No, it couldn't be that. At twenty nine I was hardly likely to be the kind of prize the traffickers were seeking. They generally sought girls in their early or even pre-teens, not what were considered geriatrics in the white sex trade. So why?

Was I grabbed by some guy who wanted to share me with his mates and in that way insinuate himself in to some secret society he wanted to join. Or was I grabbed by some nut who wanted his own pet and who would dispose of me when he wanted something new? If I were to be his pet why hadn't he raped me already? Why the delay? Unless he was one of those serial sadists who wanted to have me wide awake so he could enjoy seeing my reaction to his overtures?

I knew about weirdos. Working with them was my job. I was trying hard to think rationally, keep calm and prepare to meet whatever it was that was coming up next. I was thankful that even with that ferocious door slam I was not injured. Nothing broken, or it seemed that nothing was broken. Maybe just a little bruising on my arms but because of the dark I couldn't see. I was shaken but nothing I couldn't handle. At least I was alive and able to think. What was I to do? Should I cry out and maybe attract attention from outside? Trouble was I didn't know what was outside. I could be in the centre of Perth or I could be somewhere out in the sticks. If I cried out my captor would know I was awake and maybe come and finish the job, rape me then dispose of me. What was I to do? I was burning with anger, an anger I had to keep under control. Anger disrupts thought. It is a short from of madness that in my present circumstances would serve no useful purpose. I had to keep calm and cool and try to work out exactly why I was here. I was also burning with thirst and needed badly to go at the same time. I hadn't wet the bed since I was a toddler and I was not going to begin now. I couldn't cross my legs because of the way they were tied. I couldn't hold out much longer. I gritted my teeth. I thought I could hear some movement. Some movement outside the room.

Yes, definitely, there was a shuffling to my left. That must be where the door is. Somebody was coming. I didn't hear any door open. It must have been open already. I raised my head as well as I could to see if there was light in that direction. No light. Nothing. Just darkness. Then a torch was switched on and pointed at the floor. There was a silhouette behind it; big and broad like the silhouette I had seen when my front door had been burst open. There was something different about it but there were so many things going through my mind I couldn't figure out what it was. Now the silhouette was fully in the room. Although I couldn't see behind it I could see, or thought I could see, outside the circle of light, something hanging to the silhouette's left, towards the end of the bed. The sight of that thing caused my heart to almost leap out of my chest. I nearly cried out and would have had it not been that the approach of the silhouette was causing me to shrink into myself at the same time. I was as near to being petrified as I had ever been in my whole life. I nearly passed out. I knew from my training what was happening. My brain was suffering from overload to the point where it couldn't cope. It wanted to shut down and thus protect me from further trauma. With an effort I hung on. This was not the time to collapse. What I had seen hanging was a skeleton. I didn't know whether it was a real flesh and bone skeleton. Yes, I know, flesh hardly comes into it with a skeleton. What I mean is that I wasn't sure and couldn't be sure, from that glimpse I had, if the skeleton used to be a living breathing person or if it was one of those skeletons specially constructed for use in medical schools and teaching hospitals? What really threw me was that the skeleton was wearing my clothes. The very clothes I had on when I went to answer the door. My silk scarf was knotted round its neck; it was wearing my blouse and I could just see the top of my skirt. My watch was hanging on the fleshless wrist just below the end of my blouse's sleeve. The grinning skull, with mouth slightly agape was staring straight ahead. Was it laughing? Laughing at me? Or was it screaming in agony? Was it the skeleton of a man overcome with the relish of being inside a woman's clothes? My clothes? Dear God, I am in a living nightmare! Have I gone mad? Is this really happening to me? I had no more time to speculate, the figure now was beside my bed. The light shone on a chair quite close to my head. The silhouette sat down. The light was switched off. I was in the dark again. I was quivering with fear and the need to go. There was complete silence except that I could hear his breathing. It was very steady breathing. This person was in complete control. Every move he made was planned. Even in my fright I knew that he had switched on the light when he did so that I could see that skeleton. Part of the softening-up process. I lay still trying to control my breathing although I felt like screaming. But I would not scream. I didn't know what this monster, or whatever it was, was going to do to me but it was not going to have an easy victory. I would not yield easily. My arms and legs might be bound but he had not gagged me. That was a mistake. If he attempted to touch me or get on top of me, when I could see that all was lost then I would give vent to the rage within me and mark him for life. I would use my good strong teeth to rip him open and scar him in a way that he would never forget and would cause people to wonder what had happened to him. It might give a clue to cause the police to question him when my disappearance was noticed. Only trouble was my disappearance wouldn't be noticed for at least a month. Anyway, I would bite deep and hard and I would not let go. I would tear the piece right out. I never considered myself a vicious person but, then, I had never before been in a situation like this. I would make him sorry he kidnapped me. If I was going to be raped and murdered I would die with honour. I would not go out with a whimper. I felt like a coiled spring in suspense.

CHAPTER TWO

I was amazed when he spoke. He had the most beautiful, gentle voice I have ever heard and I recognised it instantly. It sent vibrations through me. We had all remarked in the hospital how beautifully he spoke. Silvery, would best describe it. I had heard him speak often when he soothed traumatised patients. He would put his arms, quite fearlessly, round a violent patient and talk them back down to earth. I knew who this person was. My heart thumped. This was not good. It meant that I was in grave danger, with the emphasis on grave. I was not going to be released, ever. Kidnappers avoid recognition. Anonymity is their friend. They do not seek to be known by their victim. If they are and are arrested they can be identified and sent to prison for a long time. Even I knew their only means of making sure that they stay free is to stay unknown. To remain unknown they have only one alternative - kill their victim. The only thing I could do to save my life was to pretend I didn't know him. I would become the great pretender.

His first words were, 'I trust you are quite comfortable, Nurse Bradley, in the circumstances. I regret that I had to make such a forcible entry into your home last night but it was the only thing I could do. If I had come in gently then tried to overcome you, it might have resulted in a very violent struggle between us in which you could have been badly hurt. I, also, could have been hurt. I didn't want that. I am happy to say that I have examined you and apart from a little superficial bruising, and, maybe, the initial shock, you are little the worse for wear. I had to give you an injection to tranquilise you so that I could remove your clothing and examine you and, of course, secure you in such a way that, whilst you are my guest, you would be quite comfortable whilst together we carried out a little experiment I have had in mind for some time. You know me, of course, I am Dr Wilderman from the hospital where we both work.'

Now, I really was terrified. He had told me who he was and thus his knowing that I knew who he was would very likely prove fatal. I could not see how I was ever going to get out of this situation alive. He had, undoubtedly, flipped. Sometimes doctors working in mental hospitals do lose the plot. What most people don't know is that the suicide rate for doctors is much higher than in the general population. There have been several high profile cases where doctors have murdered their patients, their wives, their servants and just anyone they felt didn't fit into their scheme of things. There was that recent case in England where a Dr Shipman murdered hundreds of his patients. Why did he do that? I don't know the answer to that question. No doubt if he were around to answer he could give, what seemed to him, a sound reason. Maybe he was completely mad? Maybe he was carrying out some kind of experiment? Some of my friends used to tell me that you had to be mad to work in a mental hospital. They believed that most psychiatrists were a bit loopy already. Now, it seemed, they were being proved right. We used to laugh in the hospital and say that insanity was contagious and had better watch out lest we were infected. Now, I was not laughing, I was wondering if maybe there was something in that. Many a true word is spoken in jest. An experiment, he had said. What kind of experiment? Whatever the experiment, it did not have first preference in my things to do at the moment. So far as I was concerned, it would have to take second place to my pressing needs. If I didn't go soon the bed would be flooded. I interrupted him.

'I'm sorry, Dr Wilderman, I need badly to use the bathroom and I need a drink of water,' I croaked. Then to placate him, 'I will be better able to take in all about the experiment you say that you and I can conduct together when I am in a better position to concentrate on what you are saying.'

'You poor dear. How remiss of me. I should have known better. Let me take you to the bathroom immediately. I must warn you, of course, that a certain amount of trust will be involved. I shall stretch the cord holding your feet just enough to enable you to walk without too much difficulty and I'll free one of your hands to enable you to perform whatever functions are necessary in the bathroom but I shall retain a hold on the lanyard on your left arm throughout. I shall not go into the bathroom with you but shall remain just to the left of the entrance where I can't see you whilst you are inside. There is nothing inside that would assist you in trying to escape. Also, the bathroom has no door. The lanyard is long enough for me to be outside the bathroom whilst you do what you have to do inside. Then I will accompany you whilst you wash your hands and have a drink in the bathroom. You will still be in darkness, I'm afraid. There is a reason for that. Please do not be difficult. I do not want to have to hurt you. That would not assist our experiment. Do you understand?'

Our experiment? His experiment had now become 'our' experiment. He was acting as if we were engaged in some joint project or other. As if we were both in a research laboratory. Maybe he wanted to win the Nobel Prize for medicine? At the moment, I just wanted to use the bathroom rather badly.

I pretended not to notice that 'our'. I could see that I was going to have to do more pretending in the immediate future than I had done in the whole of my life up to now.

'Yes, I understand.'

What else could I say? The doctor was certainly out of his mind. I had to do the best I could to keep him non-violent. It would take very little to tip him completely over the edge and cause him to tranquilise me permanently as medical researchers do with their rats and mice and guinea pigs when they become mutinous rather than act like rats and mice and guinea pigs usually do in research situations.

He took me to the bathroom then brought me back and secured me to the bed as he had before. Whilst in the bathroom I looked at my wrist where I usually wore my watch which had a reflective dial. I forgot it was now on the arm of the skeleton. So, I didn't know what time it was. In the bathroom there was a heavy curtain on the window, I tried to lift it to see if there was daylight outside but I couldn't budge it. Most likely it was morning but because everything was blacked out I couldn't tell. The tranquiliser he said he had given me could have knocked me out for several hours, maybe a whole day? I just had no way of knowing. I felt with my left hand the binding on my wrists and feet. It appeared to be made of padded leather at the end of a fine steel chain. I could tell that chain would not easily be broken. The padded leather must have been custom made for it did not chafe my wrists. Probably made for those people who indulge in bondage?

'Feeling better now, Nurse?' he asked.

'Yes, I am. Thank you, Dr Wilderman.'

'Good. Whatever we do we must always act like a gentleman. By the way, do you mind if I call you Elizabeth? It's much more informal and may assist in the experiment.'

'I don't mind what you call me. Elizabeth is what my friends call me.'

'Good! Does that mean that you consider me a friend?'

'I have always considered you a friend, Dr Wilderman. To me you are one of the best doctors in the hospital. I just don't know why you are treating me like this. This is not your way. I have never seen you treat a patient like this.'

'How right you are. I believe in helping people not hurting them. But there is a reason for it in this instance. Let me explain.'

'I am sure you have heard of the Stockholm Syndrome which is said to affect people who have been taken hostage. You, being a mental health nurse, I would be surprised if you were not aware of such a condition.'

'Of course, I'm aware of it,' I said. 'You don't have to be a mental health nurse to know that. It is that strange condition which became world famous as a result of a bank hold-up in Stockholm in 1973, I think it was 1973? On that occasion several bank staff were taken hostage and held, under siege conditions, for several days by the bank robbers. Then, when the siege was over, far from condemning their kidnappers, the hostages kissed and hugged them and refused to give evidence against them. Then, again, on a later occasion, Patty Hearst, the American newspaper millionairess, claimed she was kidnapped and held hostage in a similar manner. She, likewise, refused to give testimony against her kidnappers. That is what you mean, isn't?'

'It is, indeed. Clever girl! I knew I had picked the right person. Oh, before we go any further I think it proper if I am to call you by your first name, Elizabeth, that you have the choice of calling me by mine. My first name is Caspar. Would you like to call me Caspar?'

I couldn't see him in the dark but I felt he was smiling in his usually friendly manner just then.

'I would prefer to call you doctor. It was what we always called you in the hospital and I would feel more comfortable if I could continue to do so.'

'Of course, you may. The choice is yours. It was just that I wanted us both on an even footing, as far as possible throughout this experiment.'

'How can we be on an even footing, Doctor, when I am here against my will, am in the dark, am completely naked and am bound hand and foot?'

'That is a very good question but the answer to the binding is very simple. Were I to release you you would immediately want to leave. Hostages never have that choice. In fact, they have no choice. They are held because their captor has a power they do not have. That is something you must not forget. It may be that at some stage I shall be able to remove the bindings and set you completely free within the confines of this room and the bathroom. But that depends, very largely, on how you respond to my study of your behaviour. What you must not forget, Elizabeth, is that I am a psychiatrist and that my area of expertise is the human mind. By the time this experiment is completed I hope to know more about you than you know yourself and that you will be happy that such is the case. Together we will both have extended the borders of science. So far as the other aspects of your question are concerned let me explain that you are in the dark because most people fear the dark. I have to ensure that, to begin with, like any other hostage, you are afraid, very afraid. If my appreciation of the human mind is correct you will lose that fear totally and, very possibly, come to enjoy the dark. Yes, you are naked but, then, so am I. I have tried to put us both as I have said, on an equal footing. The only differences being that I am not afraid of the dark, I am not bound and I am in control. I can tell that you are afraid. We are also both naked because only that way will you get rid of your inhibitions about nakedness in the presence of a strange man. It will bring you closer to me. There is nothing wrong with going unclothed. I often go about my house completely unclothed. That way I have complete freedom. You, too, once you get used to it, will be glad that I have introduced you to that freedom. Losing your learned inhibitions will free your mind to the point where you will be better able to understand what I am attempting and so assist in progressing this research. I want you to be comfortable and not comfortable at the same time. Why I am doing this will become apparent to you the longer you are in my company.'

My God, he was naked, too! That was what was different about his silhouette which I had seen behind the torch as he entered the room. Why was he naked? I didn't believe it was to bring me closer to him. More likely it was to intimidate me into being more afraid of him, at first, and then as I grew used to it and began to accept it as normal I would begin to accept that being a hostage was normal too. He was using his psychiatric knowledge to bend my mind in the way he wanted it to go. If that's what he was attempting then, so far as his research went, he was cheating. A true scientist would not attempt to influence the outcome of his research by adding something that would not happen in the normal course of things. I didn't believe that the Stockholm bandits set out to turn their hostages around to the point where they were loved by them. That, surely, happened without being aimed at?

'Let me now endeavour to acquire the knowledge that I need to assist me to proceed further with our experiment. I need some particulars from you which I hope you won't mind giving. I want to know all about you, everything. I want to look into your mind and I want to do so with the minimum of compulsion. Do you understand?'

CHAPTER THREE

I understood all right. He was mad.

'Yes, I understand,' I said.

He spoke in the calm, clinical manner of the psychiatrist carrying out some kind of mind-probing examination of a patient on the couch in his consulting room. Did he think he was Dr Freud in Vienna? I gave an involuntary shudder. He displayed his expertise then by picking up that shudder, even in the dark.'

'Are you cold?' he asked. 'You shouldn't be. The heating in this room is thermostatically controlled at an even twenty eight degrees twenty four hours a day. If you wish I shall increase it to thirty even though I feel quite comfortable with it.'

'No. No. I feel fine. This whole thing is just a bit too much for me. I am finding it hard to come to terms with it. I have never been in a situation like this before.'

Even as I spoke I thought how bizarre this whole thing was. I was beginning to respond as if I were indeed a patient in his consulting room. As if this were all normal. And it was not normal. I had to keep telling myself that if I were not to become as mad as he was I had to remember that he was out of his mind and I wasn't. Maybe I was the one who was imagining all this and it wasn't happening. Had I been working too hard? No, I hadn't! He was the one who had the problem. Only trouble was, his problem was my problem.

'Perhaps it would be better if, before I obtain the particulars from you that I require I explained to you that I have had this project in mind for some time. My difficulty was that I could not undertake it alone. The very nature of the experiment demanded that at least one other person be involved. That person could not be a volunteer. No one could ever volunteer for this experiment. What I had to do was conscript someone. In this case even conscript is a euphemistic description of the person involved. Conscripting such a person could lead to all kinds of complications. You see, that person would suddenly be taken out of circulation. There could be no warning. As they say in South America, they would be 'disappeared'. Into thin air, as the cliché has it. Take a nurse out of a hospital with no notice whatsoever, not to her supervisors, friends, family, acquaintances, no one, and a man-hunt would immediately ensue.' With black humour he tried to make a joke out of that and said, 'Perhaps a woman-hunt, would be a more accurate description?' He gave a chuckle at that. 'The police would then question everyone with whom she worked or had contact of any kind: Doctors, nurses, auxiliary staff, patients, patients' friends. Alibis would be checked. Had she a boyfriend? If so where was he at the time of her disappearance? In disappearances boyfriends or husbands are the first to fall suspect. When did she disappear? Where was she last seen and by whom? Had she ever disappeared before? What was her mental state when last seen and just prior to that? You can see the intensity of the enquiries and investigations that would follow? I wanted to avoid such a situation. I wanted a nice clean disappearance, so normal and so natural that no one would notice until later. Much later, when the trail was cold, so cold that not even a Sherlock Holmes could find it. How was I to achieve that?

'I gave the matter much thought over many months. I thought of picking up a homeless person and making them the subject of my experiment but such a person did not quite fit the bill. When I had completed the project I did not want to be hugged by someone I was going to throw back on the street. I wanted my 'assistant', for want of a better word, to be the type of person I could respect and who was not and never had been a 'no hoper' and who would want to share the rest of their life with me. In other words, Elizabeth, I wanted a female companion who was interested in the same things as I was.'

Oh, please, God, tell me this is a nightmare. Send your angels to wake me up. He not only wants to hold me hostage, he wants me to become his companion, for life. I am to have no escape, ever. What am I to do? What am I to do? There is only one thing to do, say nothing. Say nothing and appear to go along with him. Something will turn up. Mr Micawber, be my friend.

Then an awful thought struck me. What if he had a heart attack or was involved in a serious traffic accident and me here alone bound hand and foot? I could die here and not be found for years. Didn't something like that happen to two little girls in America when their kidnapper kept them bound in a cellar, then he was involved in an accident or was arrested by the police or something, and couldn't get to them and didn't tell anyone where they were. They both died. Oh, please, God, keep this madman alive and safe until I find a way to get out of this. Find a way for me, God, and I promise I will be your servant for the rest of my life. I'll go to church every Sunday and I'll be a better person.

'One day I heard one of the nurses say to another that next day she was going on a week's holiday to Broome in the North West. That gave me an idea. What I needed was a nurse going on holidays for a month or even longer. A week was nowhere long enough. Going alone. Going somewhere where she would be pretty well inaccessible for the whole of her holiday. Someone who had no attachments; who would not be missed. Such a person would fit the bill admirably. I began to organise for the day I found such a person.'

'I looked for a house in an isolated area, well away from the beaten track. I searched the 'houses for sale' ads for weeks. At last I found exactly what I was looking for. It was the only house down an unmade road in Kalamunda, the suburb in the foothills to the east of Perth. I went and had a look at it. It was perfect. I already owned several companies which owned several companies so that it was easy to have it purchased by one of those companies and then get lost in a series of transactions that would have taken the most skilled property lawyer a lifetime to unravel. Nowhere in any of the transactions does my name appear. No one knows I own this house. The council rates, water rates and electricity bills are paid through a bank which bills the company. There is no gas connection, so no gas bill. There is no fixed-line telephone. I use mobile ones. The company has a registered office to which all mail is sent, so the postman never has to visit. In any case, there is no letter-box which is very convenient for there is no place to leave junk mail. I have had each room adequately furnished. This one has a queen-sized bed, the one you are now lying in. I, myself, fitted the restraints so that they would hold the person I found with complete security with as little discomfort as possible. No chance of my subject freeing themself and aborting the whole experiment, not to mention the repercussions that would follow any report to the police. Every room in this house is sound-proofed. A hand grenade could be detonated in any one of them and with the doors closed the resulting explosion would hardly be heard in the next room. That, my dear, is why you have not been gagged. You could scream your head off and no one would hear you. Anyway, I wanted you to be able to respond to my questions and you could not do that if you were gagged. Gagging is such a terrible thing. I would never do that to anyone, especially you. You are so beautiful. But I digress. There is a lock-up garage, where a car can be safely housed without being seen. The area surrounding the house is all paved so that there is no need for a grass-cutter or gardener to attend. All the windows are double-glazed and the doors reinforced. The roof is made of zinc sheeting so that entrance could not be gained by removing a tile or two. Removing a sheet of tin is a much more difficult enterprise. It would take nothing short of a bulldozer to gain entrance to this house. All the exterior doors have deadlocks. In short, the house is about as self-contained as a medieval castle. There is no moat and no drawbridge. They are not required. No one can get into this house. That, Elizabeth, is the house where you now are.'

I knew from my studies that there is nothing more cunning than the deranged mind. Several of my patients had proved that to me. Now, that was being brought home to me more forcefully than ever before. What was I going to do? If no one could get in, how could I ever get out? Even if I did manage to free myself how would I get past those deadlocks? He had thought of everything.

He continued. 'Even whilst I was searching for a suitable house and making it ready for its new resident I continued my search for my hostage. Came the day when I found the person I had been looking for. The choice was almost cast upon me, dropped into my lap, so to speak. One day, when I went to the nursing station for a file I heard Charge Nurse Enwright say to Nurse Grimwald that Nurse Bradley was going for her annual month's holidays to Tasmania in a fortnight's time. I couldn't believe my luck. Nurse Bradley, you, Elizabeth, were the ideal person for what I had in mind.'

'I had seen you almost daily on the wards and was always impressed by your professionalism. There are a lot of good nurses in the hospital but I always considered you the best. However, in addition to professionalism I wanted someone who was socially and morally acceptable as well. There are lots of good nurses and other staff in the hospital, as I have said, but some of them have involved social lives which I need not go into. A good many of them are married or have partners. Either way they were excluded. I didn't want someone who was already spoken for. No secondhand goods for me, thank you very much. In any case, their disappearance would immediately cause as much attention as poking a stick into a hornet's nest. Neither did I want a widow, no matter how young. Working widows generally have children and so were not within my ambit of choice. Hurting children is not within my philosophy no matter how pressing may be my need. I wanted someone who in today's world is unique. Someone who, in the biblical sense, had not been known by any man. I'm sure you understand my meaning. Nowadays, people of both sexes seem to jump into bed at their first meeting. That type of person would not fit in with what I have in mind. I don't mind telling you, Elizabeth, in fact I think it is important that you know, that though I am fifty two years of age I have never slept with any woman. And because of the kind of world we live in today I had better say that the feminine includes the masculine. Sex before marriage is abhorrent to me. Not that I had time for any relationships, heterosexual or otherwise; I was too deeply involved in my work.'

CHAPTER FOUR

Now I was beginning to get the picture, he wasn't a purist so far as research went, after all. It seemed that he was only a purist when it came to sex. He was attempting to combine his biological needs with his research. I wondered which came first? Had he worked so hard at his profession for so long that he had suddenly wakened up one morning and found that life had passed him by? That he was alone. That if he didn't do something fairly quickly he was never going to have a wife or children and would go into old age never having known that joy and companionship and fatherhood that sex and marriage would bring? Was it that need that had tipped him over the edge? If I kept quiet and listened carefully I might learn enough about him from him to be able to turn it to my advantage. I was going to have to use all my skill and the knowledge I had acquired in my training and years as a mental health nurse and apply it to my present situation if I was going to leave this house alive and unbroken. I was going to have to become a Freud. Even better than Freud for, as far as I knew, the great Freud had never found himself in a situation so dire as this. Then another awful thought struck me. In all the reading I had done relating to his life and his work, and I had read a lot about him, I had not read anywhere about Freud having cured anyone. There was a suggestion in one book I had read that he had cured a woman. One woman. One woman! How long he had to work on her to effect that cure I didn't know but it seemed that I was going to have to listen, collect the data, sift it mentally, analyse it and cure my 'patient' in something like a month. Oh, God! One month. Never, in my training or practice as a nurse had I read or learned of anyone being cured of insanity in a month.

But he was talking still so I concentrated to listen the better. I knew now that I must listen better or I was lost and I did not want to be lost. I wanted to leave this house the victor in a battle between a very sick mind and what I had no doubt was a very normal mind. That, I told myself, was the key to my survival: belief in self.

'I knew that, like me, you did not smoke or drink alcohol and had no health problems. No diabetes or anything that would require daily monitoring. In fact you are a very healthy person, both physically and mentally. You were always so neatly dressed, never had a hair out of place, did not wear loads of make-up, were tall and straight, and radiated confidence. Not once in the years I have seen you at work with your patients, and some of them were very difficult, had I ever seen you anything but completely calm and totally in control. You have such a beautiful smile that more than once I heard patients and staff remark on it. As far as I knew you did not have a boyfriend. I had never heard of you being late on duty and I had never heard of you having a day off other than those allocated. Always, if someone called in sick, something you never did, you were prepared to come in and work the extra shift without the least complaint. I knew that you did not live in the nurses' home, which fitted very well into my plans, but I did not know where you lived. I knew that you were from Ireland and had no relatives in Australia. Excellent! So far I could think of no better candidate to be taken hostage. You were strong-willed and would not be won over easily. Put you to the test and I might be able to establish if there actually was such a thing as the Stockholm Syndrome or if it was nothing more than a myth that had been said to happen in two isolated cases. I had to find out more about you.'

'That very night, when you had finished duty and went to your car in the staff car park, I followed you. I followed you all the way to your home in

Guildford. It was quite easy, there was plenty of traffic through the city and when we got on to Great Eastern Highway I just did as the detectives do in the detective stories that I sometimes read, I dropped into place a couple of cars behind and stayed there until you turned into the street where you live. I was delighted to see that your little single storey house stood in its own grounds, nicely away from the neighbours and well back from the road. That would make what I had in mind easier. As you turned into your driveway I drove on past, went to the end of the street, turned and went home. I knew where you lived. At last, after all my searching, things were beginning to come together. I had found my hostage.'

'I should say here that I would have liked two or three people like you as hostages at the same time. That would make it much more like Stockholm but I had to content myself with you. After all, there was only one Patty Hearst. Anyway, where was I to find two other people going on holidays at the same time as you and who were so unattached that they, too, would not be missed for at least a month? I would have to be satisfied with what I had. I didn't want my experiment jeopardised. I had to tell myself that there was only one of me. In the Stockholm case and with Patty Hearst there was more than one kidnapper.'

'I followed you several times after that. I would sometimes get ahead of you and be waiting when you arrived at your house. I came to know your routine as well as you did. On several occasions I scanned your house with binoculars. You never pulled the curtains so I was able to see inside and get a pretty good idea of the lay-out of the building. I was glad to note that you had no pets: no dog, no cat. No caged bird that might have to be given to a neighbour to be looked after during your absence. Animals can be a complication. I confirmed that you had no live-in boyfriend or girlfriend. I didn't expect either but one has to guard against every possibility. By the time the night of your departure arrived I was 99.9% certain that neither at the hospital nor at your home did you have any relationship that would place problems in my way. As far as I could tell I was going to have a clear run. All I needed to know was the time of your flight to Tasmania and then

I was all set. That was easy to find out. You probably remember my saying to you how lucky you were going to such a beautiful place for your holiday and hoping that you had chosen a decent airline. In your innocence and directness, you told me that you were travelling by Qantas but regretted you would be on the Red-Eye Horror leaving just after midnight. I said you would probably be tired by the time you got there and you agreed but said that that little inconvenience was worth it as it was cheaper than the day-time flight. I was now in possession of all the information I needed to know. You know most of what happened after that.'

'I waited until dark and drove directly to your house. I took the direct approach and drove straight into your driveway as if I had a legitimate reason to do so. Because I didn't know if you had a security chain on the door I had to make sure that, if you had, I used sufficient force to rip it out of the woodwork. Because there was no such chain my entrance was more forceful that I intended it to be. Happily, you suffered nothing more than superficial haematoma. As soon as I had applied pressure to your carotid arteries and rendered you unconscious by cutting off the blood supply to your brain, I picked you up, carried you to your bedroom and there injected you with a tranquiliser to make sure you didn't recover before I had brought you here. I then went to my car and put off the lights which I had left on to give you assurance that you had a legitimate visitor otherwise you might not have opened the door. Then I also put out the lights in the house, carried you to the car and put you in the rear seat with a blanket over you, just in case I was stopped by the police for a random breath test or something connected with police monitoring of road traffic. I also put the cases you had already packed for your trip in the boot, locked up the house, made sure everything was in order for at least a month's absence and drove here. The journey was uneventful. That brings you pretty well up to where you are now. Except, of course, when you came here I placed you on this bed, removed your clothing and examined you to make sure that the forceful opening of your door had not broken anything. It was after that that I placed the necessary binding on your hands and feet.'

CHAPTER FIVE

It was all as I had worked out except that I didn't know about his following me and keeping observations on my house. The thought that someone might follow me home had never entered my head. What a trusting fool I am. But of course the normal person doesn't go around looking for cars following them. Why should they? That is something reserved for the realms of fantasy. That is something one reads in those detective novels that Dr Wilderman seems to enjoy. I prefer autobiographies.

'Now, to get back to the particulars I need from you. I have to delve into your background.'

'Aren't you on the wrong tack there, Dr Wilderman?' I asked. 'Wouldn't such an enquiry corrupt the whole thrust of your experiment?'

'How do you mean?' he said.

'I don't know what the position was in Stockholm when those bank robbers entered the bank and took the staff hostage but I have never heard it said that they sat their hostages down and delved into their background. So why do you need to do so with me?'

'What an intelligent lady you are,' he said, 'and you are absolutely correct. But don't you see, I can't exactly replicate the conditions that were extant during the Stockholm bank siege, unless, of course, I staged an actual bank hold-up. That could lead to all kinds of complications during which someone might be hurt, possibly even killed. Such an approach is entirely out of the question. In any experiment I carry out there will naturally be some form of artificiality. Indeed, I believe that I have a much more difficult task to induce the Stockholm Syndrome, if it exists, because you know what is the position right from the outset. I have to cause you to do something you don't want to do, i.e. to love me and mean it. If I were to ask you the question, right now, "Do you, at this moment, love me?" what would your answer be?'

I said nothing.

'Well, what would your answer be?'

'My answer is that I do not wish to take part in such a charade.'

'Why not?'

'Isn't that obvious? You are holding me against my will and you expect me to assist you. Even to love you. That's a bad joke, Doctor.'

'May I take it, then, that you don't love me?'

'I most certainly do not love you.'

'Bravo! That is exactly the answer I expected, at this stage. It shows me what an honest and truthful person you are.'

'I am being neither honest nor truthful intentionally, I am stating the position exactly as it is. Honesty and truth are just there coincidentally. If I say 'yes' you will not believe me. You will think that I am afraid of you and that I am trying to please you so that you will release me. You would certainly know that I am lying. I am not given to lying. If I say 'no' you will believe that I am assisting you in your enquiry and that will give you stimulus to continue to hold me here. So, I decline to answer your question? Also, if you want me to be truthful I will say that I don't believe that you are engaged in research. I believe that you are just deluding yourself and attempting to delude me. What you are really searching for is a sex object and you haven't enough confidence in yourself to find a girl, court her and take her to wife in the normal way. Well, I will not be your sex object. I will not assist you in raping me and helping you salve your conscience by telling yourself that it was consensual. Just so you get the idea, I am not afraid to die.'

'How perceptive of you. In answering as you have you have already answered my question. I wouldn't expect you to love me after the way I have treated you thus far. As far as my finding a girl and courting her in the conventional manner, I agree that would be difficult for me. I have always found it difficult to get close to girls, apart from patients, with whom I have no trouble getting on the closest terms. I'm sure I could if I tried but I never seemed to have the time. I am not deluding myself. That is something I never do, I am a realist. When you put your arms around me and tell me you love me there will be no sham about it. You will really mean it. I believe that. As well as the Stockholm Syndrome there are a million cases on that to prove me right. Just think of all those arranged marriages in those countries where parents choose the spouses for their children. A young woman is introduced to a young man she may never have met before, and they are told that they are to marry and that is that. There may be some unhappiness between the 'happy couple', isn't that a joke, at the beginning but, eventually, they settle down, have children, get to know each other and live happily ever after. In quite recent times, in Italy, a brigand would come down out of the hills, grab a fair maiden, take her to his hideout and keep her there until she yielded. Thereafter, she would be his and would not leave him. She couldn't, really. She could not go back to her family for he would claim that it was her wish to 'elope' with him. Over time she would grow to love him and so, too, will you grow to love me. That, of course, depends upon whether the Stockholm Syndrome really exists. That is how I think. That is what I want to find out. So far as your not being afraid to die goes, I don't believe that. Every healthy person is afraid to die, or at least, does not want to die, just yet. The exceptions, of course, are those who are in despair or in unbearable pain. You do not fall into either of those categories. You are a healthy and beautiful young woman and you want to live as much as I do. So you cannot fox me in that regard.'

Then he said something that really threw me when he said, 'If you decided to commit suicide, which you won't, I don't know what I would do. I haven't thought that one through yet. That is a thought that, I must admit, had not occurred to me. One thing would follow from that, though, this experiment, with you, would be at an end.' He emphasised the 'with you'. 'But that won't happen for there is no way you can commit suicide no matter how much you might want to; you are too securely bound for that, and I will make sure that you don't. Since we began this talk, through your mind has been running the thought that where there is life there is hope. You are hoping, and I am sure, praying, that I will somehow slip up and you will be able to free yourself. I am happy to tell you, Elizabeth, that will not happen. I did not make all these preparations and take all these elaborate precautions so that I would fail. I have considered each and every detail with the greatest care. If this project does fail it will not be my fault. Just keep remembering that I am a psychiatrist; that I know pretty well how people think and how they will react in particular situations but I don't know everything. If I did how boring life would be. I don't know if there is such a thing as the Stockholm Syndrome but I intend to find out and present a paper on it to the Lancet or to Nature. Both of those respected journals would, I am sure, be delighted to add a positive result to the pool of medical knowledge. Whilst I have a great deal of knowledge, it could be properly said that at this moment my knowledge in this particular area of my expertise is incomplete. I intend to fill that gap, with your help.'

CHAPTER SIX

I don't know if he intended to frighten me but what he said was having that effect. I had never felt really frightened in my life before I woke up on this bed. I continued to quake inside. It was the way he said, 'this experiment, **with you,** would be at an end'. He was leaving me in no doubt that if I faded out of the picture, no matter how, he would find someone else. It was clear, too, that he could read my mind. What he had said was exactly how I thought. What was I to do? At that moment, if I had been free, I would, undoubtedly, have killed him. It was the only way I could have assuaged the anger that burned within me. If he was not a serial killer or a serial rapist he was on the way to being one or the other or both. Again, even though I was terribly afraid I told myself to be steady. I must not let him beat me. Or cow me. Or terrify me. I found then that it is very hard to think when almost overcome with fear. Nevertheless, if I wanted to live I had to stay aware and cool and think myself out of this. He wanted to look into my mind he said, to see how I think. Well, two can play at that game. If he could look into my mind I could look into his. He might be a very learned psychiatrist and I merely a qualified mental health nurse but that didn't mean I couldn't outthink him. Weren't all the odds against David when he faced Goliath? What I had to do was to trick him. Make him feel that he was winning. I must not do it too suddenly for he was very clever and would know what I was doing. I must play hard to get at first, then appear to come round to his way of thinking but very gradually.

He was a mental case. Just like those other mental cases I worked with every day. He needed treatment. I would provide it. So, please, God, you can see how much I need your help. I am now the soldier in the foxhole. I am in dire straits. I need your help now like I have never needed it in my whole life. Please help me.

Now he changed tack and went off at a tangent.

'My goodness, I didn't realise the time. I had hoped to be further on than this. You must be very hungry? I do want to know all about you but that will have to wait. You may be a hostage, a reluctant guest, but that does not give me any excuse to forget my manners. Would you like something to eat?'

He spoke in such an apologetic way that he made me feel that he really did care for me; that he did not want to cause me any discomfort. I didn't know what to say. I thought the longer I dragged things out the better so I said, 'Yes, that is very kind of you. Doctor Wilderman, I would like something to eat and drink. I am still very thirsty.'

'Let me fetch you a drink right away,' he said. 'Then I will bring you something to eat afterwards. Would you like a fruit juice, a mineral water or, perhaps, a glass of milk?'

'Just plain tap water,' I said.

Next thing I knew he had risen from the chair, had turned his back on me, switched on the torch and left the room. He did not close the door so I could hear him rattling about in the kitchen and then the tap running. In a few seconds he was back with the water. He didn't release either hand but held the paper cup to my lips and I drank from it, greedily. When I had finished he said, 'Feel better now?'

I said, 'Yes, thank you.'

'Okay, so far so good. Now what would you like to eat? I have several meals ready. All I have to do is pop them in the microwave. You are not a vegan or a vegetarian, are you?'

'No. Doctor, I am neither. I eat everything.'

'In that case we'll have fish and chips. I shall eat the same as you. I too can eat anything. If you'll excuse me I shall go and make it ready.'

He didn't wait for a reply but went back to the kitchen again. This time he shut the door. He was correct; the room was completely sound-proofed. I couldn't hear a thing from the other side of the door. I felt frustrated. I wanted to know as much as I could about the rooms that lay beyond the bedroom.

Here we were, apparently on such friendly terms, he asking me what I would like to eat and when I told him, dashing off to prepare it as if he were my servant. Anyone listening to a tape recording of our conversation would think that he was the considerate and attentive host having only the best interests of his guest at heart. Maybe that was what he had in mind? Could it be that when his research was at an end he would produce the tape, or part of it, to show that he had acted completely honourably throughout? If that was what he had in mind then I would have to find some way of circumventing his plan. Of course, no matter what I did he could always delete anything that was detrimental to his designs. At the same time, I wasn't sure if he would do that. He wouldn't if he were a true researcher. I wasn't sure what to do, I was so mixed up. Maybe I was becoming as crazy as he was? I must not allow that to happen. I must not allow myself to become confused. Stay focused, girl. Stay focused. No matter what, you must not let him win. Your life and the life of some other innocent may depend upon on how able you are to outthink him.

He was back placing a tray across my naked thighs. Again he released my left hand and lifted the tray whilst I sat upright on the bed. When I was comfortable he put the tray back again and said, 'There is a knife and fork on each side of the plate, I'm afraid you will have to do everything by feel, for the time being. There is salt and pepper and tomato sauce to the right of the plate. If you want more water you will have to get that separately. The plate is one of the disposable kind and the cutlery is all plastic. There is nothing there that you could use as a weapon to do yourself, or me, an injury. Bon appetit. I will now go and get mine.'

He switched on his torch and left the room but was soon back and I could hear him eating as he sat on the chair. 'I am having the same as you,' he said, 'And will do so all the time we are together.'

Each time he switched on the torch, and he only did so very briefly, I could see that skeleton at the end of the bed. It grinned and gaped at me as those eyeless sockets locked on my eyes; and I knew that it continued to stare even in the darkness. I knew it was staring at me. Was it was enjoying every moment of my ordeal? Why? Why? Why? Was it, too, a sadist joining forces with this madman who held me to strip me of what courage I had? Was that why the darkness? Was that why it was posed at the end of the bed where I could see it, just within the ambit of the torch light? Then with a jolt like an electric shock it hit me: this was a previous victim. This was the hostage before me who had given her life to prove or disprove the whole idea of the Stockholm Syndrome. Did I really think that I was his first hostage? If I did I was a fool. No researcher bases their conclusions on the result of one piece of investigation. No, they would do the experiment again and again and again to the point where they were one hundred percent satisfied that they had proof one way or the other. Pavlov did not carry out his research using only one dog. Not every dog answered to the bell. There were those dogs which did not answer. He allowed for them in his conclusions. They had what he called 'the freedom principle'. They would never salivate like their fellows when the bell told them that there was food to be had. So Dr Wilderman was using real live human specimens to 'look into the mind' of his hostages. He was undoubtedly mad. But why was the skeleton wearing my clothes? Why not her own clothes? I presumed it had been a woman. Was that to indicate to me that I was being given a peek into the future and that soon I would be hanging there if I didn't comply? 'The mind of the insane can only be comprehended by the insane', one of my nursing friends had once said to me. 'Why do you think so many of these psychiatrists are as mad as their patients?' Staff Nurse Margaret had said that as a joke. But, as my father used to say, 'Many a true word is spoken in jest.'

CHAPTER SEVEN

What was I to do? Only one thing to do, as I had already determined, play hard to get, blow hot and cold. Keep him guessing. Spin the thing out as long as possible. Pretend to fight him at first and then to gradually come round to see his point of view. I had to do it in such a way that he was completely fooled for if he had the least inkling that I was stringing him along I would take my place alongside that skeleton before the month was up.

The meal was delicious. I ate every scrap. By the time I was finished I knew how a blind person must feel when it came to eating a meal. That was something I hadn't had brought home to me so forcibly in the past. It was bad enough not seeing what I was eating but to only have the full use of my left hand with very limited use of my right made it particularly difficult. I had to lean forward and lower my head until it was almost touching the plate to ensure that I found my mouth and that none of the food went on the bed. My mother would not have approved of my table manners but my mother was never in a situation like this.

After I was finished eating I groped about the tray until I found a serviette to wipe my mouth. He was listening to everything and knew that I had finished for as soon as I had wiped my mouth he said, 'Would you like some dessert? I have ice cream with yogurt or tinned fruit, or you may have fresh fruit if you would prefer that? Just tell me what you would like.'

I opted for an apple. I thought that would be easier to handle with one hand. He went and brought it immediately. When I had finished the apple he told me that I had a choice of tea or coffee. I chose tea. Then, when all was finished, he took everything away and returned to sit in the chair again.

He treated me like an honoured guest. I could not have been better treated if I had been there of my own free will. Only my bonds and my nakedness reminded me that I was not. This, I supposed, was his way of getting me on side. My head was full of mixed thoughts. I had to keep telling myself that this man was dangerous; that he was suffering from some form of mental imbalance. Most certainly he was delusional. The psychiatrist who took my class for lectures during my training would certainly have typed him as schizoid. He was living in a world I hoped never to inhabit: a self-made world where everything in it was created by him. He was his own God. He couldn't do wrong. He believed he was the great researcher, a Freud, or a Fleming or a Pasteur who was out to save the world. The only trouble with schizoids, said the lecturer, was that they were liable to go to extremes in pursuit of their fantasy. Any person who got in their way or obstructed them would be in great danger. They should be handled with great care. Although the illness had its own distinct pattern within that pattern there could be different idiosyncrasies. Get to know what those idiosyncrasies were and a great advance would be made in returning the patient to normality. Return this patient to normality and I would live, unharmed. I remembered that lecture well. I had now been given the opportunity to study and, I hoped, to understand and treat such a person. Dr Wilderman was now my unknowing patient. I'd better be good or the results of my research would never be published in any textbook. How strange it was that instead of being in beautiful Wineglass Bay, unwinding, and casting all my cares away for a whole month, I should be engaged in mental combat with a deranged doctor with my survival as the prize. Somehow, that thought strengthened my resolve. I had always wanted to be the best nurse in the hospital, now I had been given the opportunity to discover just how clever I was. Vanity can have its own reward.

That aspect of the matter depended, of course, on whether he was fixated on research or whether research was just a by-product of what he was really after. Was his primary object the breaking down of my reserve and possessing me in every sense of the word 'possess'. At the moment he had possession of my body which he had not violated. He had me physically in his thrall but not spiritually. Did he want me so traumatised that I would give myself to him and he could then somehow salve his conscience by claiming that I had submitted of my own accord? No, not submitted, I don't think that is the term he would use. It was possible that what he wanted was for me to beg him to join me on the bed and the question would then be, would he? My training had shown me that some men who were impotent would act out their fantasies to the point where sexual union was imminent and then, because they were impotent and unable to perform, would blame their victim and use some kind of monstrous sex aid on them before disposing of their 'temptress'.

Maybe he was, quite simply, a sadist who enjoyed some kind of perverted thrill in torturing his victim into submission. Torture does not have to be of the rack or bludgeon type, with breaking of bones, tearing of flesh and the infliction of excruciating bodily pain. Torture can be a most refined thing. And certainly, apart from that bursting in through my front door, he had acted in the most refined manner. But at the end of the day was his aim my pseudo- consensual rape? That I didn't know but I was certain I would discover the answer to that question before this 'experiment', as he called it, was at an end. I would find out before too long if he really was a sexual purist and did not believe in sex before marriage. I doubted that. I am not a cynic, I believe there are good and decent men who would never, under any circumstances hurt a lady, but I also believe there are a lot of men who would find it difficult to refuse sex if it were available and offered to them without comebacks. Would they murder to conceal their 'sin'? That was something we had often discussed in the hospital, particularly when we had an alleged rapist murderer sent to us by the courts for assessment. The general consensus was that the psychological barrier having been broken by the commission of the rape they would go the extra yard and murder their victim to silence them.

I really was in trouble and I knew it.

There were two other possibilities, a) he was a psychopath and, b) he had a personality disorder. If he were a psychopath then I had no chance. Was he a 'psycho? I could see in my mind Alfred Hitchcock's 'psycho' stabbing to death his victim in the shower. I held myself rigid and tried not to shudder as I imagined meeting such an end. I thought of Ted Bundy the real life 'psycho' bludgeoning to death several girls at the same time. How could they allow that to happen? Why didn't they rise up, collectively, and attack him? Surely, that way, at least one of them would have been able to get clear and survive. But they couldn't, could they? They were petrified with fright and the emphasis was on petrified. They had had no time to think and were incapable of thinking collectively. They could no more have stood up and attacked him than they could have gone to the moon. There was one difference between them and me; I was only one. I knew something about the damaged mind, I was not completely petrified and I was still able to think even if in a restricted fashion, sufficiently, I hoped, to keep me alive. But he didn't seem to be a psycho. He hadn't that predatory gaze and the eyes with nothing behind them, as described in the literature. People said of Bundy that, for all his charming manner, his eyes were dead. Dr Wilderman's eyes were not dead. Indeed, when he was comforting a patient they lighted up. He was their guardian angel; their rock in the storm, their own personal haven. Maybe I was lucky, imagine it, lucky, in that my kidnapper was not a 'psycho' - as far as I could tell. I hoped I had made a correct diagnosis of my 'patient' in that regard. If he was not a 'psycho' was he then suffering from some form of personality disorder with the good guy and the bad guy each striving for dominance in his mind and, because they were so equally balanced neither could achieve it and, therefore, had reached an accommodation whereby they took it in turns to motivate him? In the hospital he was Mr Nice Guy. Out of it he was, it appeared to me now, Mr Bad Person. These thoughts and many more crowded my mind as I tried desperately to concentrate on his every word. My life depended upon reading him. My hope was that if he suffered from some form of personality disorder he suffered from only two. That way I might be able to assist the good one to overcome the bad. What would Freud have made of him? Probably, as was his wont, he would have put all his woes down to sexual frustration, maybe, in this case, due to overwork, hence his taking me hostage. I was very aware of the fact that he had not taken a male hostage unless that skeleton was of a male? I didn't think it was. My clothes fitted too well. No, the aim of this game was sex, pure and simple. I was quite sure that Freud would have agreed with me.

'Now, let us return to those particulars again', he said. 'We do not appear to be making much progress. We'll start at the beginning, or, rather your beginning.'

'When were you born?'

'1981.'

'So, you're twenty nine, eh. And not married?'

'No, I'm not married.'

'Never been married?'

'No.'

'You're not a lesbian, are you?'

'That, Doctor, is a rather personal and offensive question. Just because I'm twenty nine and unmarried you feel you should make presumptions about my sexual orientation? You are fifty two and unmarried. Does that mean that you are gay? I refuse to answer such a personal question. In any case, I fail to see what it has to do with the Stockholm Syndrome?'

'Elizabeth. I said earlier that I wanted to do this with the minimum of compulsion. Be a sensible girl and answer the question.'

Again there was that implied threat in his voice. I was playing hard to get. That is how I had to play it at this stage.'

I answered, 'No, I am most certainly not a lesbian. I am very much heterosexual.'

'Thank you. Couldn't you have said that without all this fighting me every inch of the way? Now, where were you born?'

'Ireland.'

'Which part?'

'Does that matter? Ireland is Ireland.'

'Please, Elizabeth,. Again you are resisting me. Just answer the question. There's no need to be difficult. You know, as well as I do, that you will answer in the end.'

The implied threat was there again. I wonder how he had worked out that I would answer in the end. If I didn't want to answer I wouldn't answer. He couldn't make me. On second thoughts, he could make me. He would torture the answer out of me by beating my mind. It would be foolish not to answer. There was always the danger that if I stopped answering his questions it would drive him into a fury and he would become physical and I would become history. Just how physical he could become was illustrated by the force he used in bursting open my door. No, I had to remember that I was treating him. He was my patient. I had to pretend to be difficult and cooperative at the same time.

'Sorry, Doctor. I didn't think where, exactly, I was born mattered.'

'Well, it does. Now please answer the questions without further argument.'

'Yes, Doctor. I was born in County Antrim, Northern Ireland.'

'That's better. What did your parents do for a living?'

I couldn't see the point of all this. The Stockholm bandits didn't, I'm sure, know or care what their hostages' parents did for a living. They didn't sit their hostages down and subject them to a question and answer session to get them on side. I had only a rather vague recollection of what had happened in Stockholm. As far as I could recall the hostages' support of their kidnappers was more a spontaneous thing at the end of the siege. I'm sure the kidnappers were just as surprised by it as anyone else. Come to think of it, the Swedish police must have wondered what was going on. So, once more, I queried the reason for the question.

'You know, Elizabeth, you are just being obtuse. You are much too intelligent a person to act in such a manner. We are into very important research at the moment. We are not playing silly games. So answer the question.'

That impatience, irritation, testiness, whatever it was, in his voice, left me in no doubt that I was trying his patience to the limit. I knew that if I did not answer I would be taking my being to the edge of the abyss. One wrong word and I would be over the edge. It was time to be more cooperative. Make him think he was winning. With pretended reluctance, I answered.

'They were farmers.'

'Were they rich farmers?'

'Hardly. They got by.'

'How close were you to them?'

I did not like the emphasis on the past tense. My parents were still alive and very well. So I said. 'I AM very close to my parents. Always have been.'

'If that is the case why didn't you go home to Ireland to share your holidays with them instead of going to Tasmania?'

For a fleeting second the thought went through my mind that I should answer: 'There was no need for me to go to Ireland to see them. You see, they were to meet me in Hobart. They must be wondering why I am not there.' I discarded that idea immediately. I knew, intuitively, that if I said that I would be dead meat. I don't know how I knew that, I just knew it. So I said 'Oh, they come to Perth at least once a year. It gives them a nice break. They enjoy the beautiful sunshine that we take for granted. You know it rains a lot in Ireland and they like to see the sun once in a while.'

He laughed at that and said, 'Yes, I know what you mean. I have been to Ireland. I've been to see the Giant's Causeway in your native County Antrim. It rained every day of my holiday. I liked the Giant's Causeway, in spite of the rain. Very interesting. If the farmers had some of that rain here I'm sure they would be very happy.'

There he was with his wonderful bedside manner again, talking as if he were in the hospital putting a stressed patient at ease, but I wasn't at ease. Into my mind had popped the question: How is he going to publish the results of his research? Researchers undertook their research for many reasons: fame and fortune or glory. To win the Nobel Prize would be something. To eradicate disease and ease the suffering of many. For the betterment of mankind in general. For the sense of achievement in a job well done. The list could go on and on but just where did proving or disproving the Stockholm Syndrome fit into that list? Were there so many hostage-takings around the world that to be aware of the Stockholm

Syndrome would assist future hostages in any way or contribute to the conviction of the perpetrators of such a crime or even prevent them from committing it in the first place? I couldn't see of what benefit such research could possibly be one way or the other. I couldn't see what use knowledge of the Stockholm Syndrome was to me. It in no way induced me to love my kidnapper. What I could see, and see very clearly, was just how dangerous was this mad doctor was, with the melodious voice, beautiful bedside manner and apparent care for his patients, this patient in particular. If at the end of his experiment, whenever that might be, I didn't throw my arms around him and hug him to me to show that I loved him, what then? Could he publish that? Hardly. My obit wouldn't even be published in the West Australian, the local daily newspaper. I would just have disappeared without trace. Oh, God, the thought of it! Mum and Dad forever wondering what had happened to me. To never see them again. To be buried in some unmarked grave in some little-trodden place where someday someone out walking their dog would be attracted by the dog's digging and one of my bones would be found. DNA would tell who the bone belonged to. Then would start a murder hunt with no hope of success. What would my friends and colleagues at the hospital think? Would they cast a tear for me? Would Dr Wilderman read the eulogy at my memorial service? From what I had seen of him since he kidnapped me he was quite capable of doing so with the tears trickling down his face and a catch in his voice. Then, again, if his experiment was a success and I did kiss and hug him and tell him I loved him, what then? Could he publish his results? Could he tell the world how he kidnapped me, stripped me naked, kept me in a dark room and held me until my mind was so turned that I now professed my undying love for him? Well, Elizabeth, could he? No he couldn't. One way or the other I was for the chop. No doubt about that. Even if I put up no resistance and allowed him to rape me I had no chance. He would tire of me. He had made a conquest. He would dispose of me for, no matter how stubbornly I resisted him, he had triumphed in the end. He would go in search of a new plaything and start the cycle all over again.

I pulled my mind back to his next question.

'Tell me about your religion, Elizabeth. Coming from Ireland you will surely have a religion?'

Once more I wanted so much to tell him it was none of his business. He really was making me more angry but I continued to hold my control and answered, 'I am a NIP.' I knew that would make him think.

'A NIP? I don't think I've heard of a NIP before? What's a NIP? Is it some form of Japanese religion?'

'Northern Ireland Presbyterian,' I said proudly. I wanted him to hear the pride in my voice. He would think my answer was spontaneous and he was getting into my mind.

He actually chuckled at that. 'That's a good one. I haven't heard it expressed like that before. NIP, indeed!'

Then he was serious again. 'Presbyterians are the difficult ones. Don't they believe that they are God's chosen people?'

'We most certainly are,' I said, again, proudly.

'I have never felt the need for religion although I concede that it brings comfort to a great many people. Is it comforting you now?'

'It most certainly is.'

CHAPTER EIGHT

He was silent then for several seconds. I wondered what he was thinking. Had I said the wrong thing? Did my answer mean that as a NIP he recognised that I was too tough a nut to crack and that he would abandon his research, ditch me and go looking for someone who was not a NIP? Did it mean that he liked NIPs? That he wouldn't do me any harm, say something like, 'I'm sorry, Elizabeth, this whole thing just got out of hand, please forgive me,' and would let me go? No. I couldn't see that happening. He was in too deep. Let me go and he would spend the rest of his days in jail. I was in a minefield. I just couldn't read him. I would have to weigh each of his questions and each of my answers carefully. The mind of the mad can be very fragile. It can be turned by the least apparently innocent word and what would happen then? Dear God, help me to win this battle against Satan. I am so alone. So afraid.

Then, thank you, God, he was speaking again.

'Tell me about your education, Elizabeth. Did you go to university?'

'No.'

'Why was that? You would surely have obtained a degree without difficulty.'

'Everyone seems to think that a degree is necessary for success in life, I happen to think differently. Ever since I was a child I wanted to be a nurse. My mother bought me a little nurse's uniform when I was five. I wore it for weeks. I even wore it to bed. My parents were delighted. They were happy to think that I might help people who were in need. They encouraged me.'

'How very noble of them. If that were the case why didn't you go to medical school and become a doctor? Queen's University in Belfast has a very good medical school. I have met many graduates from there in the course of my medical career.'

'I never considered it for a moment. I just wanted to be a nurse and wear a nurse's uniform. That was the beginning and end of it.'

'So it was all about dressing up?'

'Not all but the uniform had a lot to do with it. Doctors, as far as I know, never had a uniform, except those in the armed forces. I never thought of a stethoscope slung around the neck and a white coat as a uniform.'

'Where did you do your training?'

'I did my general practice training at the Royal Victoria Hospital in Belfast.'

'But you are now in mental health. Why did you change?'

'There were many reasons for that. I enjoyed general nursing very much. I learned a lot about gunshot wounds and busted kneecaps. I saw so much hate-inflicted injuries - that it caused me to wonder how people could be so bestial. Bestial is hardly the word. Animals do not hate. Only humans do that. One day, after a twenty three year old had been brought in with bullet holes through both patellas, I decided that general nursing was not for me. What I needed to do was to nurse some of the minds that were broken by the brutality around them that had become an every day occurrence. Maybe in nursing those minds back to health I would understand what drove people to hate with such blindness. You see, Doctor, you are not the only one who wants or needs to look into the morass that is the human mind.'

I knew that would make him think. I had to get inside his mind, make him think about what he was doing to me. I had to plant the seed. Maybe I would be able to turn him around to the point where he would have pity and stop his experiment. There was that case in Lima, in Peru, where the reverse of the Stockholm Syndrome occurred and the hostage takers identified with their hostages. I didn't recall much about it but it did indicate that the kidnappers could be turned. Could be made to feel for their hostages. I wondered how that could be done. Did that just happen spontaneously as well? What a subject for research hostage-taking really was. I had never thought of it in this light before. The trouble of course was that if my diagnosis was wrong and he were a psychopath he would have no pity. He would act the part of the caring doctor, live the part of the caring doctor; unfortunately, he would not be a caring doctor. I would never see outside this room again. My heart quailed. I was back in terror again. What was I to do? Only one thing to do, remember he was my patient. I had to fight his mind with my mind.

'Where did you do your mental health nurse's training?'

'I had to get away from Northern Ireland so that I could think straight. I made a clean break and went to London. I was lucky to be accepted into the Free London Clinic for Nervous Disorders just as a new course was beginning. There were six of us on the course and it was wonderful.'

'So you liked it then?'

'No, I don't just like it, I love it.' I was in the present tense, again. He was in the past tense. Was he doing it deliberately to jangle my nerves? To disorientate me and in so doing disrupt any plans. Keep me unsettled and he was more likely to get inside my guard.

'Better than general nursing?'

'Oh, yes.'

'Why was that?'

'There were several reasons, among them being the fact that I didn't live in fear of IRA or Loyalist gunmen suddenly appearing in the ward to finish off a patient who had somehow survived the first attempt on their life. I liked the lecturers. I liked the staff. I liked the patients, too. What I liked most of all was that I was trying to treat an illness I couldn't see. I could see symptoms all right, not the cause. The cause was there to be found. Sometimes the treating doctor would find it and tell us what it was. Sometimes I would find it and tell the doctor. Occasionally the cause was not found. Such patients were a challenge. We wanted to help them. We wanted to bring them to normality. It was as if we were detectives always looking for clues. I suppose we were in much the same position as you, Doctor, and the Stockholm Syndrome? What you are trying to discover is, is the simple act of taking a person hostage the sole cause for that phenomenon or is there some other reason for it? I was and still am fascinated by mental health nursing.'

What I was trying to do was to cause him to think I was thinking along the same lines as he was. Maybe I had gone off at a tangent and if I had that wasn't necessarily a bad thing. Two of us now searching for the same thing and I reaching out to help him in his quest. Would that make him think that I was coming round to his way of thinking? Was there just a glimmer of hope that I would go the extra yard and come round to loving him? It was somewhat early for that. Careful, girl. Go gently or he'll smell a rat.

'Which textbooks did you use?'

Why did he want to know about textbooks? Like all psychiatrists, he was not asking questions without a good reason. What was his reason here? Why this probe? Then it hit me, he wanted to find out if I was on to him. If I knew enough about how psychiatrists, and maybe even madmen, thought to know that the Stockholm Syndrome had nothing to do with his holding me hostage. What he was after was his own sexual gratification but be had also set himself a challenge, take a virgin who had no regard for him whatsoever, apart from their working relationship, and work on her mind to the point where she would throw herself at him. And if that virgin was heterosexual and at twenty nine had survived all the overtures of men up until now, then his overcoming her reserve and inhibition would prove to him what a great master of the mind he was. There must be no violence, apart from the occasional veiled threat just to jolly things up a little and keep his 'specimen' on track. Hence the gentlemanly conduct. This much I had gathered from his approach up to now. I was beginning to read him but it was early days. I must be careful how I answered this question. Give him the bare minimum in reply. Don't appear too clever even though he says, 'you're clever'. He is only saying that to get inside your armour. He is very wily.

'We used, mainly, two, with references to a host of others. I must admit, though, that there was a great deal in the textbooks I didn't understand. Symptoms, their cause, and the psychoanalysis involved in the understanding of a patient's illness which you psychiatrists find easy, I find very difficult. It's hard work but that's what I like about it; it's a challenge.'

'Which were the textbooks?'

'They were, Psychiatry and Mental Health Nursing: The Craft of Caring by Philip Barber and The Art & Science of Mental Health Nursing by Ian Norman and Iain Ryrie. I have read them and reread them and whilst they are very simply written, I suppose, from a psychiatrist's point of view, I find them difficult to comprehend. It's going to take me a lifetime to have that grasp on the subject to which I aspire, but I am going to keep on trying.'

There was no reply for a moment then he said, 'Yes, Ryrie is a very sound chap. His writings are generally very lucid. It will take time but before you know it it will all become crystal clear or as clear as psychiatric understanding ever is. When you and I are on better terms I will tutor you. I think that together we will make a great team.'

Did he mean it or was he just stringing me along? I said nothing. Must not appear too eager.

'Do you have any recurring dreams?'

Now what was he up to? What had my dreams to do with the Stockholm Syndrome? I had no idea what he was about except that I was aware that some psychotherapists are of the view that some dreams give an insight into a person's underlying problems. Should I lie to him and keep him out of my mind and my thinking or tell him the truth and see where it leads? He would probably know if I were not telling the truth and, anyway, I wanted to see what he made of a dream which I had quite regularly. I had always wondered about it. It was always the same, with minor modifications. I answered truthfully.

'Yes, I have a recurring dream.'

'Tell me about it.'

'Well, usually, I feel that I am at a great height, that I am against a barrier of some kind. There is a great force pressing against me. I resist it with all my might but it's no good, the barrier breaks and I am falling, falling, falling. Or else I dream that I am flying using my arms as wings when, suddenly, my arms are pinioned to my sides. I strive with all the power within me to break the bonds but I am unable to do so. I can't fly anymore and, again, I am plummeting.'

'Have you attempted to analyse those dreams?'

'Yes, I have, but I am unable to make head or tail of them.'

'Have you read Freud?'

'Only parts here and there. Not with any degree of application.'

'Have you read what he has to say on dreams, this kind of dream, specifically?'

'No, I haven't.'

'You should.'

'Why should I do that?'

'You might know more about yourself if you did.'

'What might I know?'

'That will have to wait until another time. I have a thousand and one other questions I still have to ask y...'

CHAPTER NINE

Whatever he was going to say was interrupted with a bang. There was a tremendous crash at the window. It was like it had been struck by a bullet. His chair was flung backwards and he was up and running with such speed that he was wrenching the door open and was standing silhouetted in the doorway whilst I was still trying to come to terms with what was going on. Then the door was shut tight. Had I not experienced it I would not have believed him capable of such rapid movement. He was still without clothes. Because of the soundproofing I could hear nothing. I just lay and wondered what it was? I prayed that it was someone trying to break in and that there would be a fight and he would have to call the police. That way I would have help. But then I thought no matter what he would not call the police. Even if he was injured he would not call the police. He dare not. How could he explain my presence there, bound hand and foot? No, there would be no police. My only hope was that there were burglars at the house and there would be a fight in which he would be overcome and then the burglars would find me and release me. Would they release me? They would probably think that I was one of those ladies who, for the proper fee, are invited by a 'gentleman' to his house and take part in kinky sex: bondage, or some other weird and intimate game. Then I might be in greater danger than ever. They might decide that if I was there for the occupant's pleasure they might as well share in that pleasure. I could tell them that I had been kidnapped and ask them to make an anonymous call to the police from a public phone and as a reward they could take whatever they wanted from the house. I would promise never to identify them. Would they believe me? They might. They might not. My mind was really going into the realms of hope and fantasy, clutching at straws, but I was brought down to earth when he re-entered the room, still without clothes, and said, 'It was just two boys with a catapult. Obviously they had been aiming at birds and one shot had gone astray. I got to the back door just in time to see them haring into the distance. I have examined the window and there is a small round stone wedged in the double glazing. No harm done. Nothing to worry about. I'm sorry if it gave you a fright. It certainly made me jump.'

He was the caring doctor again.

I wilted. All my hopes of an early rescue were gone. Ah, but that hole might have affected the soundproofing of the room. He would have to bring someone to repair the window. That way I might still be found. No such luck. He knocked that hope sideways immediately when he continued. 'I shall have to have the glaziers come and repair the window but all in good time. The hole is a very small one and I can plug it later with some liquid cement and super glue. I can have it properly repaired when our experiment is completed.'

I almost wept but I didn't. I was not going to show weakness. I would keep control no matter what. Then as the thought was passing through my mind I began to shake, uncontrollably. I knew it was shock. It was the trauma of it all. There is just so much a person can take before the cracks begin to appear. I was cracking up. I just couldn't help it. Try as I might I couldn't stop shaking and, worse still, I began to hyperventilate. I lay gasping. I couldn't get enough air. I was going to die. Well, at least, he would have been cheated out of possessing me. Would it be better to yield to him than die? Tarsey Horrigan with her infectious, deep-throated laugh, when some crisis or other was happening in the ward, would say, 'If rape is inevitable, honey chile, lie back and enjoy it. Particularly if James Bond, the Sean Connery one, is about to do the raping.' Then she would burst into gales of laughter. Not for me. Never! I would not lie back and enjoy it. I would not die either, and I would not yield. No matter what, I would stay alive. I would do something that I had never done before, I would lie, just to stay alive. He really was turning my inner moral self inside out. Lying was repugnant to me but what else could I do? Speak only the truth and die? If I died he would never be brought to justice and, no matter what, he must be brought to justice. He must be arrested, put before the courts, stand trial and be subjected to the humiliation and embarrassment of having his crimes exposed to the world at large. Let his colleagues at the hospital, the staff and his patients, see what a sham he was. He should be made to appear in the dock, stripped naked, metaphorically, and see if that engendered rapport between him and the people who would come to see this great doctor fall from grace. Would he tell how he had kidnapped me, purely in the interests of science, of course? Would he tell how he was only interested in the betterment of mankind in researching the existence or non-existence of the Stockholm Syndrome? I would be the main prosecution witness. I would take pleasure in going into the witness box and telling the world what he did to me. I would like to see his face. I would like to ask him what he thought of the Stockholm Syndrome then? Ask him if he felt then like throwing his arms around me, kissing me and telling me that he loved me? I knew it was all wishful thinking; he would never be brought to trial. He was mad. Mad people can do anything. Anything they like. They are not responsible for their actions. Didn't I know that? They don't know what they are doing. They can commit murder and get away with it. When all else fails, claim insanity. It is not work but madness that sets you free. My anger was welling over again. How I hated him. I had to get him. Bring him to justice. Please, God help me bring this monster to justice.

Then I thought, if I do get him before a court he will be found unfit to stand trial by reason of insanity. Probably everyone would feel sorry for him, say what a great doctor he was. That pressure of over-work had caused him to snap. How kind people are. They should be at the sharp end of his snapping and see if they feel so forgiving then. Really, at the end of the day, I didn't care what people said, I just wanted my freedom and him where he belonged, in a mental hospital, not as a doctor but as a patient behind bars in the locked room. The pity of it would be that his room would not be soundproofed. I would like him to be in a soundproofed room with no one to talk to. His meals brought to him in utter silence. Led to the bathroom on a leash. Have to do everything with one hand, in the dark. See how he liked that. Was I becoming vengeful? I didn't really know and I didn't really care. What I did know was that I did not feel like loving him. Where was the Stockholm Syndrome now?

Yet, here he was, as soon as he found that I was shaking and hyperventilating, being the caring doctor again. Comforting me, telling me what I knew already, that it was all due to shock. It would pass shortly. I must be strong. He knew I was strong, that was why he had selected me. He would bring me something to drink, something that would settle me. I had no need to worry. He would take good care of me.

CHAPTER TEN

I couldn't speak. I was shaking and gasping too much. He left the room, switching on the torch as he did so. I saw that damned skeleton on the periphery of its beam again. It was still gaping at me. I was revolted. Love this doctor for doing this to me? The strongest emotion I felt then was hate. Hate of the most virulent, destructive kind. There was no love in me. Had I been asked then what I thought of capital punishment for kidnapping, I would have said that I voted for it with both hands and my feet as well. I would even volunteer to pull the lever to open the trapdoor.

The door opened and closed again. He was back. He bent over me. He was holding my upper arm to stop it shaking, rubbing it with something. I felt a jab. 'Just a little something to stop the shakes. When you wake up you'll be fine again. Just relax.' Then he was rubbing my arm again where he had injected me.

I don't know how long I was asleep. What I do know is that the dream was there again. I was in a car racing up a mountain. The car was going faster and faster, it was racing towards a bridge the centre of which had collapsed. I put my foot on the brake but nothing happened. I moved my foot up and down frantically but it was no use I could do nothing to prevent the car hurtling into the void. Once more I was falling. It was then that I awoke. I didn't know where I was for a few moments, then, I recalled that

I had been kidnapped and was tied to the bed. I was mad with thirst again and it was still dark. Happily, the doctor was right, the shakes had gone and I was no longer hyperventilating. The doctor was sitting in the chair. He must have heard my movement for he said, 'Are you awake, Elizabeth?'

'Yes, I am', I croaked, having difficulty enunciating through parched lips. 'I need a drink of water badly, please.'

I was still alive and unmolested, and I was thankful for that but I felt terribly, terribly alone. That dream disturbed me and I needed badly to be comforted. What came wasn't exactly comfort but it was the next best thing. Dr Wilderman came up beside the bed. He brought a glass and a bottle of ice-cold water. I could hear him filling the glass. Then he lifted my head and put the glass to my lips. I drank greedily only stopping for breath. 'Enough?' he asked when I had drained the glass. 'No. I need another one, please.' He filled the glass again and I drank it more slowly. I drained that one, too, and asked for another. He gave me that and I drained it too. Then I lay back on the pillow and felt much better.

'You certainly were thirsty,' he said. 'Now would you like something to eat?'

Only then did I realise how hungry I was. I was ravenous.

'Yes, I am very hungry,' I said. 'I could eat a whale.'

'Sorry, we don't do whale meat but I can do you some very nice roast lamb, mint sauce and roast potatoes,' he chuckled.

There we were, back to the friendly kidnapper and the kidnapped.

I didn't know how he managed it, he must have had the meals deep-frozen or something, then cooked them in the microwave, but within twenty minutes he was back again with a beautifully appetising meal. I ate it all in no time. Then he brought dessert: tinned peaches and cream.

When I had time to think about it I was back scared out of my wits again. He had done all this before. He had it off too pat. I was becoming more and more convinced, in spite of what he said, that I was not his first hostage. He hadn't somehow found me by chance. He had had others here. My kidnapping was very carefully planned. He had probably looked up my personal file in admin and probably looked up the personal file of every nurse, clerk, ward assistant, cleaner and any other female in the hospital. This man left nothing to chance. He did not make random selections. He was a professional snatcher. He was the cat who knew how to catch the mouse and play with it. With him the mouse had no chance. I was only the latest in his carefully selected bag of females with whom he would play mind games to discover how long each held out. I noticed that for all his questioning of me he did not appear to make any notes. How could he, in the dark? Very likely, after each question and answer session he would go to his study, write it all up then do a comparison with how long other hostages had held out against him. I ran over in my mind the number of young females who had gone missing in Perth over the past ten years. Hadn't there been a young clerical assistant who had gone missing several months ago? Hadn't she left the hospital at the end of her evening shift and never been heard of again? Her bank account remained untouched; her credit cards unused. She was classified simply as a missing person who might have eloped with a boyfriend. Maybe that was her skeleton at the end of the bed? Her parents had gone frantic but she was still missing. Other females had disappeared without trace but they were not from the hospital. Was he responsible for some of those disappearances? 'Oh, God! I'm in a torture chamber. What am I to do?'

CHAPTER ELEVEN

At the end of the meal, after he had cleared away the tray and the dishes, he said, 'I have to go out for a little while, Elizabeth. I may be away four or five hours. Do you wish to go to the bathroom before I leave?' I said I did. He followed the usual procedure of extending the lanyard between my feet and freeing one arm before leading me to the bathroom. Then, when I had finished, he brought me back to the bed and secured me again as before.

I said, 'If you are going out, for several hours, Doctor, what would happen if the house went on fire or I badly needed to go to the bathroom again and couldn't wait?'

'The house is unlikely to go on fire. There is nothing to set off a fire. I usually unplug all the electric sockets before leaving. There is nothing that would ignite easily. I keep inflammables to the barest minimum. There is a lightning conductor on the roof. No chance of a strike there. There is a sprinkler system in every room. Any fire would be doused immediately. You see, Elizabeth, I have left nothing to chance. I do not need the police or any "sticky beak" to come calling before we have finished our research. As for your needing to use the bathroom in a hurry, well, that's something I could not guard against. However, if that happens it happens. There is nothing I can do about that except stay with you all the time and I cannot do that.'

'But I am very afraid and I don't like being in the dark, Doctor, and I don't like being on my own, tied up and completely naked. Can't you at least leave a light on for me?' I begged.

'I thought I made it clear already that being in the dark, naked and properly secured, is part of the scenario I had in mind. They are part of what you might call, 'conditioning'. Don't worry, nothing will happen to you whilst I am away. I have done my best to ensure you are not exposed to any foreseeable risk. Now, I'm afraid I must go. I am already late for my appointment.'

He left the room as always closing the door behind him. Now I was on my own, alone in the dark with nothing to do but think. The hateful part of it was that I didn't know if it was morning, noon or night. I was completely disorientated. That, of course, was what he wanted. Have me so unsettled that I would have to go to him for reassurance. For him to tell me that I had nothing to fear. He had already started that process. I was safe here. I was not exposed to any foreseeable risk. He was already breaking his way into my mind. That was the prelude before he broke into my body. Maybe that was his kind of foreplay? I had heard of rogue police officers before; I had never heard of a rogue psychiatrist, but rogue psychiatrist he was. He was in my mind. He was searching for control. I had to get him out of it. How? Outthink him. Thought was the only weapon I had. Why had he asked me about my dreams? I should not have told him anything about that one which kept recurring but I don't really know why I did. Maybe it was curiosity. I did want to know why it kept coming back. I was foolish. I had let him into my mind. He would use it against me. Here I was lying trussed like a turkey at Christmas with a madman in complete control of me, a madman I had to beat and yet I was actually assisting him. There's one for those people who like Chinese puzzles. Tell me how I get out of this one.

I had to stop thinking so negatively. I had to think of something to lift my spirits but what was I to think about? Well, I suppose I could pretend that

I had gone on holiday and was now at Wineglass Bay. I would have spent the night in my favourite little Hobart motel where the hostess, Mrs Panic, had been waiting to greet me. Fat and friendly, she would have flung her arms around me and greeted me like an old and trusted friend. Well, I suppose I was on the way to being just that, I had stayed there twice before. It was much cheaper and less sterile than a big flashy hotel. The staff all knew me. When I first saw her name in the holiday brochure I almost split my sides laughing. How did she ever come by a name like Panic? Was it because she lived where there was always panic or caused panic or because panic was her usual way of life? I found it hilarious and intriguing. I showed the brochure to all the staff. They thought it was hilarious too. We all wondered about that name. It was Tarsey Horrigan who came up with a reason for that name. 'What better advertisement could she have than a name like that? By showing all of us her brochure you have done exactly what she wanted you to do, given her motel publicity. Now, I suppose, you won't be able to resist visiting her salubrious establishment to see how Mrs Panic handles things. I tell you this, Elizabeth, you won't be the only guest she'll have from this madhouse. I won't be far behind you. Haven't we constant panic of one form or another here? You should feel quite at home going from this panic to Mrs Panic, the mother of all panics.' Again her loud and infectious laughter rang around the staff room. We all laughed with her.

There was no panic, except Mrs Panic, at The Blue Wine Cove motel in Hobart. It was a delightful place. Not even in Ireland had I found a more friendly place. The beds had sparkling white sheets and the food was delicious. One night when I had gone into the dining-room, Roxy, the waitress, who was waiting at my usual table, could hardly contain her delight. She had a grin a mile wide on her broad happy face when she said, 'Mrs Panic has laid on a special meal for you tonight, Elizabeth, and it is entirely complimentary. This one is on the house.' (Another good ad.) 'Can you guess what it is?' I tried a variety of dishes but Roxy shook her head to each one as the grin grew ever bigger. 'You are nowhere near it,' she laughed. 'It is Irish stew. Mrs Panic said she thought it would make you feel at home.' It did make me feel at home. Even though my mother prided herself on her cooking she had never made a better Irish stew than the one that followed. It was delicious. It made me feel that in spite of the advertising hype these people really cared. Was it any wonder I went back each year? As for the name, Mrs Panic was from the former Yugoslavia where Panic is quite a common name. It is not pronounced Panic but Panitch. The t & h were never added in Australia. The name was a better ad. without either.

They must be wondering why I hadn't showed up? I had paid a ten percent deposit in advance. What would they do about that? Would they still keep the reservation for me? I always gave my home telephone number when making the booking; I had no need to do otherwise. I never gave the hospital's. What a fool I was. What would they do about that? No good ringing my home address to see if I had been taken ill or something, all they would get there would be the standard telephone company reply after the phone had given five rings: 'We regret the person you wish to contact is presently unavailable. You may, if you wish, leave a message after the beep.' If any message was left there would be no reply to it. And that would be that. I don't think they would know to ring the hospital. I had mentioned that I was a nurse but I don't think I ever gave the name or address of the hospital. What a fool I was. If I had only told them where I worked they might have rung there. Then I thought, what good would that have done? It might have done more harm than good. I would only have been listed as a missing person, if that, and the police, without any complaint, would have more to do than chase after shadows. I might have had my own reasons for going temporarily absent. It might also have sent Dr Wilderman into a frenzy and caused him to abort his experiment, to my detriment. He might have 'disappeared' me permanently, sooner than he originally intended. I'd better not think about that. There were pleasanter things to think about, things that might save my life. I could tell myself stories about things that happened to me or my friends but those stories would have to have a happy ending. Didn't that lady in Arabia save her life by telling stories to the king? I hadn't read 'One Thousand And One Arabian Nights' but I knew about how the bored king would have killed the lady if she hadn't kept him amused with her storytelling. Every night she told him a story which ran into the next day, when she would then start another which would run into the next and so on until the king became more interested in hearing the end to each story than in killing her. Now, I must tell stories to myself that would keep me amused, maybe even make me laugh, so that my morale did not flag. Whatever I do, I must not become depressed. I could pretend to be depressed but I must not be. I hoped that I would be free long before I arrived at the end of the one thousand and first tale.

CHAPTER TWELVE

Where to start? Ah, who better than Tarsey Horrigan to begin with? I could think about Tarsey. She would lift my spirits. She was really funny. 'Laugh your cares away, honey chile,' she would always say. 'You is gonna be a long time dead and you might not do much laughing den. It all depends on whether you is going up or you is going down. I know I is going up. No God worth his salt could send me down der where it's so hot. Not after putting up with all de hassle we get around here. Mind you, honey chile, we blacks could put up with de heat better than you white guys. I is so sure dat I'm going up dat I have joined the local church choir. I is der every Sunday mawning among all dose hot gospellers singing about dat band of angels dat is acoming after me just to carry me home. I'm glad I won't have to walk. Being carried would be nice and if it is an angelic hunk doing de carrying, then all de better. I is taking lessons on de harp. When I arrive at de Pearly Gates I'll tell dat St Peter dat I is just a raring to go. I can hardly wait. But I does not want to go today. Maybe tomorrow.' Then would come her contagious laughter. I am not so sure if we laughed at what she said or how she said it or both. We all loved Tarsey.

Born in the East End of London of an Irish father, Patrick Michael Horrigan, who was a train driver, and a black Jamaican mother, Serina Emmanuel, who was a speech therapist, she was christened Theresa Kingston Horrigan but was never called anything but Tarsey. I seldom saw her without a smile on her face. Her big brown eyes sparkled and glistened from the time she came on duty at the beginning of our twelve hour shift until she handed over to the incoming staff at the end of it. She never seemed to tire. Her complexion was like black silk and she revelled in her blackness. At 180 centimetres tall and 100 kilograms in weight there was nobody and nothing in the ward, or anywhere else for that matter, that she feared. Even in the locked ward the most violent patient fazed her not in the slightest. She had the most beautiful diction, almost as if she had had elocution lessons which she never had, and often, at staff parties would mimic the BBC newsreaders using language which the visiting vicar would not have approved of. 'Good evening, this is a special edition of the nine o'clock news from the BBC with Slinky Lovealot reading it. In a special bulletin issued from 10, Downing Street this evening, England's first black prime minister, Mr John Hotwithers, has declared that he is gay and has had a sex-change operation. He, sorry, that should read, she, has advised that from now on she should be addressed as Joan She is soon to go to a well-known finishing school in Switzerland for two weeks where she will learn to walk like a lady and sit like a lady. 'No sitting with knees apart for me from now on,' she laughed. After Switzerland she is to spend a week in a high profile hospital in London where she will have her vocal cords adjusted so that she will also talk like a lady. 'If I walk like a lady and talk like a lady,' she said, 'Then I must be a lady.' The now Ms Hotwithers has advised that she and her wife have separated, amicably. She is taking up residence with the Chancellor of the Exchequer who has also had a sex-change procedure. 'Ten Downing Street is about to become a different place,' she said. She and Lady Titia Adook, formerly known as Sir Titus, will be married as soon as the bill, allowing gays to exchange marriage vows, now before Parliament, has been voted into law. 'This is a great day for gays in England and across the globe,' she said 'This great country of ours has always led the world in social and religious liberty; has always been progressive. There has been too much hypocrisy in this country. No more hiding in cupboards for anyone, except, maybe, those caught in flagrante delicto by a too soon returning spouse. Everything out in the open. My motto throughout this parliamentary term will be,

'Make your day, become a gay.' Meanwhile, it is reported from Northern Ireland, that Lord Paisley has been seen weeping on his knees outside the Ulster Parliament where he is reputed to have said, 'History is repeating itself. It is Sodom and Gomorrah all over again.' He advised all straight people to prepare for the wrath to come and take out life insurance for surely the end is nigh.

We all hooted with laughter. Tarsey was in her element. Then she would switch from the received pronunciation of the BBC to the patois of the Dublin back streets. 'Ah, now, Michael, is it yourself I'm after seeing, at all, at all? Sure, now, you'll be after having a drap o' the hard stuff? Gargle wi' a pint o' Guinness every night and you'll never get tonsillitis and you'll never go bald.'

'Sure I'm bald already, Patrick. But I'll have the Guinness anyway. I need the nourishment after standing all day in that fecking dole queue. What kind of a country is this where they won't post a man his fecking dole money anymore? I would complain to the Ombudsman but I hear he's doing time for criminal trespass. He was caught blind drunk in the ladies' bathroom in WC2 singing, 'Stranger in Paradise.'

Now she was a cockney selling patent medicines at a stall in Petticoat Lane. 'No more constipition, Lidies and Gentlemen. Two of these little pink pills first thing in the mawning wiv your weeties and you can be sure to 'ang loose for the rest o' the die. Drink two spoonfuls o' my special pepped up Viagra mixture before going to bed, gentlemen, and you'll be twice the man. Your lidey wife will neva leave ya and neva let you go. Buy two bottles, git one free, wiv a rock solid guarantee. Try a spoonful now and see but stiy well awai from me.'

And so she went on. Tarsey would have earned a living any day of the week as a stand-up comic. She was the clown of the class during lectures. But she wasn't a clown. Tarsey was very switched on. She knew about life. Knew about people. She didn't top the class in nursing theory but she did in practical nursing. And she was kind. The care of her patients was her whole focus in life. She knew when to put her arms round a patient and hug them out of a self-destructive frenzy. She knew when to keep them at arm's length and talk a language they would understand, and understand very, very clearly.

If there was a panic on and any member of staff was in danger, Tarsey would drop everything and rush to the scene. She was always loyal and true. We all felt much safer with Tarsey around. Generally, mental hospitals are quite pleasant places to work. The majority of our patients had nervous disorders which showed themselves, mainly, in an inability to cope with the stresses and strains of everyday living. All some of them needed was a haven where they could be sheltered for a time from the heartaches and the thousand naturals shocks that flesh is heir to. Usually, a few weeks, sometimes only a few days, with us and they would be restored to a state of mind where they could face up to the problems that caused their breakdown. Sometimes, there were patients with deep-rooted problems whose treatment was spread over several months. Some were so ill they could not safely be discharged and would remain with us for the best part of their lives. Some were suicidal and had to be continually watched lest they took their own lives. Keeping them safe from themselves could be stressful for the nursing staff. We could not relax for a second whilst they were under our care. None of those patients were dangerous, to us. What they needed was love, and love they got in abundance. The nursing staff was hand-picked to provide an environment that exuded friendliness and care. Patients were not mollycoddled; their independence was not taken away. They were continually supported so that their confidence was built up and they could learn to laugh again.

CHAPTER THIRTEEN

We were smug enough to congratulate ourselves every time a patient was returned to wellbeing and discharged back into the community. We thought we were good nurses.

The suicidal ones did cause us a problem from time to time. Millie X was one of them. Millie had had a bad run. She had arrived at the church exactly ten minutes late expecting her beau to be waiting there hopping up and down thinking that she had changed her mind only to find that it was the other way round – he wasn't there. Her agitated brother, who was to be one of the ushers, rushed to the bridal carriage frantically waving his arms and told the driver to go round the block. Four times round the block and there was still no sign of the groom. A search party was sent in haste to find where he was but he was nowhere to be found. He never did turn up. There never was any explanation other than a garbled message from his landlady saying that he had lighted out for the train station early in the morning and there wouldn't be a wedding. Millie collapsed. A week later she was our patient in the worst state of depression any of us had seen in a previously high-spirited young woman. She had to be placed on suicide watch twenty four hours a day. It was a slow process but she gave us the impression that she was coming out of her depression to the point where her surveillance was downgraded to ordinary. We began to think that she would be as good as new in another couple of months or so and were beginning to congratulate ourselves on another cure. Then one day, by a trick, she was permitted into the grounds of the hospital. She didn't waste a minute; she hared it straight to the scaffolding surrounding the new extension to the hospital. She sprinted past the guard at the gate. Before anyone could stop her she was climbing the scaffolding until she was right at the very top. There she calmly walked out along a girder and sat down with her legs dangling over the side. The gate-keeper was frantic. He had failed in his duty and was at his wit's end for two reasons both of which were going to cost him dearly. He was a married man with three young children and this lapse was going to cost him his job and how could he live with himself if Millie jumped? He shouted at her to stop and had begun to pursue her up the scaffolding when it came to him that he was dealing with an inmate from the 'looney-bin' and it would do no good. If he pursued her she would surely jump then he really would be in trouble. The only sensible thing to do was to dial 999 and call the police. The police, fire service and an ambulance were on the scene within minutes of his call. But what was to be done? Millie was out at the end of that girder, all anyone could do was stand and watch. Well, not totally. In these cases a trained negotiator is usually called in. An urgent call had an expert in such cases on the way but she would not arrive for at least an hour. Millie would most likely jump into oblivion before then. The fire service piled kapok-filled bags around the spot where she was likely to hit the ground whether she jumped or just simply fell. All the watchers held their breath.

Tarsey was just coming out of the locked ward when she heard someone shout, 'Millie has done a runner! She's at the top of the scaffolding!' Tarsey dropped the papers she was carrying, raced outside and looked up. She could see Millie standing at the very edge of the girder. No longer was she sitting dangling her legs over the end. A strong gust of wind and she would be over.

There was a police officer standing keeping the gawkers and gratuitous assistants away from the gate. Tarsey came running up to him, showed him her hospital identification and gasping said she had been sent to assist, that she had training in these matters. The police officer said that a negotiator was on the way and no other person was permitted access to the area. Tarsey said, 'He gave me permission,' and pointed to a police inspector standing nearby. When the police officer turned round to look where she was pointing Tarsey skipped round him and dashed for the base of the scaffolding. She was already climbing and out of his reach by the time it dawned on him that he had been tricked. Shouting, 'I'm coming, Millie, hang on!' Tarsey began to climb. Tarsey feared nobody and nothing, nothing except only one thing, heights. Just looking over Vauxhall Bridge down into the water took her breath away. She knew now that she must not look down. Climbing steadily she reached the level where Millie stood. All the time she shouted, 'I's acoming, honeychile. I's acoming. You just wait right der for me. I needs to talk to you.' Millie watched fascinated. Did someone really care this much about her? Now Tarsey was at the girder and couldn't help looking down. When she did she saw a blur of white faces, mouths agape, all looking up at her. Her whole world swung sickeningly. She found herself retching. Beads of perspiration formed on her forehead not from exertion but from sheer fright. She sat down astride the girder with a plop. She had to pull herself together else all her efforts would be in vain. If she went over then Millie would surely follow. Wrapping her arms around the metal she put her head down, closed her eyes and waited until everything settled and her world stopped swimming. Then, something strange happened. She felt a hand caressing her head and thought she was hallucinating. She turned her head, opened her eyes and looked up. Millie was kneeling beside her saying, 'There! There! It's all right, Nurse Horrigan, you're quite safe now. I won't let anything happen to you. I'm sorry. I flipped. I just wanted to end it all. I couldn't take any more but I never wanted anything to happen to you or to anyone else. Just to me. Are you all right?'

'It's the height, Millie,' whimpered Tarsey, who now saw how she could take advantage of her predicament. 'I never could take heights. I don't know how I'm going to get down now. I just can't move. I'm petrified.'

'Come on, Nurse, let me help you. Hold my hand and slide yourself backwards. We'll go down together,' said Millie.

And so it was that the roles were reversed. Instead of Tarsey helping Millie and talking her down to earth, literally, it was Millie who helped her carer back down to terra firma. There they both threw their arms around each other and shaking and weeping hugged and kissed each other until a woman police officer came and gently led both of them back to the hospital whilst all around them police, fire service personnel, ambulance crew and spectators cheered them all the way. That was the end of Millie's depression. Two weeks later she was discharged from the hospital. The hospital could then truly congratulate itself on having affected another cure.

Tarsey had the remainder of that shift off. Next day, when she reported for duty the charge nurse told her that she was to report to head office. She reported to the administrator's office. The tall, bespectacled lady was sitting behind her desk as stiff as a poker with a face as friendly as a love-starved puff adder. She told Tarsey to be seated. When Tarsey sat down there was a deathly silence for about ten seconds. Not a paper was shuffled. Not a pen was straightened, just a silence that was thunderous. Tarsey wondered what was coming but looked at the floor, said nothing and waited. She feared the worst.

Then the lady spoke.

'What you did yesterday, Nurse Horrigan, was a very brave act. A very brave act indeed, in view of the fact that I understand you have a morbid fear of heights. You very likely saved Miss X from doing herself irreparable harm. In the normal run of things what you did would, undoubtedly, have called for an award of some kind. I have been authorised to tell you that the entire hospital board is most impressed by what you have done and each member sends you their congratulations and thanks. However, that being said, we have a problem. You see, at the moment, because of the privacy laws appertaining to the treatment of our patients, Miss X is protected, rightly protected I might add, from any publicity that might reflect on her mental state to the great embarrassment of her and her family. All the media in its many forms know at this stage is that a young female was rescued from the top of a tall building yesterday. They may have heard many stories but they have no exact knowledge of what actually happened. We have had many enquiries from the local press, radio and television about the matter and, up until now, we have fended them off one way or another as diplomatically as we can. You see, if this story gets out not only will Miss X be embarrassed but so will the hospital. All kinds of questions will be asked and I have no doubt that no matter what we say any comment made will be turned in such a way that we might very well end up with a commission of enquiry on our hands. All for no good purpose. All that happened was that we dropped our guard for a moment and a very depressed young lady thought to take advantage of it and so end her depression. I am advised that that depression is now under control and it is very unlikely that we shall have a repeat of what she did. It is also most unlikely that we will drop our guard again, although I am aware that our staff is human and that keeping up one hundred percent vigilance one hundred percent of the time is well nigh impossible. But we do our best. Now, Nurse, what I am asking is that you, so far as it is possible at this late stage, advise no one, and I mean no one, of what happened yesterday. That way the hospital will avoid a great deal of unwanted and unnecessary publicity and we will be able to do what we do best, get on with looking after our patients. What do you say to that?'

Tarsey didn't have to think. She replied immediately. She raised her head and looked into the long pale face of Miss Haffard staring unblinking at her and said, ''Sfunny thing, Miss Haffard, I can't remember what happened yesterday. You see I keep getting these bouts of amnesia and I lose a whole day now and then. I'll have to stop drinking that home-brew they make in the nurses' quarters. I think it might have something to do with it.' And she laughed that deep throaty infectious laugh of hers.

For the first time since the interview began Miss Haffard visibly relaxed. The stiffness went out of her body, the long face cracked into a smile, the smile became wider, then she threw her head back and laughed with relief. Her immediate worries were at an end. She knew, like everyone else, that Tarsey could be relied upon. Tarsey looking at her thought, 'The old biddy is human after all. If she carries on like this her spectacles will start laughing in a minute.' When they had both stopped laughing Miss Haffard became serious again and said, 'There is another matter that the board asked me to bring up with you Nurse Horrigan. I could not bring it up with you before lest it be thought I was offering you some kind of inducement. But I have it from your supervisor that you have been doing exemplary work on the wards for a considerable period of time, sufficient in itself to earn you a medal but you will not get a medal. What you will get, with the blessing of the board, is a two week holiday on the Greek isles with air-fares, hotel accommodation and food, fully funded by the hospital. You can begin that holiday anytime you like, at your convenience. What do you say to that?'

'What a wonderful offer that is, Miss Haffard,' replied Tarsey. 'But I must decline it. You see, all of us on the wards do our best to look after the patients who become our friends. Their recovery is medal enough and reward enough for all of us. None of us would have it any other way.' Then she said with a roguish grin on her face, 'There is one thing, though, I would like Miss Haffard, after that climb yesterday,' and she waited long enough to cause Miss Haffard to ask, with a quizzical look on her face, 'And what would that be, Nurse Horrigan?'

'A new set of lingerie,' replied the impish Tarsey.

CHAPTER FOURTEEN

Apart from those patients who were likely to do themselves harm there was one class for whom the greatest care of all was required, as much for the safety of the staff as for the wellbeing of the 'guests'. They were the involuntary patients who were extremely dangerous: alleged murderers, rapists, arsonists, drug addicts and the ones given to violence. People who had been referred to us by the courts for assessment. These were people who were either genuinely mad or who pretended to be mad to escape the consequences of their crime. A murderer who was genuinely mad was dangerous because of the strong likelihood that they would murder again not knowing that what they were doing was wrong. They sometimes thought they were under threat and had to protect themselves from some wild animal or demon that had existence only in the dark recesses of their extremely disturbed minds. But the most dangerous of all was the murderer who was not mad but pretended they were to cheat long years of imprisonment. They were extremely cunning and watchful. They studied each member of staff until they knew, almost, how each member of staff thought. They had nothing else to do. Every little idiosyncrasy of staff, how they moved, walked, talked, breathed, coughed, laughed, stood, bent, straightened, was all noted, absorbed and filed away for future use. Those patients looked for strengths and weaknesses; those who could be manipulated and those who couldn't. Particularly did they watch for the new trainee who was more trustful and who would be sure to drop their guard sometime during that long twelve hour shift.

The violent and dangerous patients and those who would not stay in an open ward and wanted to run away were kept in the locked area where only the most experienced staff was ever allowed to work. All staff carried three alarms that would bring help at the double as soon as one or the other of them was activated. Of these the most important was the snatch alarm which, when the cord was pulled would alert every member of staff anywhere in the hospital that there was a violent act occurring which required urgent help immediately. Then there was the alarm with the yellow button which, when pressed, would alert staff near at hand that help was needed. What was called the 6666 alarm was reserved for medical or psychiatric emergencies, such as when a patient had a life-threatening physical collapse of some kind or violent psychiatric episode. I don't know why it was but in all the time I had been at the hospital I knew of no instance where Tarsey had activated any of her alarms. Maybe it was just good luck, maybe it wasn't? Maybe it was the way she was able to handle people? She had that happy knack of being able to be friendly without being familiar. She had that aura about her that exuded confidence and strength. Nobody would ever want to take Tarsey on. There were less formidable ones to be groomed or hoodwinked into vulnerability.

Two nurses, one male, one female, the male older and experienced, the female on her first day in the locked wing, were in the exercise yard with an alleged murderer in for psychiatric assessment. Young Carla Mason was being shown the ropes by James Oakford. James was an old hand. He kept a firm but light rein on his charges. Didn't crowd them too much. Gave them a little room. The object was to make them feel free when they weren't. James and Carla walked one on each side of their man. Usually, patients were taken into the exercise yard for safety reasons one at a time so that they could have a glimpse of the sky. The supervising psychiatrist believed that all patients, so far as possible, should have a look at the sky at least once a day. To deprive them of that was likely to hinder their recovery and drive them further into the darkness that would destroy their sense of reality. 'Let them taste the day' she said. 'No human being should be kept in a cage in the darkness of the interior of a building for longer than 24 hours without the opportunity to walk and talk with another human being. Feeling the day was important to every animal; the human and non-human alike. We must not lose sight of our humanity and deprive those in our care of their's.' The supervising psychiatrist was a wonderful lady, with the greatest regard for those under her care. Occasionally, very occasionally, those in her care would attempt to take advantage of her humanity. They were not psychiatrists and did not think like psychiatrists. They were very cunning animals. This day was one of those rare occasions when a very cunning animal sought to take advantage of the humanity extended to him.

It was his fourth week in the locked wing. He knew the routine very well. He was walking up and down apparently quite docile when, almost nonchalantly, he withdrew his handkerchief from his trousers pocket to blow his nose. He had a sideways glance to his right and left as he wiped his nose. Then he dropped the handkerchief and bent down to pick it up. As he straightened he kicked the legs from under Carla on his left and with both hands bunched together punched James with great force under the chin. James heard the crack of his own jaw breaking even as he dropped to the ground unconscious. Then the patient kicked Carla in the face as she scrambled to get up and pull her snatch alarm cord at the same time. She pulled the cord just as the shoe connected with her chin. She fell backwards across James's prostrate body. Now the patient was running at the twelve foot wooden wall that gave on to the street and freedom. He was a tall man, 186 centimetres, skinny and very agile. He had managed, by some act of extreme agility, to grasp the top of the wall and was in the act of pulling himself up and over when Tarsey entered the fray. She took in at a glance her fallen comrades then, without a break in her stride, she threw herself at the legs trying to kick themselves up the wall. She locked her arms around them then threw herself backwards. She didn't have to worry about her fear of heights here. The patient's reluctant fingers were torn from the top of the wall and he came with her. Tall and well-padded she might be but she was as agile as an Olympic-trained athlete. Nobody was going to assault her friends and colleagues and get away with it. Care had two aspects, there was care for the patients and there was care for the carers. The cared-for must learn that they, too, must be caring. That surely was part of their rehabilitation. As soon as she hit the ground she did a roll on to her face, was up on all fours, then on her feet as the patient began to rise. Tarsey was just that fraction ahead of him that gave her the edge. As he regained his feet Tarsey threw her arms around him in what was not a loving embrace and kneed him hard in the groin, then she kneed him again, just to be sure. He gave an uggghhh! and began to slide to the ground. It didn't seem that he wanted to climb that wall anymore. Tarsey was too old a fox to fall for old tricks. She knew there was a possibility, faint though it might be, that in spite of that double knee type immobiliser he was pretending to some extent and still had some fight left in him. She still kept her arms locked around him and was preparing to give him another sleeping draught in the groin when two male nurses followed by two doctors arrived on the scene. Then she released her grasp on him and went to the aid of her two prostrate colleagues, saying as she did so, 'What took you so long?'

The assessment of the patient, for the court's better understanding of his mental state, was delayed whilst he recovered, under armed guard, in the local general hospital, from the damage to his lower appendages. Then he was transferred to another mental institution, lest it be suggested that any further assessment in his present environs might be less than impartial. Six months later he was found fit to stand trial, was convicted by a judge and jury of murder and sentenced to life imprisonment.

And he is still there. I wonder if he is thinking of the Stockholm Syndrome? I wonder if he is falling in love with his jailers?

James Oakford had several weeks taking nourishment though a tube whilst his broken jaw healed. Carla, after three weeks off duty, during which her swollen face returned to normal, and she received counselling she said she didn't need, was happy to be back on the wards again. Next time she walked a patient in the exercise area Tarsey was by her side.

There was an internal enquiry. Tarsey appeared before the Board. That same Board which had offered her an all expenses paid trip to the Greek islands. She was asked if it had been necessary to use such force to deter the patient.

Very quietly, in her best accentless English, Tarsey said, 'I would respectfully ask members of the Board to look at it this way, there was an alleged murderer who had just assaulted two members of staff, my friends and colleagues, who was scaling a twelve foot wall and was on the point of escape. To allow him to escape would probably have put at risk other innocents. I could not allow that to happen. I used such force as was necessary to prevent his escape and restrain him. Care of the patient is one thing, idiocy is another.' The Board smiled. End of enquiry.

Publicity was again kept to a minimum lest it would in some way have influenced the trial jury or caused the general public to lose confidence in the security of its mental hospitals so far as the holding of dangerous criminals was concerned. Tarsey was given a two hundred and fifty pound bonus and the height of the wall increased to fifteen feet. Things returned to normal.

CHAPTER FIFTEEN

Casting my mind back to the thrills and spills of being a mental health nurse and working with people like Tarsey kept me focused. Oh Tarsey, if you were only here now, what would you do? What could you do? Would you have accepted being tied hand and foot by a sex maniac? I could almost hear Tarsey's reply, 'Hold on, Elizabeth, honey chile. Watch him, as those wily patients watch us. He'll drop his guard sooner or later, have no doubt about it. Give him confidence. Make him think he has complete dominium over you, body and soul. Cause him to drop his guard. Work on his vanity. Look for a weapon. There must be something you can use as a weapon.'

How can I look for a weapon in the pitch blackness, Tarsey? I can see nothing. Nothing at all. I can't even see to the end of my nose. I'm a miner down that goldmine I told you about in Kalgoorlie. Restful to the eyes the darkness might be but is it not restful to the mind. I'm a trapped animal. I have no hope of rescue. I am going to die. When I do see the light I'll be dazzled, blinded, and I won't have any sunglasses.

Am I losing my marbles? I'm beginning to think I am lost. I must not think that way. Capitulate after one or two days as a hostage, not me. I had willed Tarsey there to give me strength and that's what she was doing. I was not going mad. One mad person in this house was enough. We didn't need two. Tarsey was here in this room with me. I could see her laughing eyes, now full of concern for me. I tried to will her back at the hospital to know that all was not well with me. To know where I was and come and rescue me. I knew she would if she could. Tarsey was a peoples' person. Is there such a thing as telepathy? The Tibetan monks seem to think there is. I knew I was clutching at straws, but there was nothing else to clutch at. There had been times in the past when my mother had told me that she had been thinking of me at the same time as I was thinking about her, and us both on different continents. I lay and concentrated. If will-power could achieve what I wanted then Tarsey would come.

Aches and pains were intruding themselves in to my thoughts. I was becoming stiff and sore from lying very much in the same position. I was pinioned on my back. I needed exercise. If I didn't have exercise, when an opportunity presented itself to attempt an escape I wouldn't have the strength to take advantage of it. I needed to keep my strength up. Lie like this for too long and I soon wouldn't be able to walk to the bathroom then I really would be out of the contest. How could I exercise tied as I was? I could bend my knees very well even though my feet were tied together but as my arms were tied to each side of the bed I could move them very little. Never say die, Elizabeth. Move the parts you can. Breathe deep, big breaths. Think positive. Be brave. Tarsey would have found a way.

I moved my legs up and down, up and down, up and down. Slowly at first then faster and faster. My breathing speeded up. My heart began to beat faster. I was fighting back. I stopped moving my legs and worked on my arms. I could move them only a few inches but that was enough. I had to move them one at a time but I was moving them. I moved my head up and down, rotated my neck, I took deep breaths. I was not going to lie quietly like a sheep waiting for its throat to be cut. I was not a sheep. I was a healthy, resilient young woman. No madman, no sadistic sex maniac, for that was what he was, was going to beat me. Not without a fight. I would keep my strength. I stopped and lay exhausted. I was perspiring. That was good.

Then I thought about my bonds. If I could only reach them with my teeth, my good strong teeth, I would chew through them like the fox caught in a trap. My father had often told about the fox he had shot. He said it had one foot missing. Obviously, it was the fox to which that foot belonged that had been found in the trap several months previously. What animals will do just to live? I shuddered at the thought. Even if I could have reached my bonds with my teeth I wouldn't have chewed my hand off. My hands were precious to me and I would need both to fight back with when the time came. Oh, how I would love to free myself and be waiting for him when he came through the bedroom door. Wouldn't he get a shock? A shock like the one he gave me when he burst through my door.

I was a trained mental health nurse. Trained in how to treat the sick mind. How to be kind and, above all, caring. Yet here I was lusting after revenge. How I hated him for doing this to me. My anger was welling up again. I had to keep it under control otherwise I would be blinded by it and destroy myself. Nothing like being in the position of the victim, the hapless, hopeless, innocent victim to have a better perspective. I had to stay in charge of my own mind no matter what. And that recurring dream, what about it? It kept coming back into my mind. Dr Wilderman obviously knew something about the reason for it, or thought he did. What did it mean? How many times had I promised myself I would go to the local library and request one of Freud's books on dreams but always found I had something more pressing to do? I would ask Dr Wilderman to tell me what it meant. Maybe that was what he wanted? He really was screwing me up. I didn't know what to do. I didn't want to ask him but I did want to know.

Now, I needed to go to the bathroom again, very badly. That kept me focused. What was I going to do? I held my breath and counted to one hundred, then I started all over again. I was becoming desperate when the door opened. He was back again. I was very glad.

'I'm so sorry, Elizabeth, that I was longer than I intended. There was an traffic accident on Great Eastern Highway. A motorcycle had collided with a truck. The pillion passenger had a ruptured artery in her leg and I had to assist. I couldn't get away any sooner.'

Now he was the good doctor again, showing me how much he cared. Someone whom he doesn't know, whom he meets at random on the road, receives the benefit of his medical knowledge and care whilst I, with whom he works every day, he keeps locked up, tied up and in the dark. What category of diseases of the mind does that put him in? Robert Louis Stevenson wrote a story about a person like him. He called it 'Doctor Jekyll and Mr Hyde'. It was an illustration of two personalities, the good and the bad, in one person. Was Dr Jekyll a stereotype for Dr Wilderman and, if he were, how did that help me? Apart from showing that I had, very likely, placed him in the right box, not in the least. I had it right only if he were telling the truth and I doubted that. There may have been no accident and his telling me that there was one was only to throw me off track. Keep me confused so I couldn't figure him out. Blow hot and cold, show what a good guy he was and I would be in a constant state of disorientation. I had no sooner worked out that he was one thing when he sought to show that he was another. If I had attended to anyone injured in a road traffic accident where there was a spillage of blood, the first thing I would have done when I arrived home would be to jump into the shower and scrub. I would scrub, particularly my hands and arms which would have been in closest contact with the blood. Doctors and nurses and all other people involved in the health industry are only too well aware of the danger of contamination from blood-borne diseases: Aids, HIV, hepatitis, are too prevalent too ignore. Yet I couldn't smell any soap off him. He appeared to be naked again, for I couldn't hear the rustle of clothes but that would have enabled me to smell, more acutely, any soap or antiseptic substance, such as methylated or surgical spirits, that a doctor would use at the earliest opportunity after such an incident. And he didn't smell wet. I took what he had to say about an accident with a pinch of salt. Maybe he had never left the house? I wondered just then if it were possible for him to see into this room from another part of the house? Was there a window, a tinted window, through which he could see every move I made?

No, there couldn't be, he couldn't see what I was doing, not in the dark. Oh, yes, he could. He could if he had a pair of those night-goggles that soldiers use to see in the dark. No. No. He couldn't do that. I'm becoming paranoid, he is driving me crazy. No, he isn't, he's just making me think. Anyone who would go to the lengths he has gone to to make sure that he had covered his tracks in every way would find no difficulty in obtaining night-goggles. All he would have to do would be to go to the Army and Navy Stores and make enquiries. If they didn't have them, I'm sure they could get them for him. This man thought of everything. Of course, I had to be careful I didn't overestimate him for then he would have achieved complete dominance over me. I wouldn't be able to move even when he was not in the room. I would be spiritually hamstrung as well as physically so. I wondered if he had been watching me all the time when he said he had been out. If he had, then he would have seen me exercising. Now, more than ever, I would have to listen more carefully to everything he said just in case he let slip the least indication that he had me under observation all the time. I thought grimly that I could not afford to be complacent, after all it was only my hands and feet that were bound, not my mind. 'I suppose you need to go to the bathroom' he said.

'Very badly,' I said.

'You poor dear. I'm so sorry,' he said. He took me there immediately. Then he fetched me something to eat; another delicious meal. Every time he switched on the torch I saw that skeleton at the end of the bed. It really was beginning to get on my nerves. It was beginning to be that I hated it as much as I hated him and I didn't care if it were the sad remains of a previous victim. It was intimidating me. When I had finished he asked me if I were comfortable.

I answered, 'How could anyone be comfortable tied hand and foot, naked, in the dark? No, I am not comfortable. Would you keep a patient tied up like this in the hospital?'

'I most certainly would if it were necessary,' he replied. 'In your case it is necessary. I think I've already told you that and I am not going to go into it again. I am sorry you are not comfortable but it is all part of the research. I am sure that the hostages in Stockholm were not comfortable. They didn't know what was going to happen to them. They didn't know if their captors were going to kill them. There was always the chance that if the Swedish police decided to rush the bank they would be killed either deliberately by their captors or injured by a stray bullet in the process. There is no danger of you being killed by a stray bullet here; neither the police nor anyone else, except you and I, know that you are here. So, just in case you are hanging on to the hope that you will somehow be rescued I can tell you now that there is no hope of that happening. The sooner you begin to cooperate, Elizabeth the sooner all this discomfort will be over. Do you understand?'

'I understand.'

'All right. Let's get on. I have many questions to ask. The first is, 'Do you think that there is such a thing as the Stockholm Syndrome or do you think it is all a myth thought up to give psychiatrists and psychologists a reason for being?'

Was he beginning to have doubts? Or was this just his way of giving me the impression that he needed my help? He didn't need my help. If there was one thing I was sure of it was that he most certainly did not need any help from me. What he wanted was my cooperation in his possession of me. That, he was not going to get. He would have to break me first, spiritually, and I did not feel like being broken. What I had to do was to give him something to think about. I didn't answer for a moment to give him the impression I was thinking. I counted slowly to twenty then I said, 'You are the psychiatrist, and you are a very good one. Your skill in handling people is almost legendary throughout the hospital, so you should know better than me. I am just one of the lower echelons. I hadn't thought much about those hostages in Stockholm up until I found myself here but

I have thought a lot about them lately. I think I know why they sided with their captors. I think there were two reasons, a) they were relieved at being alive and uninjured when the siege was at an end and b) they were kind people and felt sorry for their captors who were likely to go to prison for a long time. It may be that their captors told them all kinds of sob stories during the time that they were in such a close relationship and got them on side. I just don't know. I can't answer unless I have a full account of what happened during the time they were under siege.'

'I suppose that is a fair answer but you have referred only to the Stockholm siege; what about Patty Hearst?'

I thought I could see what he was doing. He was seeing how much I knew about both kidnapping incidents and what effect they had on me. At the same time he was confusing me with questions that made me curious. He was confusing me so I didn't know where I was. Was I being softened up? I must go carefully. I was under examination by one of the most gifted of psychiatrists who had gone rogue. I would have to make him think and show him that I, too, could think. Had been thinking. I pretended to ponder again. He knew I knew about them but how much did I know? I told him.

'As far as I remember Patty Hearst claimed that she had been kidnapped by the Symbionese Liberation Army who had held her for two months and made her take part in bank robberies with them. When caught by the police she claimed the Stockholm Syndrome. The court wasn't satisfied. She was convicted and went to prison. Is this what this experiment is about? Are you are trying to prove Patty Hearst really was innocent and actually was under the influence of the Stockholm Syndrome?'

'I am trying to prove nothing of the kind. My research is not about Patty Hearst. My research is simply to see if there is such a thing as the Stockholm Syndrome.'

'I can tell you now, there is no such thing, it just doesn't exist and because it doesn't exist your reason for holding me here is baseless.'

'Why do you say that?'

'Isn't it obvious? Look at all the people who are taken hostage and who do not fall in love with their captors. In fact, they hate those who hold them.'

'What people are they?'

'Slaves, for a start.'

Lots of slaves came to love their owners. Some of them laid down their lives for their masters.'

'One or two maybe? A lot more didn't. As far as I remember lots of slaves ran away. That did not show much love.'

'A lot didn't.'

'That was because they were in despair. They didn't know where to run. They also knew that if they did run they would be retaken, brought back and flogged. Some of those, after being flogged, committed suicide rather than live as slaves.'

'Perhaps you have a point there. But slaves are in a different category to hostages who are being held as pawns in a game where their captors are often attempting to extort something from a third party who is not loved by either captor or hostage. The hostage takers who take on a bank want instant riches and, possibly, want to have a kick at the bank at the same time. Nobody loves banks. Nobody cries, except the bankers, when a bank gets done over, not even the people who work for them. Maybe that common dislike of money grubbing bankers and their big bonuses for their fat cat executives is what caused the hostages to hug their captors in Stockholm?'

'The Stockholm siege is the only case, as far as I know, where such a phenomenon occurred. The only case. Can you base any kind of theory on one case only?'

'That's what we are trying to discover.'

'I think it is such an unusual occurrence that nothing can be based on it. Not one of the lecturers in any of the lectures I attended in the course of my training ever based their contention on one solitary instance alone. I'm sorry to say it, Doctor Wilderman, but I think you are wasting your great expertise in chasing after smoke. Just think of all the convicted prisoners in jail. Aren't they, in a sense, being held hostage? Do they hug and kiss their jailers when they are released? All those conscript soldiers who were held hostage in the army. Did they love their captors and kiss and hug them when they were released? I don't think so. Do you think that I will love you when you have released me? Well, do you?'

CHAPTER SIXTEEN

His answer made me shudder.

'Yes, I think you will. You will be so glad when I release you that you will kiss me for it.'

'Be honest, Doctor, is it that you want more that I kiss you than that you care about whether there is such a thing as the Stockholm Syndrome? If that is only what you want then I will kiss you now, if you release me. I will kiss you and hug you and then go on my holiday and never breathe a word of what has happened between us to anyone.'

I had shaken him. I knew I had. He couldn't help the audible intake of breath. He didn't expect that. I had got under his armour. Now what would he say? I had a fair idea. He would prevaricate. What else could he do?

He recovered very quickly and said, 'You don't seem to understand, Elizabeth. At the end of the day I don't want you to kiss me and hug me just to please me. If that were the case I could have had you do that at the outset. What I want is for you to kiss me and hug me because you want to. I want you to never want to leave me. To be my companion for always. I thought I had already made that clear?'

'And if I tell you that is never going to happen, what then?'

'The thing is, Elizabeth, it will happen. Not only that but you are the one who will want me to put my arms around you and hold you. Be sure of this, I will not lay a finger on you until you make it clear that that is what you want. You think I am going to force myself upon you, violate you without your consent. Isn't that what you think? Well, isn't it?'

'I don't know what to think. Isn't that usually why a man kidnaps a female? I certainly don't think you have taken me hostage purely to discover if there is such a thing as the Stockholm Syndrome. I believe there is more to it than that. You have surprised me by what you have done to me. I had thought better of you than that. I had always thought that you were the best psychiatrist in the hospital but no psychiatrist would do to anyone what you have done to me. To strip someone naked, tie them hand and foot and keep them in the dark is to strip them of their dignity and self esteem. Hardly the way to cause them to love you. Do you think I am going to love you for this?'

'Yes, I do. You see, Elizabeth, I know more about the human mind than you do. Have you ever thought why bondage is practised by those ladies who sell their favours? I don't suppose you have. Well there is something for you to think about. I'll leave you to consider that whilst I attend to other things. I have to go back to the hospital later, that road traffic accident took up a lot of my time. I'll look in on you again before I go and make sure there is nothing you need.'

'Before you leave I would like you to tell me about my recurring dream. What does it mean?'

He chuckled. 'You know what they say about curiosity, Elizabeth, it killed the cat. The meaning of that dream is something I don't think you should know.'

'It is you who have made me curious. Did you make me curious deliberately?'

He didn't answer. I could almost hear his smile.

'Now I know you are tantalising me. I must know. Please tell me what it means.'

'I think it best that you don't know.'

'It's my dream. I am entitled to know.'

'Very well, if you must know, I suppose you must. Don't blame me if it is not what you wanted to hear?'

I should have known better, He had set the trap and I had walked into it. I was doing exactly what he wanted me to do. He laughed quietly. 'According to Freud, dreams where the feeling of falling is involved indicate you are contemplating giving in to a sexual urge or impulse. Now, tell me, Elizabeth, what is your view on that?' He didn't wait for an answer. I could hear him chuckling as he got up from the chair saying, 'Now I must be off.'

I said nothing as he switched on the torch and left the room. For a second I saw the skeleton gape at me, then the door closed and he was gone. I was left speechless. I had done exactly as he knew I would. He had excited my curiosity to the point where I had to know at any price. All he had done was answer the question I had begged him to answer and in doing so he had gained a victory over me. Oh, he was so clever. So manipulative. At every step he was gaining ascendancy over me. He knew so well how the human mind works. He certainly appeared to know my mind.

I was back in the dreaded dark, again. Alone. My mind was in a turmoil. He had, indeed, told me something about myself that I would rather not have known. He could forever claim that he had tried to save me from myself but I had insisted that he tell me. I had no doubt that what he had told me was a Freudian truth. What a fool I was. I felt like crying but I wouldn't. How I longed to have my Mum and Dad there. They would certainly have sorted out this torturer. Yes, torturer he was. How I longed to have Tarsey there or Byron Osborne. Tarsey would have loved to give him a knee massage where it mattered and laugh as she was doing it.

I lay thinking about all the things he had said. He had talked about bondage and asked me to ponder it. What had bondage to do with the Stockholm Syndrome? What had bondage to do with me? In spite of my recurring dream, or Freud's analysis of it, I wasn't one of those ladies who distributed their favours for cash in hand. Nor did I contemplate being one, either for cash or pleasure. Bondage may have provided sexual gratification for those ladies and the persons who placed the bonds upon them but it was not for me. Was he insulting me? Was he humiliating me? Was he planting seeds? Was he suggesting that I was some kind of bimbo and that this whole thing was some kind of sexual game in which, subconsciously, I wanted to be involved? Was he intimating that I would come to see that and willingly enter into the spirit of it and that, eventually, I would satisfy my as yet unrecognised cravings, play the part of the fair damsel in distress and he the knight in shining armour would ride to my rescue? Was that what he meant when he said I would be the one to kiss him and hug him, and mean it, and want him to kiss me in return? I thought I had read his thinking, now I was beginning to wonder. But then, who knows the mind of the deranged? I was not a psychiatrist. I was but a lowly nurse who had much to learn about at least one brilliant human mind gone awry.

What am I going to do? Please, God, help me to think my way out of this.

The door opened. He was back again. He brought me food and drink, took me to the bathroom and then was gone. He didn't say when he would be back.

The trouble was I didn't know what time it was or whether it was day or night. I guessed that what was happening was that he worked in the hospital during the morning, did his rounds, saw his patients then came home for the afternoon. Now he had gone back to work from 6 pm to 10 pm.

I didn't know what day of the week it was or how long I had been a hostage. I had had two periods of unconsciousness, the first when he had burst into the house and had drugged me, the second when I had the shakes and he had drugged me again. I could have been here four or five days. I didn't know. I knew that the hostages in Stockholm where held for five days. I knew that Patty Hearst said she was held for two months by the SLA. I knew that Dr Wilderman said he would hold me for 'as long as it takes' but I wondered about that. Was that just to terrify me into submission? He couldn't hold me indefinitely. If he didn't break me he would become either bored or frustrated and then… I mustn't allow that to happen. Time to make a move.

Carefully, girl. Carefully. You are dealing with a very knowing psychiatrist well versed in telling the true from the false. He might be mad but that makes him all the more dangerous. Remember, this guy wants to get into your mind; is getting into your mind but wants to get into your body; wants to control you from the inside. Is pretty sure he can do that. Wants you to be his puppet without strings. You must make him think he is gaining the upper hand. You must make him think you are crumpling. Whatever you do, tell yourself that that is what you really want to do. For you pretence does not exist – pretence is reality. Relax. Loosen up. Don't lie petrified with fright. You're a nurse. Take control of your 'patient'. Take control of yourself. No good all the time asking God to help you. You know He will but He needs you to help Him get you out of this mess. You must not forget 'God helps those who help themselves'. Forget the mad doctor for a moment, think of something funny. Visit some of your friends. Get them to cheer you up. Your body might be hobbled; your spirit isn't.

CHAPTER SEVENTEEN

I'm back in London again, at the Free London Clinic for Nervous Disorders. I'm in Byron Osborne's class. It's a Wednesday afternoon and Byron is in his element. He is the centre of attention and he loves it. There is nothing about psychiatry or the inner workings of the mind here. This is a very physical class in every sense of the word. It is all about survival, about gaining control of the body. Not your own body, someone else's. We are in the gym and Byron is putting us through our paces. It is his first of six lessons. Byron never called them lectures, he wasn't that arrogant.

'My friends,' he said, in his thick Scottish burr, which even I had difficulty understanding at times, even though I came from County Antrim and we speak the nearest thing to a Scottish dialect in the British Isles without being Scottish, 'let me introduce mesel. My name is Byron Osborne. Ye can ca' me Ossie or, if you like, Jock. What you canny ca' me is B.O. Ca' me by that name an' ye will no like what I'll do to ye by way o' revenge. I might try oot one o' they new size seventeen suppositories just tae tickle your tonsils. I hae never tried one mesel but I'm sure ye'll no find them as soothing as the manufacturers claim them to be. Everybody understan' that?' There were no dissenters, so he continued. 'Good! Now, pay attention. What ye are about to learn might save ye from ending up in the general hospital or maybe even on a marble slab in the morgue. Dinny worry, I havnay lost one o' me fan club yet.' He laughed then for those of us who understood him must have been looking somewhat worried. 'What we are aboot here, the noo, is how to defend oorsels when someone has turned a wee muckle unfriendly. Some of they boys, aye and the lassies, too, ye serve, will no see ye as nurses; they will see ye as crocodiles or alligators or big hissing cats who are oot tae destroy them. They will want tae destroy ye first. Some, o' course, will be quite sane and because they are in trouble wi' the law will want to pretend that they really are mad and will just be as dangerous, maybe even mare sae. Dinny hesitate, take control o' the situation and do it as if your very life depended on it as it might very well do, ye ken. Nae matter what ye do, never trust a patient. Any patient. Ye must monitor their every move. The least apparently innocent move may hae an ulterior motive. So ye never turn your back on a patient. Dinny let them get too close either physically or emotionally. Too close physically and you might get a knee in the stomach or a head-butt on the nose. Reconstructive surgery on the nose can be embarrassing and painful. A knee in the stomach, particularly for the men, can spoil that romantic weekend in the country with the girl o' their dreams. Someone straightening up wi' lightning speed from a stooping position can smash your lower mandible. So you need to watch the position of your patient at all times. Do not relax your guard. You may get the frontal approach where they charge you. That's pretty easy tae deal wi'. Just turn aside, stick out your foot and when they hae run themselves into the ground, pull your snatch cord and jump on top o' them. You will hae enough help within seconds to make sure you are no in any great danger. Watch out for the hidden weapon. If, by some mischance, your patient gains possession of a knife and comes for you wi' it, run, and pull your snatch cord as you do. The last thing you want to do is allow yersel' or your patient to be injured but there are times when there is nothing else ye can do but use force. The rules are that ye only use such force as is necessary to regain control of the situation. If, somehow, a patient grabs ye by the throat from the front wi' both han's dinny try to release the han's. Throw up both your arms under theirs and kick them on the knees at the same time. If you are grabbed by the hair, go wi' the pull. The more ye resist the more painful it will be. If ye are grabbed around the neck from behind, throw your arms into the air and drop to the ground. Don't try to wrestle. Remember, they will hae the strength o' the psyched up and you will no. So ye need to be able to counter their every move. When all else fails gee it to them in the goolies. If your assailant is a male, that will take the wind oot o' his sails. If it is a female, well, she'll hae a sore stomach. But ye will have stopped them until help arrives.' It took a few moments for me to work that one out. I wondered what the rest of the class who were not familiar with the lingo of a native from Robert Burns's country made of that? He gave a hearty chuckle then before continuing with: 'All joking aside, what I want to impress upon ye is that we are, above all else, carers. It is no' for us to scratch mental rashes and make them worse. It is no' for us tae break bones or bodies, we are here solely for the purpose o' soothing frayed an' tattered nerves and healing broken or damaged minds. Do not allow yersel to become emotionally involved. Become emotionally involved wi' a patient and the next admission to our esteemed establishment and getting fitted oot wi' a nice tight fitting jacket will be ye. Feel sorry for them if you must but dinny let your compassion cause you to drop your guard. Do that and it may very well cost ye mental trauma that ye will never recover frey. We must never forget that we are carers. We are no' agony aunts or uncles. We are in charge here and we stay in charge even in our most relaxed moments. In spite of what the man in the street says, the patients are no' in charge and must never be. Now, let us try oot some o' they moves ye'll need to make second nature if ye are tae survive unscathed in this topsy-turvy world.'

Ossie selected several students, one at a time, and demonstrated how to counter all kinds of moves. Then he had us practise on each other. After six weeks, all of us had a pretty good idea of how to defend ourselves.

We all listened to Ossie. He was a senior nurse and he was one of us. He had spent enough time nursing the sick of body and of mind to know a lot about people. He knew most of the tricks in the bag but he was always prepared to concede that you never knew them all. 'Aye, there's a'ways somebody waiting in the wings to spring a new one on ye. That's why ye must never become complacent. People dinny realise what a dangerous an' stressful job we do here. Well, at the least the government does, that's why they pay us extra money and allow us to retire at fifty five. O' course, that early retirement's nay use to ye or me. Ye have to be in mental health nursing right from the beginning to qualify but it does show the government gets some things right.' Then he would laugh and say, 'Ye and me are no in it for the money though, are we?' He would give that droll look of his and say 'We are in it purely for altruistic reasons; for love o' oor fellow man and woman. That's why I'm told a' mental health nurses go tae heaven when they die. Although how the guy who told me that found that out I dinny know. Maybe he's been there and back?'

Ossie had spent twenty two years in the Royal Navy as a Sick Berth Attendant before retiring on pension and beginning a new career, and a new pension path, as a Registered Mental Health Nurse. Martial arts were a hobby of his and he passed on what he could to us to keep us safe. He wasn't only interested in modern martial arts he; liked the medieval ones as well. His favourite weapon was not the nun-chukka but the quarter-staff. His eyes would light up with excitement as he described how Robin Hood and Little John sharpened their skills with jousts against each other. On one occasion he brought a couple of quarter-staffs and asked for a volunteer to attack him. One of the male nurses did. The male nurse came at him very gingerly until Ossie dared him to hit him. 'There's a quid in it if ye can touch me,' he said, as he tickled his opponent under the chin with his staff. We all hooted with laughter. Then the nurse really went for him. He had us all entranced by how easy he made his defence look. He blocked and jabbed, turned, twisted and twirled so that his opponent never got near him and laughed whilst he was doing it. He had us all in the hollow of his hand. We all wanted to be martial artists, just like him. His classes were great fun.

'Nae matter where ye are,' he would say, 'always look at your immediate environment and know what is there that ye can ca' in aid if you ever need it. An umbrella, a broom shank, a hard piece o' footwear to the ankle, may just save your life. And if you are going to use an umbrella or a broom shank jab wi' it. That way you are likely to cause more pain and repel your attacker and a short, hard jab is harder to get under than a weapon raised to strike.' Ossie never had an absentee from his classes. Pity that every mental health hospital didn't have someone like him.

I loved being on the same shift as him and hearing some of his tales about his time in the Royal Navy and what sailors get up to when they go ashore in a foreign port. He would chortle as he rhymed off, 'Absence makes the girls grow blonder, forget about the girls back yonder, now's no the time to stop and ponder, grab one now or forever wonder.' 'The trouble was,' he said, 'that if some of the young innocents on their first trip abroad had stopped to ponder it might have saved them much pain when they were back at sea and that exotic sweet young thing who had taken them to her bed on that first date was just a memory. Many of those young sailors had reason to thank God for penicillin.'

I hadn't realised that so many sailors became seasick and so many suffered from that worst of all sickness, homesickness. Eventually, Ossie said, all recovered from both but there were times when homesickness drove young men to the edge of suicide. The trouble was that there wasn't a lot that could be done for them. Homesickness wasn't a disease that the Royal Navy recognised as meriting medical discharge. It was only when suicide was attempted that notice was taken. Ossie said that it was his keeping observations on young recruits going to sea and being away from home for the first time that awoke his interest in mental health.

He told me about the two young sailors, both stokers who served on the same cruiser as he did. When they had been at sea for three weeks and the remainder of the crew had got over their seasickness and their homesickness and all were pretty well settled down the two young stokers kept coming to the sickbay on some pretence or other. They complained of pains here, there and everywhere. He examined them but couldn't find anything physically wrong with them except that they were both desperately lonely and unhappy. 'Lonely on a ship among hundreds of men. Imagine it, Elizabeth. After they had both called at the sickbay seven days running I began to dig deeper,' he said. 'This wasn't physical, this was mental. They couldn't sleep, they couldn't eat, they couldn't concentrate, they cried most of the time. All they could think of was home. Each was almost a mirror image of the other. Lack of sleep caused them to make mistakes in the engine room. They were a danger to the ship. Their chief petty officer stopped them both from coming to the sickbay. Refused his permission, he did. Said they were both malingerers who didn't like the idea of work. Thought their mates should do their work for them. Either that or they were just a couple of wimps still tied to their mammy's apron strings. Well, he would cut those strings pretty damned sharpish. He wasn't going to have a couple of gutless shirkers in his engine room. He put each of them on report to the officer of the watch. The officer of the watch ordered additional work as a punishment, which, of course, only made matters worse. He told them it was time they got their act together or they would be in real trouble. When I heard they had been put on report I was troubled for I knew that those two lads needed kindness, they didn't need to be beaten about the head by a bullying CPO and an officer of the watch who had no knowledge of their background. I went to see the chief poker to find out what was going on. He was in no mood to listen. More or less said that I was making matters worse by mollycoddling them. What they needed was backbone. Anyway, who did I think I was, a doctor? The ship didn't carry a doctor, Sick Berth attendants were the only medical people aboard at that time. He wondered what I was doing in his engine room. Wasn't my place in the sickbay? There were bound to be lots of malingerers who needed a softie to give them chits saying they were fit only for light duties. What the hell was the Royal Navy coming to? It wasn't like that when he had joined.

Well, the two 'malingerers' or wimps or whatever they were got their act together that same night. The night watchman found them both lying in each other's arms under a table on the mess deck. The night watchman saw two empty whisky bottles lying beside them and wondered where they had obtained the drink. He thought they had drunk themselves into oblivion. That was, undoubtedly, their intention but not in the way the night watchman thought. There had been no joy in their drinking. Suicide was their aim. He tried to rouse them but couldn't. He sought help. When they were carried to the sickbay I examined them and found that they were both suffering from acute alcoholic poisoning. Neither of them were drinkers yet they had managed to down a full bottle of whisky each. I pumped out their stomachs and did my best to save them; then I prayed. I had done all I could. They were lucky, they survived. When I asked them both afterwards why they did it and, playing the religion card which sometimes worked, wondered aloud if they were not afraid of going to hell when they died, each said the same thing in a different way. They said that they were in hell already and any other hell had to be better than the one they were in.

'The story ended happily, Elizabeth. I managed to write a report without any mention of attempted suicide in it. I said that they were both suffering from extremely high levels of stress and as far as I could see, mental health nursing not being my area of expertise, these young men were psychologically unsuited to life at sea and never would be suitable and should be returned to their families as quickly as possible lest they became a liability on the service and maybe the subject of a public enquiry. The powers-that-be got the idea. I think that they feared there might be a leak to the media and that scared them. The armed services don't like commissions of enquiry. With a nod here and a wink there the report went through a lot of channels, including protracted psychiatric and psychological examinations. What to do with them was the question? One thing was certain, nobody wanted a couple of potential suicides on their watch. Five months later they were both discharged, 'Medically Unfit For Naval Service'. They were home again. I know this only because I had a letter from one of them telling me what had happened and thanking me for what I had done. I had done nothing but my job, Elizabeth. Looking back on it afterwards I realised why they came to me in the sickbay every day. They found someone there who was kind and who cared about them. Can't beat a little kindness, Elizabeth. That's something none of us in this work should forget. It was that little episode that brought me into mental health nursing.'

'There was one little aside to that episode that never got into the official reports. What wasn't said was that the two bottles of whisky had been stolen from the chief petty officer's little stash which he kept secreted in his locker. In view of the part he had played in the episode he thought it better that he keep quiet on that. He never again, during my time on his ship, stopped any of the crew under his supervision in the engine room from coming to see me in the sickbay.'

Ossie's story kept me from thinking of myself and my dire situation. I was lucky to have a friend like him. Oh, if only he were here now! He and Tarsey together would soon bring my life back to normal again.

CHAPTER EIGHTEEN

My thoughts turned to Tarsey again and that time when the drug addict had cut up rough and… The door opened. He was back. Tarsey would have to wait until later but she would never be far away.

Without any introduction at all he said, 'Time to eat, Elizabeth. I don't know how those other hostages did for food and drink but I can assure you that whilst you are my hostage you will be well fed. Would you like to go to the bathroom before you eat?'

I said I would and after I had washed my hands and face and returned to the bed he brought me another beautiful meal. After I had eaten he cleared away the tray and sat down.

'Do you know a Theresa Horrigan?' he asked.

My heart leapt. Did I know Tarsey! What was he up to now? Was he able to read my mind? I began to wonder. Maybe he drugged me when I was asleep, injected me with a truth drug and then questioned me so that I told everything? 'Don't be silly, Elizabeth,' I told myself. 'You're letting him get to you. He has done nothing of the kind. Don't think that way. Take it that you are aware of everything that is going on and that you are ahead of him. Go with the flow. Lie back and listen. You know that Tarsey was still in London last time you heard from her. He didn't know her.' I steadied myself. As far as I could recall, I had never mentioned Tarsey to him. I wondered how to answer then thought, 'What's the use, I'll go with the truth, whatever he's up to will soon become apparent.

I said, 'Yes, I know Theresa Horrigan.'

'I know you do,' he replied. 'She has applied to us for a nursing position at the hospital and has given your name as a referee. Says she would like to join you in the sun.'

My heart leapt again. My breathing quickened. Tarsey had received my calls for help. I knew she would. Telepathy really does work. I could hardly believe it. I had to take command of my breathing. I mustn't let him see how excited I was.

'I am surprised at that, Doctor. She has never mentioned it to me at any time. Last I heard she was very happy in London where she was near her parents. I didn't think she would ever leave the Free London. She was so happy there. I can tell you, Doctor, you will never meet a better nurse.'

'I already have. I have met you. Maybe Nurse Horrigan didn't want to tell you she was thinking of joining you here although she must have guessed that in giving your name as a referee we would have to contact you. I am, of course, unable to tell the Hospital Board that I am presently in contact with you but I shall agree to her application being progressed as far as possible before you return from your holidays and if everything else is in order then, and you support her application, she will be here in no time. What do you think of that?'

I still could hardly believe it. It was really too good to be true. Was he blowing hot and cold with me? With his labyrinthine mind it was hard to know when he was telling the truth or otherwise. Now was my time to begin to turn him around.

'I think it's wonderful. Oh, you are so good, Caspar. I knew I had assessed you properly. You *are* a good man.'

I slipped the Caspar in as if it had come out spontaneously. There was no better time than now when he thought I was excited about the possibility that Tarsey would be joining the staff at the hospital. I had thought about it very carefully. It had not been my intention to call him by his first name until some more time had passed. Be too quick and he would be suspicious. He would still be suspicious but I might overcome it by appearing to act without thinking about it. I knew I had struck a cord for he responded immediately.

'Did you call me Caspar, Elizabeth, or did I just imagine it?'

I thought I could detect the slightest quaver in his voice. I had to play it carefully now. Appear confused, unsure.

'I'm.. I'm.. I'm sorry, Doctor, I didn't intend to. I wasn't thinking. It just slipped out. I'm sorry...'

'Please don't apologise, my dear. I am delighted. Do you think you could do it again?' and he laughed, an easy, almost infectious laugh.

So it was 'my dear' now. Maybe I had him fooled? Softly. Softly, Elizabeth.

'Well, I'm really not sure. It's rather difficult to call someone by the first name who has taken you hostage. I'll have to think about it.'

'Take as long as you like, Elizabeth, but remember this, the longer you take, the longer you will be my hostage, not my friend.'

'But I am your friend, Doctor. I was always your friend and I thought you were mine. I had always thought of you as a kind man, the kindest in the hospital. I always looked up to you. I am sure that your research means a lot to you and I am sure you are a very dedicated researcher but I have to repeat that your research is flawed. The setting can't be anything like Stockholm. In Stockholm the hostage-takers were as trapped in the bank as their hostages. They were all together and had the opportunity to study each other and understand each other. Here you can come and go as you like. I can't. I am in the dark. So are you.' I put a tremor in my voice then. It wasn't too difficult because I really did hate and fear the dark. I was sure he would pick that tremor up. I knew he was analysing me continually. Maybe the darkness helped him to do that. He could catch every quaver in my voice as well as keeping me in terror. I hoped he didn't realise that I had baited the hook. I had my anger under control. I would get him under my control, too. This madman was not going to beat me. I continued, 'We are both naked, yet we can't see each other. What is that going to prove? Only the fact that I saw you at work in the hospital allows me to know what a good man you are. I just don't understand any of this. I just can't see how there can be any rapport between us under these conditions? Why don't you at least untie me and put on the light so that we can see each other. I don't think I would mind the nakedness so much now. I have seen many naked people in the hospital, including the most virile of men. You can keep the doors locked. I won't try to escape. If I am to be the guinea pig in an experiment I would like the experiment to be as close to reality as possible. That way it might be worthwhile and it might be over much more quickly?'

He didn't seem to realise I had stopped speaking, or maybe he was assessing what I had just said for he didn't speak for what seemed like a lifetime then he said, 'As usual, you may be quite right, Elizabeth. You are a clever girl. But then, you see, you are the nurse, I am the doctor. I know what I'm doing. We will continue as we are. You have called me Caspar once although you didn't mean to - things are coming along nicely. I am sure you will call me Caspar again, and it won't just slip out, you will mean it.'

Even as he spoke I was analysing what I had said, and what he had said. Did I get it right? I wanted him to think I was so afraid of the dark. I would

have done almost anything to be in the light. I had told him that. That was
what he wanted to hear - him, the best doctor in the hospital. Everybody
loves flattery. They may not admit it but they do. It takes a very aware and
very strong person to resist flattery. The expression of fear and flattery
together would make him think that my will was being overborne by his.
I hoped I hadn't overdone it. You see, what he wanted was for me to be
utterly dependent upon him. He wanted to destroy my persona and for
me to be completely dominated by him. He wanted my thinking to be his
thinking. He wanted me to be his slave, his owned thing. That, I would
never be.

Now I had to try a little more psychological massage.

'It's not fair that you leave me here on my own for such long periods. That
didn't happen in Stockholm; the hostage-takers were always there. Why
don't you stay and talk to me more; tell me about yourself?'

His answer was instantaneous. 'Because, Elizabeth, this experiment is
not about me, it's about you. You see, I know myself. I don't know you.
Not the way I want to but I will. And, of course, the hostage-takers in
Stockholm did not have to go to work like I do. That is why I have to leave
you on your own for long periods. Believe me, I would love to be with
you all the time. I can think of nothing I would enjoy more. You are such
an exceptional person.'

It was then that I began to notice the pain in my stomach. I had the slightest
touch of cramp. As we spoke the cramps grew in intensity. Then I badly
needed to go to the bathroom. I interrupted our conversation to tell him. I
said that if I didn't get to the bathroom quickly we would have a problem.
He didn't seem surprised. He quickly unhooked me and led me to the
bathroom, just in time. When I was finished he brought me back to the
bed but I was no sooner in it than I had to go again. Five times in quick
succession he had to take me there. I found it extremely embarrassing.
Strangely enough, he didn't seem to mind. Had he put something in the

food? Was this another way of grinding me down. Weaken me physically and I would be weakened spiritually as well.

The exemplary bedside manner was back. He couldn't do enough for me. He knew that my diarrhoea was genuine. Well, he would, if he had induced it. If he hadn't it would be quite obvious to him that I was not pretending.

'You poor thing. You really have caught some bug or other. I'll get you some Imodium' He left the room but was quickly back with the Imodium. He held up my head whilst I took it. Then he gave me a glass of water. That day he never left me except to fetch more Imodium. Had I been in the intensive care unit of the best general hospital in the country I could not have received better care. The diarrhoea eventually did stop after I had taken enough of the medication to block the Channel Tunnel. I lay exhausted.

'You poor dear,' he said. 'I'm so sorry you are ill but I think you are over the worst of it. Now you must try to get some rest. Just close your eyes and relax. I will not leave you. I'll be right here beside you should you need me.'

No wonder we all thought he had the best bedside manner in the hospital. Pity he was mad.

CHAPTER NINETEEN

I closed my eyes and drifted off into a deep sleep. Now I was walking a tightrope far above something indefinable that attracted and repelled me at the same time. I didn't know what it was but I urgently wanted to know; needed to know. I wanted to know whether I should love it or hate it but at the same time I was afraid. Something inside me was telling me that I had no need to be afraid, that whatever it was was just like a nettle which, when touched lightly, causes irritation. What I had to do was reach out and grasp it fearlessly and firmly and it would be like grasping silk. If I did that all my fears would be allayed. I would know happiness like I had never known it before. Still, I couldn't bring myself to make that leap. Then, suddenly, the rope snapped and I was falling again. I yelled out and awoke with a start.

I heard a voice saying, 'That dream again, Elizabeth?' Dr Wilderman was still sitting beside the bed. He was into my mind again. I'm sure he knew what I had been dreaming. He didn't wait for an answer but continued, 'It's about your inner self and an inhibition you will have to shrug off. Take that leap, Elizabeth. Come into the world where I live. Let me get rid of that dream for you. In my world you will have reality. When you reach out and touch what for you has been the untouchable up to now you will never have that dream again. You see, I know about these things.'

I didn't know what to say. What could I say? I was in the Never Never Land where I was a lonely, innocent, little girl. I knew nothing. I didn't respond to what he said. I just asked to go to the bathroom again and he took me there using the flashlight to guide the way. That damned skeleton still grinned at the end of the bed. When we came back he brought me a glass of iced water. I let its iciness trickle down my throat. It tasted better than champagne. I began to feel better; at least that awful diarrhoea was gone. He sat at the side of the bed and said nothing. My thoughts turned once more to Tarsey. Would she soon be here? Would I ever see her again?

I thought of her as I remembered her in the Free London going round the patients, weighing them up and telling me during break-time what she thought of them all. She seemed to know the ones who were putting on an act, for whatever reason, and the ones who were genuinely ill. The women suffering from post natal depression; the young mothers who had had half a dozen kids, one on top of each other, and just couldn't cope any longer; the high-powered executive who worked night and day to make a profit for the shareholders then collapsed in a heap when the pressure became too much; the genuine hard-worker who battered their way out of the blue-collar and into the white collar area, an area to which they were completely unsuited and as a result crashed. Tarsey had a feeling for those people and wanted nothing more than to nurse them back to health again. A large part of a mental health nurse's work is the application of kindness and that part Tarsey knew from A to Z. Sometimes a spontaneous hug does more good to the distressed than all the medication contained in hypodermic syringes and little white pills, or electric convulsive therapy, or ECT as we generally call it. There were other times, happily rare times, when no medication, hugs or cuddles had the curative powers of a firmly applied word of warning. Just stop where you are, right now, or suffer the consequences! Tarsey was very good at applying that form of treatment as well. I saw her in action, once.

Smoking was not, as a general rule, permitted anywhere in the Free London. It was bad for the health of patients and staff alike and hospitals are all about health. However, there were times when it was recognised that a quiet drag on 'a suicide stick' might soothe a badly stressed patient who had been a heavy smoker all their life. A quiet puff and the patient would relax and begin to think that somebody cared. Still, the hospital worried about health and attempted to keep any damage to the absolute minimum. With this in mind a smoke room was provided from early morning to midnight when it would be locked. The patient, who was allowed that one-off puff, that one cigarette, would enter the smoke room with a nurse, usually also a smoker, who had volunteered for that duty, have their smoke and feel much better for it. Extractor fans sucked the polluted air into the atmosphere where it would be scattered by the four winds and less likely to do damage to innocents outside the hospital. One of the nurses had entered the smoke room with a very stressed patient who had just lit up, was sitting back in an easy chair and after that first deep drawn drag could be visibly seen to be more at ease, but not for long. Suddenly the door, which was never locked whilst a patient was using the room, was thrust open and a scrawny young woman drug-addict, under assessment at the request of the criminal court, entered, pulled out a cigarette and began to light up. The nurse told her to stop and leave immediately. In reply she had a blast of cigarette smoke blown into her face and was told to go and do something that just wasn't nice. She made a mistake. Instead of pressing her yellow alarm button there and then for close staff assistance she reached out, grabbed the cigarette, threw it to the floor, stamped on it and told the interloper to leave the room. She was up close, too close, against the wouldbe smoker who reached out swiftly, put her hand behind the nurse's neck and pulled her forward into a vicious head butt which flattened her nose. Then the nurse pressed her yellow button. The legitimate smoker tried to help by getting between the nurse and her assailant who was now kicking furiously at the nurse's legs. Help came swiftly and the attacker was dragged away. The nurse was taken to the general hospital for treatment, the legitimate smoker was returned to his ward more stressed than ever and the out of control druggie placed in a padded cell and kept under observation until she calmed down.

Several hours later I was with Tarsey when we went to that padded cell to release the druggie and return her to her locked area. As soon as the door was opened the druggie began to shout and spit and curse us both. She used some language I had never heard before. Tarsey eased me gently to one side and then stood, all 180 centimetres and 100 kilos of her, framed in the doorway. She waited until the storm had blown itself out then she spoke, very calmly, with her great brown eyes flashing.

'Now, you listen to me, honeychile, you can shout and spit and use dat bad language, and even catch trusting people unawares and break der nose but one thing you should know, I am not trusting and I can give you forty kilos any day of de week. If you want to stay here in dis padded cell indefinitely, fine, I can shut de door and let you fester, then send you back to de court and tell dat nice judge you is just a violent, vicious, malicious bad chile who has nothing wrong with dem except being plain mean-spirited. Den you will go to de prison, among all dose other nasties and see how many noses you break den. Now, tell me what is it to be?'

There was silence for about twenty seconds then the druggie began to weep silently at first, then to shake and sob loudly and uncontrollably. "I'm sorry, Nurse, I'm sorry. I didn't mean it,' she stuttered. 'I just wanted a smoke. I don't want to go to jail.'

Tarsey stepped into the cell, threw her arms around her, held her tight, ran her hand through her hair and said, 'There! There! Honeychile. It's all right now. You is just clean stressed out. Come, and you and I will go and have a nice cup of tea together, then we will both feel better. Maybe you won't go to dat nasty ole prison after all.'

And that was that. The druggie, with Tarsey's arms safely round her, went like a lamb back to the locked area. Tarsey made her a cup of tea with lots of sugar and that was the last outburst we had from her whilst she was in our care. On the day she left to go back to court she came, with tears flooding down her cheeks and kissed Tarsey and said that she would do her best to stay off drugs now that she had managed to get clean.

I don't think any of the Board of Managers of the hospital would have approved of Tarsey's tactics but Tarsey was not a great believer in political correctness. She was a doer not a talker. And she loved to return to that patois learned at her mother's knee and let those around her know where she came from. I think it somehow made her feel comfortable. Helped keep her feet firmly on the ground as she took herself back to her family and the love her mother poured on her. Back at court the druggie was placed under a supervision order and given community work to do. It kept her out of the free university where the 'students' learn better how to be more anti-social than ever. As far as I know she was never back in court again.

I longed for Tarsey to be here with me now. Just thinking of her gave me strength. She would have found a way out of this. So must I. Already a plan was forming in my mind. There was a weapon in the room. A weapon I thought I could use and Ossie would approve of. That weapon, and what Ossie had taught me, would surely be enough to get me out of this. How could I get to it? I would have to resort to some of those subterfuges which our patients knew so well. Give me a couple of days to get my strength back and I might be in a position to put my plan into action. In the meantime, I would do my exercises. I needed to keep fit if I were ever to get out of here alive.

'Could you release on of my arms so that I can massage my other one? I'm becoming stiff and sore from lying in the same position all the time and I'm getting a touch of cramp in my left leg as well,' I said.

'No, I won't do that,' he said. 'But if you like I will massage your arms and legs for you.'

Got him! That's exactly what I thought he might say.

'If you wouldn't mind,' I said.

Apart from when he was feeding me, giving me water, or taking me to the bathroom, this was the first time he had touched me in that kind of way.

He massaged my arms and legs with a gentleness I had never experienced before. I bunched the muscles in my left leg to make it appear that I had a touch of cramp. How could anyone who could be so gentle treat me with such mental cruelty? Even though I didn't need the massage I felt much better after it. I said, 'Thank you, Doctor, you are so very kind.'

He said nothing but went back to sitting in the chair. I think he was waiting for me to say something else. Did he think I was cracking? I hoped so. People who are nervous want to talk to the point where they sometimes gabble. So I would gabble, say anything as long as I said something. I had to make him think that I was mixed up. So mixed up that I didn't know whether to hate him or love him. That he was on the verge of gaining complete ascendancy over me. That soon the hate would go and there would be nothing left but love. I had to make him just that little bit less alert and he was very alert. Very perceptive.

'How long have I been here, Doctor?' I asked. 'I have lost count of time, completely.'

'Only six days,' he said. 'We still have just over three weeks of each other's company. Three weeks before you are missed and people begin to wonder where you are.'

'What will you do then?'

'What will I do then? Why nothing, of course. Nobody knows you are here. I will carry on with our experiment for as long as it takes. A dedicated researcher does not give up easily. I don't intend to give up, no matter what the price.'

I shuddered then. I hoped he didn't notice. What he was saying was that I didn't count. If I died it wouldn't trouble him. He was the dedicated researcher who would carry on researching even if the guinea pig died in the process. That beautiful bedside manner was just a means to an end. He wasn't in love with me; he just wanted to prove to himself how clever he was. Now I knew why he had selected me; he wanted someone who would be a challenge to him. Someone who was not easily broken. He wanted to fight and fight hard for the prize. Me. Fooling him, causing him to drop his guard, even a little bit, would not be easy.

'What if the police find me here and I tell them that you kidnapped me and that I do not love you? What will you do then?'

He laughed, almost merrily. 'The police find you here! The police find you here! My dear Elizabeth, you don't know what you are saying. There is not the least teeny weeny little hope that the police will find you here. To find you here they would have to search every house in Perth and they have neither the manpower nor the will to effect such a Herculean task just for a missing person who might be off in Tahiti with her boyfriend. Even if they did start a large-scale search, I as a concerned doctor at the hospital would know about it and make sure that I kept not just one but many steps ahead of the police. As I said before, Elizabeth, there is no hope of someone coming to your aid here. I will be able to complete this experiment, unimpeded. I want you to understand that.'

'And what if you discover that I am not going to love you, ever. What will you do about that?'

He chuckled throatily again. I had said something he thought funny. 'Come, now, Elizabeth,' he chortled, 'you are not that silly. This experiment will end when you decide that life is worth living and begin to cooperate. I'm quite sure that that is how those hostages in Stockholm saw it. The siege was over, they were alive and they were free. They would have hugged and kissed a crocodile or the most venomous snake in the world just then. You know, Elizabeth, it's great to be alive. I'm sure you understand that now. Don't you think it is time you started seeing my side of this experiment the same as those hostages in that Swedish bank saw their captor's side of things? I am sure that they had, unanimously, come round to their captor's way of thinking long before the siege was over. Doesn't that tell you something? Maybe they had come to embrace that slogan of the sixties, 'Make love not war'? It is much better to love and be loved than to fight. I am sure that you want this experiment to be over. So do I. It will not be over whilst you have the least resistance in you. What I am looking for is complete surrender. When I am sure that stage has been reached, that you will support me against all those who would question my motives, that you will never betray me, then you will walk free to do as you wish. But I have to be certain, beyond all doubt, that that stage has been reached before I free you from your bonds and allow you to walk out of here of your own volition. In fact, I am quite sure that when that stage has been reached you will want to stay with me and never leave.'

CHAPTER TWENTY

Now he was beginning to show his real colours. My kidnapping was not about the Stockholm Syndrome, it was about me. I had no doubt about that. The Stockholm Syndrome was just an excuse to own not only my body but my mind as well. Well, he would never own either. I might cause him to believe that he did but he wouldn't. I'd make him think again. One way or another I would change his thinking. I would own him. I didn't want his body but I certainly had to own his mind if I were to survive.

'I need to go to the bathroom, Doctor,' I said. 'Sorry.'

'It's quite all right, Elizabeth. Let me take you.'

He unhooked one arm, as usual, and we began to walk towards the bathroom. During all of the time that he had held me hostage I had never voluntarily touched him. He had touched me on several occasions when he was helping me to eat or drink or when he was massaging my pretended cramp. Now, as we walked side by side, although it revolted me, I leaned against him very lightly just for a fleeting second. It could have been an accident, it could have been intentional. I knew which. He didn't. I felt his response. It was to lean towards me. I pulled away. He leaned towards me. I pulled away further. He didn't pursue. Then we were at the bathroom.

On the way back I leaned towards him again. He did not respond. He wasn't sure. I was confusing him, just a little. That's what I wanted. Begin slowly and build up. Make him as unsure about my beginning to capitulate as he thought I was. Make him think I wanted to and didn't want to touch him at the same time. Do it in such a way that he thought he was breaking down my reserve. He wanted me to come to him. I would but in such a way as to convince him that he was beginning to control me. His talk about my wanting to live and making love not war had me thinking. If I ever wanted to get out of here alive I would have to come to him. Yes, I would come but only so that I could dominate him. He would be sorry he took me on.

I noticed he had stopped asking me questions. He no longer seemed interested in my background. All he seemed interested in was our relationship. Our relationship! We didn't have a relationship. Not so far as I was concerned. Now I felt very drowsy. I wondered if he was drugging me. Was he putting something in those beautifully cooked meals? Knocking me out. If so, what was he doing to me whilst I was unconscious? I didn't feel violated. Now I was becoming paranoid again. I had to tell myself that he was so sure that he could dominate me by the force of his personality that he wouldn't resort to drugs. This was a duel between his mind and mine and he was so sure that I was going to submit that he could even chuckle with delight at some of the things I said.

CHAPTER TWENTY ONE

When I awoke he was still sitting beside the bed. I couldn't see him but I could hear him breathing.

'What's happening at the hospital?' I asked.

'Oh, things are going on much the same as usual. Someone mentioned your name today, wondering how you were enjoying Wineglass Bay and wishing they were with you.'

'If they were with me they would wish they were back in the hospital.'

'Don't be quite so sure, Elizabeth; there are those who would like to be involved in an experiment like this. They would soon realise how lucky they were. Just as those people in Sweden did. They took only five days to come to love their captors. What's wrong with you, Elizabeth? Why are you taking so long?'

'There's nothing wrong with me. Those hostages in Stockholm were not bound hand and foot, naked and in the dark. Release me and see what effect that has on my thinking, Caspar.'

I threw that Caspar in just for confusion's sake.

'Oh, sorry, Doctor. That Caspar just slipped out again. I don't know why I said it.'

'I can tell you why you said it, Elizabeth. You just can't help it. You are falling in love with me. You should stop fighting yourself and go with your inner desires. Why don't you call me Caspar all the time? What have you to lose by it?'

'Because I don't want to. I feel that I am being pushed against my will. If you set me free I will call you Caspar and I won't try to escape. I promise. Why don't you think about that?'

That was a promise I had no intention of keeping if he accepted it. Promises made under duress cannot be classified as promises but I'm sure that he knew that as well as I did.

'I'll think about it.'

'Thank you, Doctor.'

'Now, I'm sorry, my dear, but I must leave you again. I have to get back to the hospital.'

Fifteen minutes later he was gone and I was on my own again staring into the dark and wondering what I was going to do. My mind was turning in a hundred different directions. I thought of home and of my gentle father. Would he have known what to do in this situation? I didn't think so. Cruelty, violence and hurt were not for him. Blood sports he abhorred. He couldn't understand how anyone would delight in hunting, hooking and playing a big fish. If they were going to eat it he could understand but to catch it and then, after they had had their fun with it, to kill it and put it on display in a glass case in some bar or other was something that filled him with anger. What did it prove? That the great angler was a great sportsman? Hardly. The fish wouldn't give them any votes on that score.

The bullfighter who stood in a circle of sand and tormented a noble bull to death whilst a roaring, adulating crowd cheered his every immaculate move, likewise filled him with horror. My dear father would not keep pigs because to kill them would have been an act of betrayal. When the time arrived to send them to the bacon factory he found that he had come to love them so much he could no more have had them killed and eaten than he could have his friends butchered. If he could tell me what to do now, what would he say? I think I know. He would say, 'Elizabeth, you are in the hands of a madman. What you have already decided to do is the best thing to do. Play him along like those anglers play the big fish. Cause him to think that he is dominating you completely; that he is winning the cerebral battle between you. He is very, very clever but he will drop his guard and when he does you must be ready. When that happens do not hesitate; use the moment to turn the tables. Of this you can be sure, my daughter, this man will never let you go on your terms.'

Now the question is, how do I organise things so that he drops his guard?

I must try to have him do that as soon as possible. The longer I am here the more dangerous my position becomes. If I remain here to the end of my holidays and it is found that I have not been to Tasmania, other enquiries will be made and when the police learn that I have never done anything like this before and that my bank account has not been touched, my parents will be advised and be over in Perth like a flash and a full scale hunt for me will begin. No matter how he tries to brush it off that will surely make Dr Wilderman nervous and for all his bravado he might decide to cut short the experiment, and me with it. Then he will wait until things settle down before selecting another victim and starting all over again. Unless I keep my head he will murder me and he will never be suspected or detected. Oh, God, I'm so afraid. I only wish Tarsey were here. I must keep the battle going. I must keep him engaged. I must keep fit. I must keep mentally alert so that when the least opportunity arises I will be able to grasp it and turn the tables. To keep fit and to keep a grip on myself I continue with my exercises, limited though they are. Knees up, arms up, arch back, twist. Start again.

I must have dozed off for suddenly he was at my bedside again. I hadn't heard him come into the room. He spoke.

'I got back earlier Elizabeth so that I could be with you. I was afraid you might be depressed.'

'Oh, Caspar, I am so glad you came back early. I felt so frightened and alone. I feel like a prisoner in solitary confinement: no light, no television, no radio, no books, no people. All I have is a voice in the darkness and I don't know what is going to happen to me. Please don't leave me again. I feel so abandoned. So without friends. I think I am going to die here,' I said in a voice that was that of a little girl lost. I stretched out my hand, as far as the bonds would allow me, in the direction of his voice. I was in luck. I found his bare arm and ran my hand down it to his wrist then to his hand, I grasped tightly. I began to weep half in pretence so that he would think I was beginning to crack and half in the genuine need for a good cry. I hadn't cried in years. His response astounded me. For a moment I was so taken aback that I almost forgot to keep up the weeping. The hand that I grasped so tightly responded with a tenderness I had never before experienced. It was that of a loving mother comforting a hurt child or a lover gently reciprocating a call for love. I had not had much experience with men on a one to one personal basis. Generally, those that I had been close enough to to the point where there was intimate touching had never touched me like this. Stressed though I was, I found myself shocked by the experience. Shocked that I actually enjoyed it. Even as the contact was taking place I wondered if the thrill of it, there this no other word for it, for thrill it was, was caused by some deep need I had been seeking all my life. Was it a primeval longing for something I knew not what, or was it simply the need for something to comfort me in my distress, no matter from whom that comfort came? At the same time I was alarmed that the conduct of my kidnapper could have such an effect upon me. I wanted to confuse him, leave him uncertain, now it seemed that I was the one who was being confused. Maybe this was what being taken hostage does to people. Does it cause them, in the face of almost certain death, to want to experience those things which they had wondered about and been curious about all their lives? Does it cause them to regret not having lived life more intimately? My recurring dream and a host of conflicting thoughts hurtled through my mind and, before I could stop myself, I gasped, 'Oh, Caspar!' It was completely involuntary. No pretence. When he spoke his voice was a balm beyond description; so gentle, so caring, so reassuring. It lifted me out of the dread abyss into which I had sunk and transported me to another realm. I was no longer a hostage bound hand and foot; I was Sleeping Beauty being awakened from a nightmare by the loving touch of Prince Charming. He had come solely to rescue me from the evils of the Underworld.

'It's all right, Elizabeth. I am here. You are quite safe. Don't be afraid. No one can hurt you here. I am looking after you. I will always look after you, my dear. The fact that you are in the dark without clothes or books, or television, radio or people is not to torment you; it is all for a purpose. A purpose you will appreciate when you come to understand it fully.'

Even as he was speaking I wondered how this could be happening to me. How I could feel so elated, so excited, almost ecstatic, when all he had done was respond to my grasp and he was the one who had placed me in this position. There was no doubt about it; a change was coming over me. I didn't know what it was. I didn't understand what it was but something was happening to me. When he had said earlier that I would come to love him, would beg to be held by him, had he then planted a seed that had taken root and was now beginning to play havoc with my emotions. Being a very skilled psychiatrist he knew about these things. If that were the case then I had to pull myself together and resist his overtures, otherwise I was in greater danger than ever. This was a situation I had to play to my advantage. With a struggle, and still holding his hand in what must have seemed to him a grasp of desperation, I said, 'Oh, Caspar, you are so kind. Please don't leave me. Just hold me and speak to me for a while. I am so afraid.'

His grip on my hand tightened almost imperceptibly but was still the tender touch of an angel's wing as he leaned closer to me and whispered, 'I shall be here for as long as you wish. Elizabeth. It has never been my intention to hurt or frighten you. Quite the reverse. All I seek is understanding of the Stockholm Syndrome and this is the only way I can do it. I have a feeling that we are making progress. Another few days and it will all be over. Until then I will leave you alone only when I have no other option.'

'Thank you, Caspar. You are so kind and gentle. I am beginning to understand now what it is you are attempting. I want to help you. But how can I do that?'

'One step at a time, Elizabeth. These things cannot be rushed. Just relax and remember you are a hostage in the hands of a hostage-taker and do not know what will happen next. I can assure you even I do not know. That is all part of the experiment. Just follow your feelings.'

There it was, in the midst of his comfort and consolation that veiled threat. I wondered if he intended that or if it were just a Freudian slip? He didn't know what was going to happen so I'd better be careful. No monkey business from me. More than ever I was aware that I was playing a game, a deadly game, the only prize in which was my life. If I lost I would never see the light again. I would go from the dark into the dark. Oh, God!

I took a deep breath, held it and steadied myself. I brought myself back on to an even keel again. By using his first name now instead of Dr Wilderman, I was, I hoped, getting inside his defences. But I had to be very careful. He was too aware, too clever a mind manipulator to be easily fooled. I knew that I was now on more dangerous ground than ever. I don't know why I knew it but I knew that whatever else I must do, I must keep my honour. If I lost that I feared he would have won the contest between us and I would have lost my appeal to him. If I slipped up now I would be finished. I would never get back to this level of rapport with him again. When that happened the experiment would be at an end and so would I. There could be no turning me loose.

'Would you like something to eat?' he asked.

'Yes, please,' I replied.

'Then I will leave you but only long enough to prepare the food.'

Placing his other hand on top of mine he held me in a gentle clasp for a moment then gently released himself and left the room.

CHAPTER TWENTY TWO

I lay in the dark with my eyes wide open wondering what I should do next. Should I go back to being more formal again, call him Dr Wilderman and not attempt to touch him, or should I continue to call him Caspar and touch him when I could? I decided. I had got inside his thinking, I would move forward. 'Caspar' and touching it would be from now on. Deep down in my subconscious was the thought that maybe I liked the touching. Well, I had been excited by it like never before. Maybe it depended on the person doing the touching? Elizabeth, what are you doing! What are you thinking! Oh, Tarsey, if only you were here! I'm alone. So alone. So confused.

He was back with the food. He placed the tray across my thighs and then again released one hand so I could eat. He was not yet making any concessions.

I had to engage him in conversation to show my need of him. 'How can you make these delicious meals?' I asked. 'Have you had cooking lessons?'

He chuckled. 'No formal cooking lessons for me. I have my ways.'

I'm a very good cook,' I said. 'I'm very fond of cooking. I could make very nice meals for you, if you would let me.'

'To make meals for me, Elizabeth, you would have to be unbound and I would find it difficult to control you. You see, I know just know strong and resilient you are. I think I need a little more proof that I can trust you not to run for the door or, worse still, attack me, before I can set you at liberty. As I have already said, when you come to me with need of me, and I will know when that is, then I will release you. Till then you will remain my hostage. Do I make myself clear?'

'Yes, Caspar, you make yourself very clear.'

There it was. No doubt about it. He wanted me in complete surrender. My tears and touching may have got inside his armour a little but it was a very little. I had a long way to go. I would continue.

'Oh, Caspar, I am surprised at you. I thought I had made it clear that I wanted to help you with your experiment. What more can I do?''

'Not clear enough, my dear Elizabeth, and there is a lot more you can do, Now, I have things to do. I'll leave you to ponder that whilst I attend to some pressing matters. Don't worry, I shall not be far away. Call if you need me.'

With that I could hear him getting up and leaving the room. At least I was having time to think and I needed that.

The plan I had thought of earlier was taking shape in my mind. It was a desperate plan but it was all I had. I would put it into operation soon. I would hasten slowly. I continued to exercise my legs, feet, arms and hands as much as I could. I would need all my strength if what I was going to do was to succeed. I lay quietly for a time then I called to him. 'Caspar, I need to go to the bathroom, please,'

He was in the room beside me in a trice. 'Certainly, Elizabeth.'

He unbound one arm, as usual, and began to lead me to the bathroom. As we walked side by side I again leaned in towards him until we were touching. When I made contact I did not draw back. Now, he leaned against me until we reached the bathroom door. His touch had the same effect on me as before. An electric thrill ran through me. I was transported. There were butterflies in my stomach. I leaned even harder against him. We were at the bathroom door too soon. I found it hard to withdraw myself from him. He pulled away and allowed me to enter. There was no sham about what I felt. I really had need of him. I wanted more. I was cracking. I knew I was. I wanted him. I wanted him badly, and I didn't want him. I wondered if he knew how I felt. Deprivation of human contact does strange things to people. I knew that from my studies. In the world I was then in there was not another soul but him. His was the only contact I had and I needed him. I didn't want to but I did. I had to do something soon or I was lost. He remained outside still holding the cord. When I was finished I washed my hands in the dark. Even so, I found it all very embarrassing. I was glad that he couldn't see me when I touched him for I knew that I was blushing. On the way back I leaned against him again but only for a moment before drawing back. I had to be careful. I must not throw myself at him. That would make him suspicious. He must not get me all at once. I must not lose my resolve and I was in grave danger of that. Back on the bed he tied my free hand to the bed again then left me without saying a word. I wanted the light on, not so much now because I was afraid of the dark but because I wanted to see his reactions. I wanted to gauge how my proximity and touching was affecting him. With men it is easier to see their physical reactions than it is with women. Maybe that was why he was keeping me in the dark? Oh, yes, that was it. He didn't want me to be able to read him.

I don't know how long I lay thinking in the dark, turning everything over in my mind, wondering about myself and him then, suddenly, he was back again.

'Would you like something to eat?' he asked. I said I would and soon I was enjoying another delicious meal.

He didn't speak during the time I was eating. When I had finished he began to take the tray away. As he was lifting it his hand touched my thigh. I immediately placed my hand on top of his and said, 'Stay with me and talk to me, Caspar, I am so lonely. I think I'll go mad if you don't speak to me.'

He continued to lift the tray, saying as he did so, 'I'll just put these things away and then I'll return and we can talk.'

He left the door open and there was some light but not enough to see anything other than silhouettes. I thought I could hear water running. Then I could see his outline coming into the room. He shut the door and sat down beside me.

'I'm back, Elizabeth. Now we can talk.'

I was struck dumb. I could think of nothing to say. For a few seconds, very long seconds, there was a silence that was as impenetrable as the dark. I was beginning to think that he would get up and go out of the room again when he spoke and what he said really threw me. I couldn't believe it. Now he was out in the open. The Stockholm Syndrome experiment was gone. Here was the real Dr Wilderman. 'Do you think you could ever love me, Elizabeth?' he asked, in a voice that I hadn't heard before. It wasn't so much a question as a plea, a display of great need. Thankfully, this time it was his need. This man, who in my experience, had brought so much comfort and tranquillity to so many people, was more in need of love and comfort than anyone else I had ever known. That's what this experiment was all about. Nothing to do with Stockholm; nothing to do with the advancement of mental science; nothing to do with other people; this was solely about him and me. This was about the need for love. His personal need for the love of a woman. He knew how to handle his patients' needs and ills; he did not know how to handle his own. He was just a little boy lost. What was I to do now?

The answer to that was simple; I had to offer him the same care and sympathy that I had given to my patients since the first day I had entered into the sacred trust that is mental health nursing. That all added up to love. I would give him love.

CHAPTER TWENTY THREE

My hand went out towards him again and, as if he knew and could read my thoughts, his met mine and we clasped each other in a tender loving embrace that again sent that indescribable thrill bursting, pulsating, vibrating through me again. I held him thus for how long I do not know. Then I was pulling him towards me. I moved backwards as far as my bonds would allow to give him room to sit beside me. Next I knew, his arms were around me and he was kissing me on the lips. He was kissing me with a passion I had never before known. I wanted to burst my bonds and throw my arms around him and hold him to me. I wanted him to continue kissing me and never stop. I found myself weeping uncontrollably. I didn't understand it. Here I was a hostage in my captor's arms in an ecstasy that knew no bounds and I was weeping. My sobbing caused him to stop kissing me, hold me even closer to him and whisper, 'It's all right, Elizabeth. I love you, too. I have always loved you but I could never tell you. Please don't cry.'

Then he was kissing me again, on my lips, on my closed eyes, on my cheeks, on my neck and now he was sliding down the bed to kiss me where I had never been kissed before. I could feel him hard against me. This brilliant psychiatrist whom I had always known as a quiet, gentle, somewhat introverted doctor, who had, by force, kidnapped me, stripped me naked, bound me hand and foot, kept me in the dark for days and driven me half-crazy with fear was now driving me crazy with desire; setting me on fire. How could this be? Was I a wanton who had desired this all my life preferring to be taken by force rather than admit that I had yielded to any man or was it that in the depths of my psyche I knew that I was never going to be freed unless I came to him? Was this what that dream was all about? I didn't know. All I knew was that he was not hurting me. Hurting me! This man! Far from it. All he was doing at the moment was making me glad that I was alive to experience a loving such as I had never before experienced. But even in the middle of my ecstasy I knew that this could not last. I may, wittingly, or unwittingly, I knew not which, have done something to allow me to find a chink in his armour which I must exploit to the full. I had to get out of this situation alive. If I did so, then I could discover, when I was free, if he really loved me and it wasn't just lust that was driving him. I must not allow myself to forget that he might be mad. He had to be deranged in some way to do to me what he already had. And I was still his hostage. No mention in the midst of his passion that he was going to untie me and treat me as a precious equal. Now was the time to strike when the iron was hot.

'Oh, Caspar, I love you!' I said. 'Please untie my hands so I can love you more.'

His kissing continued for a few seconds more, then, he stopped abruptly and with his breath coming in gasps said, 'I will, indeed, untie you but not just yet, Elizabeth. We must hasten slowly. Some things cannot be rushed. We still have not completed our experiment and I must be certain that I am not mistaking my passion for your desire to end our research. I hope that I have not embarrassed you and gone too far in the ecstasy of the moment?'

'No. No. You haven't embarrassed me. I want you just as much as you have demonstrated you want me. Surely it has been proved by what has just happened between us that such a thing as the Stockholm Syndrome does exist. The hostage does come to love her hostage-taker. There is no longer any need to continue with your research. All I want is to be free to prove my love for you.'

'The experiment is very close to conclusion but before I am completely satisfied that that is the case, I must have complete surrender. Do you understand? Are you prepared for that, Elizabeth?'

I was stunned. He had stripped me naked physically but that wasn't enough, he also wanted to strip me naked, spiritually. He wanted complete and total surrender. Total control. Nothing less. Then, when he had achieved that, what would he do - make another skeleton out of me to put beside his other trophy at the end of the bed? I needed time to think. I was confused again. Every time I thought I understood this man he did something to throw my thinking completely awry. I was back at the beginning. My thinking was correct then. The good doctor was no more interested in research than I was in going to Mars. He was just another of those most carnal of all animals, man. He simply wanted me physically, but consensually, so that any feelings of guilt he might later have would be assuaged. How could there be consensus from a subject who was bound and gagged? Then, later, after his conquest, when he had tired of his plaything, would he find reasons to convince himself that this woman was so lacking in morality and had led him astray to the point where she must pay the ultimate price. She must not be allowed to live to corrupt other easily-seduced men. And to think that I thought he loved me. He almost had me. It was stalling time again.

With all these thoughts racing through my mind I found it hard to collect myself. I managed to control myself enough to reply, 'But, Caspar, I thought you were a gentleman, a gentleman I am beginning to love deeply; how can you ask me to give myself to you when I am not completely free? Isn't the whole idea of loving and being loved one of freedom to decide, without the least compulsion? I need to be free so I can demonstrate to you that my need for you is not dependent on being set free because I will already be free. Can't you see that?'

'What I see, Elizabeth, is that you are my hostage and will stay my hostage until I am sure, in every way, that you love me unreservedly. And that means whether you are bound or free. I don't think you have yet reached that stage. I will say you are close but I need to be satisfied beyond all doubt.'

That was clear enough. He was never going to let me go. Oh, dear God, give me strength. This man is going to rape and murder me, no matter what. Thank you, God, he won't. I will make sure he does not triumph over a craven, cringing female whom he has terrified into submission. I am not going to yield to him. I now understand myself. I will take no more of his grooming or his blandishments or his attempts to control me by force of his personality. This man is two persons: one evil, one good. Obviously, he can control both of them and seeks also to control me. I am revolted. I cannot keep this pretence up much longer. I must do something. Time to put my plan into action.

'Oh, Caspar, how can you be so cruel? Can't you see that you have won and that I love you. Kiss me again. Oh, please kiss me again, I beg you.'

Now he was on the bed beside me again, his mouth searching for mine. He held me in such a tender embrace that I wondered at it. How could he be two people at once? One so loving, the other so lecherous and cruel. The only answer to that was that he was blowing hot and cold with me. What he was doing was keeping me so confused, so disoriented, that I couldn't think straight. But he had picked the wrong victim; I could think straight, I would think straight and I would outthink him. Even as I felt him throbbing and pulsating against me and my whole being cried out for even closer contact, I knew that there was a line I must not allow him to cross. As his hands began to move down my body I stiffened and gasped, 'No, Caspar, you mustn't. I will not let you do that. Not until you release me. You will not possess me whilst I am bound, even though my whole being aches for you.'

'Then you will remain bound,' he said. He instantly got off the bed and left the room.

CHAPTER TWENTY FOUR

I was alone again, shaking and gasping. I was in torment. I wanted him. Needed him. Craved him. At the same time I despised him for what he was doing to me. He was causing me to see a side of myself I had never known before. He had awakened me from a deep malaise from which I had unwittingly suffered all my life. How could someone, a supposedly caring doctor, be so evil? How could he do this to me? How could I allow this to happen? Did I want it to happen? Deep down in my deepest self was I a harpy waiting all my life for someone, some alpha male, to come and titillate me? Thrust upon me the delights of the flesh. Show me that I really was part of Eve's sisterhood just waiting the opportunity to lead another Adam to the Forbidden Fruit and hence to oblivion. Had I, as I walked around the wards in the hospital, in some unconscious way flaunted myself so that I had driven him mad with the desire to possess me?. A desire of which I was totally unaware. Was my predicament all my fault and mine alone? Was it all because I didn't know myself like the Ancients said we all should? But who does know themselves? Is it that we are all just playthings of Fate and have no command over which direction our lives will take? Oh, dear God, am I lost no matter what I do? Would it really matter if I drop my defences and let him do with me as he pleases? Is there really no such thing as free will? Are we all prisoners of forces over which we have no control? I lay on the bed naked and ashamed. The tears welled in my eyes and cascaded down my cheeks. I was quite unable to stop them.

I was closer to being broken than I had ever been in my entire life. Was it because I wouldn't allow myself to have him?

I'm not quite sure what happened then. I think I may have fallen asleep. What I do know is that I was no longer weeping and a stream of new thoughts had entered my mind. It wasn't my fault. Not my fault at all. How could it be? I didn't ask to be kidnapped. That skeleton at the end of the bed, was it really one of his victims and if I didn't do something about it, and soon, would I be his next. I only wish that Byron Osborne, dear, good, caring old Ossie, were here. I know that he'll be with me in spirit in what I am about to do. 'Aye, lassie, dinny lie doon and dee. Gee the mongrel a run for his money,' he would be sure to say. And Tarsey would cheer me on. I psyched myself up: 'I've got to do it! I've got to do it! I've got to do it! If I don't do it he'll rape me and kill me! I'll never see home again! I took a few deep breaths and exercised my legs and arms furiously as I prepared for the next scene in this ghastly play.

When I was as ready as I thought I could ever be and with my heart sending my blood bursting through every artery and vein in my body, I called, 'Caspar, I badly need to go to the bathroom. I can't wait.' Make him hurry so that if he is even just a little bit off guard it will give me an edge of some kind.

Although I was staring wide-eyed in the direction of the door the darkness was so impenetrable that I didn't see him coming. I could just hear the scuff of his bare feet on the carpet.

'I am here, Elizabeth', he said as he began to untie my wrist from the bedpost. Then, with him again holding the cord I rose from the bed and stood beside him. I leaned against him as we came to the end of the bed. I judged that we were in line with the skeleton which I couldn't then see. As he leaned towards me, I took a deep breath, grabbed his arm, stepped sideways, dropped to one knee and pulled with all my might, just as Ossie had taught me. The result surprised even me. He, taken completely by surprise, came flying over my shoulder, landed with a thump, an explosion of expelled air and an exclamation as his back came into contact with the bedpost to which my left foot had so recently been anchored. He was winded. Good! I had fractions of a second to complete my attack. I knew very well where the skeleton was sited. I fumbled for it in the dark. The bonds at my ankles so restricted my movements that I now wasn't sure whether I was near it or not. Oh, God! Was I not going to be able to find it after all? If I can't, what will I do? I can't run because of the restraints on my feet. He'll surely kill me after this. All the surprise will have gone out of my planning. I waved my hands frantically through the air in front of me. I thought I could hear him stirring. If I didn't find it soon he would be up and I would be down and I would never be up again. I took another step forward. Oh, Lord, help me! He is on his feet and coming for me! No he isn't. It's the skeleton. I had brushed against it. I had been feeling ever so slightly in the wrong direction. I put my arms around it and felt for the stand on which it was hung. Found it! I grabbed and pulled. I was in luck, it came with me. I feared it might be fixed to the floor but it wasn't. It was anchored to a heavy piece of metal at its base. With a physical strength I didn't know I had I lifted the metal pole, base, skeleton and all and lunged forward. My bare feet came into contact with Caspar's body lying where it had fallen. I lifted the frame up and brought it crashing down on him several times. All my anger, hate, fear, and loathing went into those blows. The skeleton rattled as I struck. It seemed to be laughing as it joined with me to exact its revenge and assist me in my preservation. I was scared out of my wits. I didn't care if I killed him. I had to make sure that he was not going to be in a position to kill me. After I had struck several times, still holding the frame, I turned towards where I thought the door was. I found myself against the wall. I followed it round. Now I could feel the wood of the door jamb. I ran my hand up and down the wall around it. Found it! I pressed the light switch and the room was flooded with an explosion of light. The effect on me was unbelievable. I had been in pitch blackness for days and was unprepared for the shock of such a bright light. It was like a thousand suns hitting me at once. I reeled away blinded for several seconds. There was a searing pain in my eyes. I let go the skeleton and clapped my hands to my eyes. I held them there for a few seconds until I had partially recovered. Then I opened my right eye and squinted towards the bed. The pain was intense but I knew I must bear it if I were to save my life. What I saw caused me to open my other eye. I was overjoyed. Caspar was lying at the side of the bed with his mouth wide open and blood streaming from his head. He was obviously unconscious He must have been knocked out and split his scalp when I had thrown him over my shoulder. Thank you again, Ossie. The pounding with the skeleton frame would certainly have assisted in his lack of interest in what was happening around him. I had no time to rest on my laurels. I had to finish the job. I hobbled towards where I thought the kitchen must be. I walked across a corridor and there it was. I switched on the light, had a swift look round. Yes, there was a set of drawers near the sink. I opened the top one. Bingo! It was the cutlery drawer. I selected a large carving knife and cut the straps holding my legs together. I cut the straps from my arms. I was free. And I had a knife. Now let's see what we can do to make the not so good doctor less dangerous to the female population at large. I re-entered the bedroom. He was still lying as I had left him. Maybe I had killed him? Still holding the knife I felt for the pulse at his wrist. It was weak but it was still beating. He wasn't dead. Into the bathroom. Grab a towel from the rail beside the hand-basin. Cut it into strips. Back into the bedroom. Down on hands and knees beside him. Bind his hands and feet. Use the remainder of the towel to tie around his head to stem the bleeding. I must take no chances. I had to be quick. He might come to at any moment and then what would I do? I didn't want to kill him but I would if it proved necessary. He must not get the opportunity to make me his hostage again for then I would surely die. Even though he was a big man fear gave me strength and I pulled him up on to the bed. Once I had him there I proceeded to tie his hands and feet to each of the bedposts as he had done to me. At last, I could relax, a little. The skeleton was beside the door where I had left it. I took my clothes from it and dressed myself. I would not dress him. He would stay the way he had kept me. The roles were now reversed except that I was clothed and the light was on. Where, dear Caspar, is the Stockholm Syndrome now?

Now was the time to look at that head injury again. I ran my hand through his hair. I could feel no irregularity. I looked closely at the wound. His scalp was split. I'd have to fix that. Then I looked at the rest of his body. There were several red blotches on his trunk and thighs. That would be where the end of the skeleton frame had come into contact with him. It didn't seem that anything was broken. Bruised he was, yes, and, probably, very badly concussed from the contact with the bedpost but I didn't think there was anything serious. I am only a nurse and did not have the depth of medical knowledge of a doctor; even so, I felt quite certain he would sleep his way out of this. The longer he slept the quicker would be his recovery. Taking people hostage can be a hazardous occupation, particularly if the hostages turn the tables. At last, I could relax. I needed to think what to do next. Of one thing I was certain; my violence against him was at an end. There was no need for it anymore. My anger was gone, too. I was just glad to be alive. He was now in my power. Apart from the initial bursting through my front door, grasping me by the throat and squeezing me into unconsciousness, he had not hurt me. Indeed, he had always appeared very solicitous regarding my health. I would act just as caringly towards him. I had had to use force against him to free myself but no more. I must find out what I wanted to find out by means of gentle persuasion. Violence had never formed any part of my make-up, I had always abhorred it. I must not let it become part of me now. Yet, in my heart I had to admit to myself that this whole experience had done something to me I couldn't understand. I was not the same person I had been a week ago. There lingered, at the edge of my subconscious, the feeling that he had awakened something within me that I had never known before. That thrill, that desire that ran through me when our hands had met. What was it? Was it some kind of yearning for that which I had never known? Then there was exquisite thrill when our unclothed bodies met. The burning passion when he took me in his arms, placed his lips on mine, caressed me in a way I had never been caressed before. He had transported me to the Never Never Land. A land I'd never been in before. I didn't know what to think. I wasn't sure if I should like these thoughts. The trouble was that I did. But I wasn't sure if I wanted to know myself quite so intimately. I am not a person who is easily confused. I always knew exactly what I wanted and where I was but he had me confused. I was confused now and didn't know where I was. With an effort I cast these thoughts aside for now. There are some things in life that are best not thought about; best not looked in the face. I'd think about them tomorrow. Time to come down to earth. Time to think about the here and now. Time to think about this very minute I was living in.

CHAPTER TWENTY FIVE

First thing was a shower. Taking the knife with me I went to the bathroom, closed and bolted the door, turned the shower on full blast and revelled in the deluge that torrented over me. God! I was feeling better. I was alive and the odds had changed in my favour. I dressed again and had another look at Caspar. He still seemed to be unconscious. The longer he was comatose the better. Now where were my shoes? Ah, there they were, against the wall near a bedside chest. I put them on. Time to have a look round the house. The deep freezer in the kitchen was stacked with precooked meals. All they needed was heating up. That was how he was able to produce all those beautiful meals so quickly. I checked the exterior doors. I was able to open them all. A door led from the kitchen to the side of the house. I undid the bolt and left it unlocked so that if necessary I could exit at speed. Where were my suitcases? They must be here somewhere, unless he had already disposed of them. Back into the bedroom again. I opened the walk-in robe. There were both suitcases sitting side by side. I checked. They had not been opened. So far, so good. Now where had Caspar slept? He hadn't slept in my bed. I checked the next bedroom. Ah, there it was - the bed he slept in. I would give that room a good search when I had checked other things I felt were more pressing. I checked the next room. What I found there surprised me. I had never thought of Caspar as the athletic type, yet this room was a miniature gymnasium. It had everything a good gym would have: treadmill, mini-trampoline, exercise bike, punch-bag, weights and all kinds of fitness gadgets. Little wonder he always seemed so agile, so supremely fit. The speed with which he moved when those boys broke the window when they came hunting birds with their catapult should have alerted me to his supreme fitness. I did a quick check of the next room but it seemed to contain mainly junk, boxes, piles of books and general odds and ends. I went outside and checked the garage. His car was inside. But where were the keys? They can't be too far away. He had used the car often to go to the hospital so they must be close by. I'll probably trip over them if I'm not careful. Behind the kitchen door hanging on a hook is a bunch of keys. That must be them. I'll try them out. Back to the garage. Yes, they fitted. All going nicely. I can pack my suitcases in the car and keep the keys with me at all times so that I can take off any time I want. But I don't want to go. Not just yet.

Lying in bed I had thought about what I would do if I did turn the tables on him. Go to the police? Have him arrested for breaking into my house and kidnapping me? Those were the sensible things to do; what the normal, sensible person would do. Get out of there fast and into the safe arms of the boys and girls in blue. But were they? He was good at covering his tracks and had, no doubt, a ready answer to any charges the police might bring against him. He would have a high profile lawyer standing by just waiting to jump in and say how it was that I had engineered the whole thing. I had fallen head over heels in love with him, a love that was unrequited to the point where he couldn't beat me off. I had arranged my Tasmanian holiday as a blind so that I wouldn't be missed whilst I enjoyed a whole month alone with him. Just imagine it – a whole month tasting the delights of the Forbidden Fruit. He was Adam, I was Eve the temptress. With the world already lost in Eden we had nothing and no one to betray. I had never had any intention of going anywhere near Tassie. I was into bondage and all kinds of kinky sex. I had made all kinds of sexual overtures to him during the course of our work together at the hospital. He had begun to fear that I was so obsessed with him sexually that if I couldn't have him I would destroy his career. He had yielded in the end in the hope that he might be able to help me get him out of my system and effect some kind of cure. After all, he was a psychiatrist and people with mental problems were within his sphere of expertise. Never in his life had he been involved with any woman in any kind of male/female relationship. If he had felt drawn towards me in that way it would have been easy for him to ask me out. He just wasn't interested in me, sexually. Kidnap one of the nurses at the hospital! Him! What nonsense! Was there a mark on me? No! Not one. Was there anything to indicate that he had molested me in any way? Not a thing. 'I'm sorry for the girl, Your Honour. I always considered her a most efficient nurse, full of care for her patients and, indeed, everyone else around her. Most charming. That is until she showed signs of this obsession. It had to be some kind of mental breakdown? It could be that she had been working too hard. As I have said, I tried to help. Tried to save her job. Now it seems that all I have done is make matters worse. I feel so embarrassed by it all. I never expected to find myself before a court of law. This is a new experience for me. I should have discussed the matter more fully with her. Advised her to have herself admitted as a voluntary patient. Now, I'm afraid, it is rather too late for that. Hindsight is a wonderful educator, Your Honour. I do most unreservedly, apologise to this honourable court for this unpardonable waste of its time.'

Yes, he was a master of the sweet talk. The charmer who was forever play-acting. My father would have said he had kissed the Blarney Stone. Now that I was on to him I wasn't going to risk making a fool of myself by dashing off to the police and plunging into a situation that would set the media into a feeding frenzy. I was now in control and I would make sure that the good doctor put to rights the great wrong he had done me. He would make a signed statement setting out exactly what he had done and how he had planned it. And if he had committed rape and murder of another or others then I would have him confess. I had about three weeks to work on that. Now he was my hostage but I wasn't interested in the Stockholm Syndrome. I was interested in knowing the truth. I was interested in retaining my honour, which I had very nearly lost. I wanted to know about that skeleton and if there were any more in Dr Wilderman's closet. The not so good doctor had a lot of questions to answer.

Where to begin? Well, I had my scoot-hole ready and could bolt to the police at any time but I would do that only as a last resort. Time to see just how deeply unconscious he was.

He was now lying where I had lain, trussed as I had been trussed. The only difference was that I was now clothed whilst he was still naked and we were no longer in the dark. I could see him clearly and would now be able read his reactions much more clearly. I wasn't in the least embarrassed about his nakedness. I was a nurse and had seen naked males many times in the course of my work.

I patted his cheek. 'Time to wake up, Caspar. Time for you to answer *my* questions.'

There was not the least response. Not the least little twitch of any kind. His mouth was open, his breathing deep, almost stertorous. Maybe that bang on the head had done him more damage than I at first thought? I ran my hand through his hair again. Nothing. No irregularity. Definitely no sign of a fracture and he wasn't foxing. Maybe I had hit him too hard around the heart with the base of the skeleton? I checked there. Bruising in other places but nothing around the heart that would indicate damage there. What to do now? I know. I'll leave him for a while. Make myself a cup of tea. I suddenly felt the need of something to eat, some comfort food. There was plenty of food, so why not?

I made myself a delicious meal and was able to eat it with both hands. I finished up with ice cream and tinned pears and a several cups of beautiful hot sweet coffee. I was beginning to feel human again. Now, I'd have another look around the house and see what I could discover about Dr Caspar Wilderman. See if I could find anything that would assist me to ascertain how he ticked. I'd go back to his bedroom, that place in the house where he lived when he wasn't trying to break me, and check it thoroughly. I had just entered his bedroom and was about to open the top drawer of one of the bedside chests that stood on either side of the bed when I thought

I thought I heard him calling. I went to him immediately and found him trying to sit up in the bed. When he saw me he said, 'What have you done to me, Elizabeth? What have you done to me?'

'Exactly the same as you did to me, Caspar,' I said. 'Now, you will know how I felt when I was in the position you are now in. All I have done is reverse the roles. What's sauce for the goose is sauce for the gander.'

'But I never banged you on the head with a blunt instrument and caused you to bleed. My head feels like a bomb has gone off inside it. What have you done to me?'

'And I never hit you on the head with a blunt instrument. I would never do such a thing. You wouldn't free me, so I had to free myself. To do that I had to use necessary force. You probably don't remember but I tossed you over my shoulder and your head hit the bedpost. That caused rather a lot of bleeding as well as making you unconscious. I'm sorry, I didn't want to do it but it was the only way I could get out of your clutches. I also hit you with the skeleton frame from the end of the bed. I didn't want to do that either but I had to make sure you were not in a position to exercise control over me again. You see, you can't take people hostage and not expect them to attempt to regain their freedom, can you?'

'I can understand that but I was engaged in an experiment. I told you that.'

'Yes, indeed, but I was not a volunteer. You kidnapped me. In case you don't know, Caspar, that is against the law. People go to prison for a long time for committing such a crime.'

'Wouldn't that also apply to you, Elizabeth? Haven't you now kidnapped me?'

'I don't think so, Caspar. I have applied self-help and freed myself. Now what I intend to do is to ask you to assist me in discovering the real reason for kidnapping me. I want the truth. Consider this; I am not a psychiatrist, as you made clear to me you are when you said you would know when I was lying. But what I have is a woman's intuition which I think is better than any of your psychobabble and I will know when you are lying. Do you understand that?'

'I'm not sure that I do. But what about our experiment, the Stockholm Syndrome? What about that?'

'Don't make me laugh. You know as well as I do that that was a lot of twaddle. All you wanted was to get into bed with me and have me as your sex slave. And, as you know, you very nearly succeeded in that, too. That's the truth from my perspective. Come now, Caspar, how about you telling me the truth, also?'

Even as I spoke the words something inside me almost willed him to say that the Stockholm Syndrome counted for nothing. I don't know why I was thinking like that. All I know was that I was. What I wanted to hear him say was that he loved me but didn't know how to tell me. Didn't know how to say the words. But it was not going to be that easy. The expectancy went out of me and I almost sagged when he dodged the question and said: 'Can you do something about my head, Elizabeth. I really am in great pain.'

I took control of myself and decided I'd leave the questions for the moment. After all I had plenty of time. I would be kind to him. Wanted to be kind to him and I was not a sadist. I was not into torture.

'Yes, Caspar, I said, 'I will certainly do something about your head. Just give me a minute.'

I went to the bathroom where I found a pair of scissors and a razor. There was a medicine cupboard there and I found in it some sticking plaster, cotton wool and antibiotic cream. Then I set about cutting the hair and shaving the area around the wound in his scalp. I cleaned it with the cream and smoothed the edges of the cut together then applied the sticking plaster. I put on a thick padding of cotton wool and wound a bandage over it. I removed the pillow and the blood-soaked towel and as I eased his head back on to a new pillow he said. 'You are very good to me, Elizabeth, but my head is still bursting. There are some tablets in my medical-bag, could you please bring me two of those.'

'Where is your medical-bag?' I asked.

'It's in my bedroom. That's in the next room. It's in the wardrobe there.'

I went to the room. Found the bag and the tablets and brought him two with a glass of water. After he had taken the tablets I made him as comfortable as his bonds would allow then sat down on the chair beside the bed and was just about to begin asking him questions, when he said, 'Elizabeth, would you kindly release my bonds? I find them most uncomfortable.'

I was almost dumbstruck. The cheek of him! He had held me bound for days, yet here he was complaining because I had done exactly the same to him.

I laughed derisively. 'Set you free! Set you free! You didn't set me free even when I promised I would help you in your research. No, Caspar, I will not release your bonds until you have answered my questions. I want to know...'

'But I have set you free, Elizabeth,' he interrupted. 'In a way that you don't yet fully comprehend. I have freed you from yourself. That is something you will thank me for in the years ahead. There is no need for me to be bound,' he interrupted. 'You see, I now believe the experiment to be completed and completed successfully. Weren't you, aren't you now, calling me Caspar? Weren't you kissing me? Begging me to kiss you? Didn't you want me? Yearn for me. Didn't it take all your willpower to resist me? Another day or so and you would have surrendered to me totally.

And I mean totally, and willingly. Without reservation. You know that is true. All that was stopping you from taking your desire to its natural conclusion was one last vestige of inhibition, no doubt caused by your NIP indoctrination. You want me with every fibre of your being. Why don't you admit that, Elizabeth? Release me and we can start a completely new life together. I will take you into a world you have never known and could never before have imagined. A world where self is king. A world where your every desire can be fulfilled. A world where being you carries no guilt. Now that you are free and have nothing to fear from me, why don't you come to me and say you will be mine and me yours forever? What have you to be afraid of?'

He was indeed a brilliant psychiatrist. He was also Satan in the flesh. I was in the desert being offered the world if I would only concede. He knew how my religion had shaped my thinking. He was into my mind. Almost had control of it, but not quite. I was in no doubt about that. I thought at that very instant that he knew me better than I knew myself or anyone else had ever known me. He had overridden my thinking almost completely and was making it crystal clear to me what it was my subconscious sought. But I had no intention of yielding. No intention of allowing my most innate desires and inhibitions, no matter what they might be, to be wrenched from my control and placed in the hands of a manipulative puppet-master. I had never looked that deeply into my soul and despite the Ancients and their 'know yourself' I was not yet ready to take that step. Maybe the truth was that I did not wish to know myself. The person I needed to know more about was Dr Wilderman. When I knew how he thought, when I had looked into *his* mind, maybe then I would know as much about myself as I would ever want to know. What I wanted most of all was to clear my mind of its confusion. Only then could I return to what was formerly normal for me.

I dodged his questions and requests as he had done with mine. I had questions to ask and I would ask them.

'You never did care about the Stockholm Syndrome,' I said. 'All you wanted was my body, at any price. You never cared about my feelings. You don't kidnap someone and treat them as you have treated me if you cared in the slightest about them. What you wanted was a challenge to test your medical and scientific skills and your powers of conquest. As you said, you didn't want a homeless person, they might have proved too easy. You didn't want a male because you are not into homosexuality. You wanted someone like me whom you had studied very closely and thought that if you could break me spiritually then you could break anyone and have a sexual plaything as your reward at the end of it. Isn't that correct?'

'You are, indeed, very intelligent, Elizabeth, very insightful, but you are quite wrong. I wanted to test the Stockholm Syndrome purely from a research aspect and if, at the end of it, you agreed to become my life partner then that would have been my reward. You see, I still had to work out how I could present my findings to a professional research body. I had hoped you would help me in that regard.'

'I would have thought that that would have been the first thing you would have considered. There wouldn't be much point in carrying out research which entailed the breaking of some innocent, physically and spiritually, if you could never publish your findings. I think you are stalling. You are not telling me the truth. I'll tell you what, Caspar, I'll promise you this; if you tell me the truth, no matter what it is, I will release you and allow you to go back to your work at the hospital and I will go off to Tasmania for what is left of my holiday and never will I breathe a word to anyone of what you have done to me. Remember my woman's intuition. I will know if you are lying. Tell me.'

CHAPTER TWENTY SIX

I waited for his response. There was none. I saw that his eyes were closed. I thought he was thinking. I decided to give him a little longer to contemplate. Next thing I knew he was breathing deeply and regularly. He was asleep. It must have been the pills I had given him. If that was the case then they had acted very quickly indeed. I hoped that they were not some kind of drug that would kill him and that I had, unwittingly, assisted in his suicide. How stupid of me not to have checked what they were before I gave them to him. But I never thought that he would want to do himself harm. I had never been in a situation like this before. Nothing I could do now but wait. Even though he was bound and I was not I felt he was still manipulating me. I almost wept with frustration.

I sat beside the bed then wondering what to do. I looked at his long, slender, naked, well-muscled body; at his pale handsome face, at those lips which had set me on fire and thought that there were many women who would have been made ecstatic by his courtship. He could have had almost any woman he wanted with very little effort. Why then did he have to kidnap me? Was it really that he couldn't relate to members of the opposite sex? Was it that courting a girl would have been too easy for him? Did he prefer the challenge to his professional skills and in some twisted, perverted, insane way think to grab a girl, totally alienate her and then see if, by reason of his superior psychological skills, he could cause her to love him? What, really, was he up to? I also wondered if he was really asleep at all. Maybe he was testing me out to see what I would do? Well, I wasn't going to wonder too long; I knew what to do. I leaned over and kissed him full on the lips. Don't ask me to explain why I did that. I don't know. I just did it. Everything else had gone out of my mind. I just wanted to kiss him. My heart thudded against my ribs as my lips touched his.

There was no response from him. Not the slightest. Yet that touching of his lips sent the blood surging tumbling, bursting through every part of my body again. How could this be? How could I touch a sleeping man and be so turned on? I pulled away from him in shame. I knew this was wrong. I was breaking every aspect of the moral code I lived by. I was becoming a wanton. This was not me. What had he done to me? What was I doing to myself? All I knew was that some psychological barrier within me had been broken and I would never be my old self again. I also knew that he was my hostage and I could do with him as I liked. Had he felt the same way about me? I got up and left the room before I did something else even more silly.

I went to check out those tablets which seemed to have such a soporific effect upon him. Now that I had time to think and had seen how quickly they had knocked Caspar out I hoped, now that his game was up, he hadn't decided to take himself gently out of the picture. People with deranged minds can do all types of things to themselves but I didn't think Caspar felt the need to commit suicide, not whilst he thought he could still win me over. I didn't know what to do. However, there was nothing I could do except maybe get in touch with the Swan District Hospital and ask their advice. To do that would mean I would lose my anonymity and the whole story would come out and I was not prepared to do that for a whole lot of reasons. I told myself that there were many questions to which only he held the key and I would not let up until I knew the answers. I took his medical bag out from the wardrobe again and examined the tablets. The little bottle did have a descriptive label on it but the writing was in a language other than English. It wasn't French, German or any of the other European languages with which I might have come into contact at some time or other. Now, that I had time to think I thought that unusual. I had certainly never seen anything like this before. Maybe it contained some ingredient peculiarly within the knowledge of a psychiatrist. I just didn't know. Stumped, I would have to wait and see if they appeared to have any deleterious effect on Caspar. If they did, then, as a last resort, I would seek outside help. As I was putting the bag away I notice a tripod at the back of the wardrobe. It had a camera mounted on it. In all the time I knew him at the hospital I had never heard Caspar mention photography. What was that doing there? I had never before connected Caspar with photography. He never mentioned it. All my life I had shied away from having my photograph taken. I always thought that if it isn't narcissistic it is a subtle form of vanity. Only twice in my life had I set out deliberately to have my photograph taken. The first was when I needed a passport and the second was when I graduated as a nurse. Mum and Dad had wanted a picture of me in my nurse's uniform to put with all the other family photographs in the living-room. I put the tripod back where I found it. I thought it unlikely that the camera would contain anything of interest to me. I'd leave the camera for the moment and have a closer look at it later if I found nothing else of interest in the room. It seemed that the more I learned about Caspar the more mysterious he became.

I went back and had another quick look at him before I began that search of the drawers in his bedroom which had been interrupted previously when I had heard him calling. He was still sleeping peacefully. I took his pulse and studied his breathing. Both appeared fine. A good sleep would help him recover from his injuries. As I was tucking the blankets in around him it occurred to me that the hospital would be wondering where he was if he didn't show up. They would try to contact him and when that failed the administration would have to call in someone else to replace him. Would they know how to get in touch with him? Presumably they would try to do so on his mobile? What would they do if he didn't turn up at all? Would they come to the house? My heart missed a beat just then and I gasped. Then I recovered myself. They wouldn't come here. They couldn't. This was his own private little hidey-hole that no one knew about but him, which he had gone to great lengths to keep only within his knowledge. If he didn't turn up and the hospital couldn't get in touch with him would they go to the police? They surely would. They would have to. Then what would happen? A search would surely follow. But it would fail. He had covered his tracks so well so that he could apply his undivided attention to me that no searcher would have a clue about where to begin. I was safe here for as long as I wanted. His mobile phone. I must find his mobile phone and switch it off. I searched the room. It wasn't there. I searched the next room. Not there. I went to the kitchen. Ah, there it was on the window ledge. It was already switched off. That is why I hadn't heard it ring since I had freed myself. I took it and hid it behind the bedside chest. I would not tell Caspar about it. So far as he was concerned we were completely cut off from the outside world. There was no way anyone could now contact us. If there were ever to be contact it would only be through me. I had gained a little more control. I felt the stronger for it. It was Caspar who had chosen the isolation. I hoped now to use it to my advantage.

I started my search with the wardrobe where I had found the tripod and camera. I went through it but could find nothing that seemed unusual. Next to the dressing-table. I went through all its five drawers, three big ones and two smaller ones. They contained mostly men's stuff: shirts, underwear, socks and handkerchiefs. Nothing that told me anything about him. I put them all back as I had found them. I turned to the bedside chests. The first one yielded nothing. I went through its three drawers. Nothing. I went to the one on the other side of the bed and there it was that I found something that sent my heart pounding: a scarf, a neatly folded lady's scarf. It was in the first drawer which was otherwise completely empty. It contained only the very faintest whiff of perfume. It must have been there for some time. I opened the drawer. I picked it up and held it in my hands. What was Caspar doing with a lady's scarf? What was that scarf doing in an otherwise empty drawer? I couldn't stop myself, I ripped open the second drawer and the third. Now my heart really was thumping. In the second there was nothing except a lipstick. The third was empty. I sank to my knees, leaned against the chest and gasped. My mind was blown. The skeleton! The skeleton! These items or at least one of them belonged to that skeleton. That must be it. That could only be it. Wait, girl! You're getting way ahead of yourself! These could have belonged to anyone. They could be keepsakes: his mother's, sister's, niece's, anybody's. Just steady yourself and think. But I couldn't think. Not of anything else but that young clerical assistant who had gone missing from the hospital several months ago and was still missing. She had left work just after 6 pm, when it was dark, to walk to the train station but she had never arrived there. She was to go to a concert that night and her mother thought that maybe she had worked late and had decided to go directly to the concert with one of her friends. It was after 11 pm and she still hadn't come home when her parents, Mr and Mrs Adams, became very worried about her. They rang work and found that she had not worked late. They then rang several of her close friends to see if she was with them or if they knew where she was and when all their enquiries drew a blank they had phoned the police. When the police were told that this was quite unlike Sally, that she had never done anything like this before, they took a very serious view and began a full scale search for her. The first thing they did was seize the close circuit television tapes from the local train station. Examination of them showed that she was not on any of them, had never come within the ambit of the railway security area and had not caught the train. The surrounding area was searched but nothing found. The search went on for days. No hint of her whereabouts was discovered. It was quite clear that something bad had happened to her. Hadn't her mother gone on television and given a description of her and the clothes she was wearing the day she disappeared: 162 centimetres, slim build, wearing a blouse and skirt. I couldn't remember the colours of either but I could remember the scarf very well. It was a blue square of Cambodian silk which her mother had bought for her at a silk farm on the outskirts of Siem Reap in Cambodia when the mother, father and daughter had been on holidays there a short time before. The scarf I was now holding was a blue silk square. My head swam. The room around me blurred for a moment. I couldn't breathe. Had Caspar kidnapped her also and murdered her? Was that truly her skeleton at the end of the bed? Was it her scarf and lipstick I was now looking at? Were they trophies? I was aware that murderers sometimes retained intimate items belonging to their victims which they regarded as trophies and kept near them so that they could handle them again and again and relive the ecstasy of their crime and conquest. Was that empty drawer waiting to receive maybe my watch or some item of my clothing? Another trophy? I shuddered, slammed the drawers shut and ran into the kitchen. I was again shaking like a leaf. I stood at the sink and held on to its sides until I stopped shaking. For a moment I thought to grab the car keys and drive straight to Kalamunda police and tell them the whole story and to the devil with the consequences. I was actually at the back door when I managed to bring myself under control. I had already decided I would get the answers to those questions which I hadn't yet asked. I would be strong. I told myself I had a life to lead, that I had determined on a course of conduct and nothing would stop me doing what I resolved I would do. Caspar Wilderman had shown me a side of myself I had never known. Maybe it was time I knew the whole self. I would not be afraid. There might be a logical explanation to all this. Caspar might be innocent. I dearly wanted him to be innocent. Anyway, I had him under control. I would keep him under control. I had the knife. I would get the truth out of him. I had shown myself that kidnapping was a game at which two could play. On my own I would take this thing to its ultimate conclusion. I returned to the bedroom where he lay, seemingly, still asleep.

CHAPTER TWENTY SEVEN

The first thing I did was to retrieve the skeleton from where I had dropped it after I attacked him with it. I studied it before I placed it at the end of the bed so that it was facing Caspar, as it had faced me. What height would the living person have been? Not tall. A female, or a small male? Would it have been more than 162 centimetres? I wasn't sure but I didn't think so. My flesh crawled. Was I alone in the presence of a murderer and what remained of his victim?

Had the murderer intended to make a skeleton out of me when I had whetted his appetite? I was fortunate that Byron Osborne had taught me enough to be able turn the tables on Caspar otherwise … Well, I didn't want to think of that. I went back to his bedroom, fetched the scarf from the chest drawer and placed it on the floor beside the bed. If he could play psychological tricks so could I. Now, I would see how deeply asleep he was. I had already placed the knife on the bedside chest, where he could not reach it but I could, just in case he tried to exercise some form of violence. Then I stroked his face.

'Come on, Caspar. Time to wake up.'

Then he did it again, he caught me completely unawares. I couldn't believe it when he began to laugh. I reflexively jerked my hand away. No complaint of an unbearable headache anymore: laughing at me as if he hadn't a care in the world. I couldn't believe the change in him. When he spoke I didn't know whether he was taunting me or whether he really meant what he said. 'Don't take your hand away, Elizabeth. I was rather enjoying that massage. You have such a gentle touch. So caressing. The touch of an angel's wing. I would love you to touch me like that all over and never stop. Say you will, Elizabeth. Say you will turn my every waking hour into a dream. Be my own personal angel and I will stay tied up for ever and bless you for it. Please, touch me again. Kiss me again.'

I was shocked. Was he only pretending to be asleep the last time I had kissed him or was he referring to the time before that when his kiss had sent me into ecstasies and I had asked him to kiss me again?. I was so nonplussed that all the questions I had to ask went out of my head. All I could think to say was 'I thought you had a very bad headache and were deeply in a curative sleep.'

'No more headache. Completely gone. I'm glad I wasn't asleep. Or am I? Am I still dreaming?'

My heart was racing again. I couldn't believe it. Here he was tied up and restrained, as I had been, yet telling me that just because of me he was enjoying it. He was making it difficult for me to think straight. I was doubting myself again. He was again making me hate, admire and, yes, even want him, all at the same time, in spite of myself. He had me in his thrall. I had to break out of it. I knew I had to resist him. He might be a murderer? How could a person I thought was very likely a murderer exercise such power over me? Had he hypnotised me or mesmerised me or something. This couldn't be happening, yet it was. I knew I had questions to ask. I must ask them or I was lost, completely lost. Maybe I was lost already?

'No, you are not asleep,' I said. 'You are wide awake and I have questions to ask which you must answer. Look at that skeleton at the end of the bed and tell me that it is not what now remains of a young female clerk who used to work in the same hospital where you and I also work.'

He was in complete control and quite calm when he replied, 'Ah, you have become an investigator, a researcher just like me. We would make a great team together, Elizabeth, you and I. Researchers must be curious and you are now so very curious. I knew that in picking you I had picked the right person. The problem is you want to know about the past. At the moment I am not the least interested in the past. I want to talk about the present and the future. I want to talk about us, you and me, and the things we can do together in the future. Exciting things. Let me ask you a question; if you say you are now free from my hold over you why are you still here? Why haven't you run to the police and had me arrested for kidnapping you? I'll answer that question for you; it is because you like what I have done for you. You want to come to me but you don't know how to do that and not betray your previous teachings. You are finding reasons why you shouldn't give yourself to me. I am a kidnapper. I might be a murderer. I cannot be trusted. You can't be sure of me. What you are really doing is fighting yourself. You are still fighting that last vestige of inhibition from your former life. Let it go, Elizabeth, and be totally free. Free from all those things that have kept you from being yourself. Don't be afraid. Take the step. Take your clothes off, every stitch, without me having to do it again for you and that last vestige of inhibition will be gone. Release me from my bonds, come into my arms and discover what loving and being loved is really like. Do it. Don't think about it. If you think about it you will never do it. Do it now. Come.'

He had me gasping again. Had his invisible tentacles around me again. Was causing me to doubt myself. I was no match for him. I was but a lowly nurse. He was one of the foremost psychiatrists in his field of expertise. He was right; my last vestige of inhibition was slipping. I knew it was. I couldn't think. Couldn't stop myself; I yielded. Yielded because I had been deprived of such intimacy all my life. I flung myself at him and kissed him on the mouth, urgently and impulsively and without restraint. The thrill of it. The exquisite thrill of it! I was on fire again. He couldn't put his arms around me because he was pinioned but I wasn't and I wanted him. Wanted more than anything else in the world to be held by him; to give my all to him, to be his no matter what the price. To be his for always, in his world. With him. I didn't care about my world. Why should I deny myself any longer that which I knew in that instant I had craved all my life? Now I knew what that dream was all about. He had opened my eyes. I could see clearly. This man knew me better than I knew myself. I wrapped my arms around him and pressed him to me with a desire and abandon I had never before experienced. Thrill after thrill sent messages to my brain that blew away every restraint of the self I had previously known. It was as if I were on some kind of drug that burst through me, sweeping me into his world where every inhibition, physical and spiritual, was shrugged off. For the first time in my life I wanted more than anything else to be known by a man. I wanted to be fulfilled. He responded by pressing against me with all his manhood. Oh, the touch of him! In that moment, that mad, mad moment, I didn't care if he was a murderer, a double murderer, a multiple murderer. I just wanted him. He rubbed his lips backwards and forwards across mine. Then he broke off to whisper, with his lips close to my ear, 'Untie me, Elizabeth. Untie me and know the joy of a love that has no bounds. Now, you are truly free; you have nothing to fear.'

I lay for a moment with my breath coming in gasps and my heart convulsing. I was truly free at last. I had found myself. I knew who I was. I wanted to taste what I had never tasted before. I was a woman, a mature woman but I wanted to be a full woman. I had denied myself too long. I searched for his lips again. I found them. I needed him. I crushed my mouth against his. He responded with a passion I had never known. He throbbed beside me. I held him even closer. It was beyond description. My whole body ached for him and I could feel his aching for me. I was in delirium but I could hold the kiss no longer, I had to breathe. His mouth followed mine as I pulled back. At the same time he pressed as close to me as his bonds would allow. I pressed back. Oh, the joy of that pressure. I never wanted it to stop.

'Untie me, Elizabeth,' he whispered again. 'Take off your clothes and come to me. You are now free from all those inhibitions, every last one of them, that have kept you from being a woman, from knowing yourself up till now. Let me hold you to me. I don't care, have never cared about the Stockholm Syndrome. It was only a means to an end. All I wanted was you. Let me take you to the rainbow far above the cares below. Let me set your heart aglow. We were made for each other. I always knew it. Now you know it. There is only you and I in the world. Nobody and nothing else matters. Let us kiss each other into oblivion. Let me show you what love really is.'

Such passion. Such desire. In all the time I worked with him at the hospital I never for a moment thought that under the façade of the tall, always calm, dignified doctor who walked the wards, seemingly oblivious to everything but the care of his patients, did such fires burn. To me now he was the sleeping volcano which had suddenly erupted and could not be contained. I was in its path and it was sweeping me with it. And I wanted to be swept along.

CHAPTER TWENTY EIGHT

I unwrapped my arms from around him and pulled away. I would undress myself, take the knife, cut his bonds and set him free; would take my life into my own hands and enjoy it. This man would not harm me. I had been too suspicious, too untrusting for too long. It was clear now that he was not interested in the Stockholm Syndrome, at all. Hadn't he just said so? He was interested only in me. I know that now. He loves me. He has told me what I wanted to hear. All right, so he took me hostage, but he hadn't hurt me. Not really. Only that grasping of my throat when he had entered the house but he had cared for me with great gentleness since then. What else could he do? He was too shy to approach me directly. I might have rejected him. How could we have worked together after that? Yes, I would release him. We would both be free. Then I would join with him in unrestrained lovemaking.

I tore off my blouse and bra, my skirt and panties and flung off my shoes. I was now like him, completely naked but of my own free will. I stood beside the bed looking down at him. I could see his need of me. He said nothing. He just smiled at me. I smiled back. I reached for the knife to cut him free, then, like a thunderbolt and a flash of forked lightning Tarsey Horrigan jumped into my mind. She was looking at me in horror. The image was so vivid I thought for a moment she was actually in the room.

'What are you doing, Elizabeth? Have you gone crazy?' she shrieked. 'Have you caught that craziness from our patients that we so often laughed about and said was contagious? Are you going to give yourself to a man who may have murdered little Sally Adams? Remember, little Sally? She worked at your hospital. Then one day she disappeared never to be seen again. Sally was seventeen and in her first job. Get rid of your inhibitions, be totally free if that is what you want, but before you give yourself to Dr Wilderman make sure that that skeleton at the end of the bed is not now all that is left of Sally. Ask him again about her and about that scarf and that lipstick. Search the whole house thoroughly, every inch of it. When you are satisfied that he is innocent then you can jump into bed with him. If you don't do that I may never see you again. You might be the next skeleton.'

Tarsey seemed so loud, so immediate, so afraid for me, that I wondered if Caspar could hear her and see her as I could. I looked at him. He was looking back at me with a puzzled look on his face. Obviously he was wondering why I had stopped so suddenly. I stood transfixed for a fraction of a second.

'What is wrong?' he asked. 'Why haven't you freed me and come back into my arms? Surely you are not having doubts now? Surely you are not going to wreck this moment?'

All that had happened since the night I had been taken went through my mind like a flash. I must play this carefully. He was the expert angler who had played me so beautifully that I was just about to lose control of myself forever. He would then be my master to do with me as he wished. I would be his slave. This was the defining moment. I teetered on the brink. Here was where I had to make my stand. If I were the free, knowing woman that I thought I had become then I must be able to control myself; must not allow passion to overwhelm me. I knew now, without a shadow of a doubt, that I wanted to be made into a full woman, wanted it more than anything else in the world. Freud was nearly right in his analysis of my recurring dream. Now that my eyes had been opened, had been opened by

Caspar, I could see that it wasn't that I was contemplating sex, there was no contemplation about it; I desired it, urgently, impulsively, immediately, now. I was the drug addict in extremity - I needed my fix, my very first fix. But what about that skeleton?

CHAPTER TWENTY NINE

I didn't take up the knife. Instead, I sat down on the side of the bed and, with my heart thumping again, said, 'Yes, Caspar, I cannot lie to you, you have made me a free woman. I have never felt so free in my whole life. I want to live, live as I have never lived before. I would be lying if I didn't say that I am thankful to you for that. But before I do anything foolish I want to know about that skeleton at the end of the bed. Look at it and tell me it isn't what remains of Sally Adams?'

His reaction was immediate. He actually jerked almost upright - as far as his bonds would allow. I did not anticipate such a powerful response from him; he who was always so in control of his every action. He was actually shaking. He opened his mouth to speak but no words came. I had certainly struck a raw nerve. It took him a moment before he could gather himself sufficiently to speak. When he did speak I knew he was lying. For the first time I was certain that he was not telling me the truth. At last it seemed that I was gaining control over him. I certainly hoped so.

'Elizabeth! Elizabeth! This is preposterous!' he blustered. 'How can you even think such a thing, let alone express it. Are you suggesting that I have committed murder?'

'That, Caspar, is exactly what I am suggesting. Did you?'

'No, I did not! I have taken the Oath of Hippocrates, as all medical doctors do. The taking of life is forbidden by that oath. It is the role of doctors to save and nurture life, not to take it. Shame on you, accusing me of such a thing. Of breaking my oath. After I have set you free.'

'So are you saying that no doctor has ever committed murder?'

'No, I am not. I am simply saying that I did not commit murder. Now, stop being so untrusting and set me free.'

'No, I will not do that. You are not going to get control of me again. If I come to you it will be on my own terms, not yours. I would be more prepared to believe you if I did not know you to be guilty of kidnapping me. You admit you are guilty of that?'

'I suppose, technically. I am guilty of kidnap but that was in pursuit of science.'

'Which science is that, Caspar? You have already told me that you were not interested in the Stockholm Syndrome, that it was me you wanted all along. Are you now saying that you lied to me as well as kidnapped me?'

'No, I am not saying that. I did want you above all but if I could have proved or disproved the Stockholm Syndrome at the same time as I won your affection, your love, that would have been a bonus, a fringe benefit for both of us to share. Now, you are wasting time. Stop interrogating me, put your arms around me and tell me you love me. I need you so much, Elizabeth.'

He was applying his charm again. So smooth. This time it was not going to work. I had control. I would exercise it. Thank you, Tarsey.

'If you didn't kill Sally then tell me, whose is that skeleton at the end of the bed?'

'I have no idea.'

'What is it doing there?'

'There are two reasons for that, Elizabeth. The first is that it seemed a convenient place to hang your clothes. The second is much more complex. I wanted you to be aware of your mortality. You know, Death is a horseman who begins riding the day we are born. The nearer we come to the finishing line the faster he rides, or so it seems. At twenty nine you have lived maybe a third of your life and yet you haven't lived. I wanted you to know the richer side of life. I wanted to take you in my arms and show you that side of yourself which you would never have known but for me. I wanted you to come to me of your own free will. You still can, Elizabeth. I won't force you. Release me now. Allow me to take you in my arms and fulfil you beyond your wildest dreams. If you don't do it with me when will you do it? I can tell you now, you never will with anyone else. You belong to me, girl, body and soul. You know that. I know that. So why prolong the agony? Come to me.'

CHAPTER THIRTY

This man was tearing me in two. He knew me so well. Knew that my whole being ached for him. He had obtained such a grip on my mind, on my will, that I had the greatest difficulty restraining myself from flinging myself into his arms, crushing my lips against his again, and letting him do with me as he willed. Even then I wondered why I felt like this. Would I, at that moment, have jumped into bed with any man? Any man, that is, who wasn't a criminal. At that moment I needed fulfilment more than I needed life itself. I was prepared to taste that which I had never tasted even if I died the very next moment. Had Caspar Wilderman made a nymphomaniac out of me? Was that his intention all along? Find an innocent, destroy her inhibitions, turn her loose and see what happens. But he hadn't turned me loose. I had turned myself loose. Maybe we could both see what would happen? I felt so vulnerable. From moment to moment I didn't know what I was going to do. One minute I was on the brink of saying yes but found myself saying no. I truly feared I would say no and at the same time yield. Did all women when they were awakened feel like I did then? There were so many things about life I didn't know and I wanted to know. I was floundering again. Almost lost. But I wasn't lost. I wasn't yet beyond redemption. Maybe I would give myself to him but before I did I would heed Tarsey's words and find out all I could about him. After all he had delved into my mind and knew so much about my inner being to the point where, even now, though I had physical control of him, I was finding it hard to resist him. I took a deep breath, held myself for a moment then continued with my questions.

'Tell me,' I said 'Where did you get that skeleton?'

There was a moment's hesitation, a hesitation that told me much, before he stuttered, 'Where did I get it? Where did I get it?' I had rattled him. Then he said, too quickly, 'I got it from the hospital! From the hospital! We are allowed to use such aids when lecturing to students at the hospital.'

'At the hospital, perhaps? But what is it doing here? What was it doing at the end of the bed dressed in my clothes when I awoke after you kidnapped me? Was it being used as an aid to your lectures then?'

'It seemed like a convenient place to hang your clothes. I meant no harm by it. I'm sorry if I offended you.'

'I believe it was there to intimidate me. To frighten me out of my wits so you could gain control over me.'

'Nothing of the kind. I did not think you had such a suspicious mind. You surprise me.'

'What kind of mind do you think I have?'

'I thought you were gentle, loving and kind. If that is not the case then maybe I don't need your love after all?'

'And maybe I don't need yours either, Caspar. How could anyone love someone they can't trust?'

'You can trust me. Have I hurt you since you came here?'

'Well, not physically but you have tried to take control of my mind. In that, Caspar, you have failed. You have not control of my mind and you never will. That I promise you.'

He actually laughed then, a deep throaty laugh, as if I had told the funniest joke in the world. 'You are deluding yourself, Elizabeth. You know that what I have said is correct. You know you can't resist me. Right this minute you are just a breath away from setting me free and kissing me again on the lips. I know that's what you want. I also know it's what I want. Why are you fighting so hard? Come to me.'

We were going round in circles. He was playing for time. He was trying to wear me down. The longer he kept me in an agony of spirit and in desperate physical need the more sure he became that I would yield. Yield, driven by my own desires whilst he lay tied hand and foot. I had to ask my next question or he would have me.

'Forget the skeleton for a moment, then. Tell me where did you get this?' I produced the scarf and held it in front of his face.

He didn't answer for at least ten seconds. I could almost hear him thinking. Then he said, 'I have had that for a long time. It was given to me by one of my patients. A grateful patient. Where did you think it came from?'

I ignored his question and said, 'And this, Caspar? Where did this come from?'

I opened the second drawer. Took out the lipstick and held it, too, in front of him. 'Was this also from a grateful patient?'

'Elizabeth. I don't intend to answer any more of your offensive questions. If you don't want to release me so be it. I have tried to give you a fuller life. What are you trying to give me?'

'What I am trying to give you, Caspar, is me. You know that even better than I do, don't you? But before I do that I want to be sure I know the person I am giving myself to. You say you want me. Fine. If you really want me then you will prove your innocence to me. Let me go back to the scarf again. Tell me the name of the grateful patient who gave it to you and when she gave it to you? Then, when you have satisfied me on that you can tell me where you got the lipstick? I don't suppose you use lipstick yourself, do you? You see, you know all about me but there is so much about you I don't know.'

I was showing my hand and I knew it was very foolish but what else could I do. I wanted him. My whole body ached for him. All I wanted him to do was to prove to me that I had nothing to fear from him and he would be free and I would be in his arms in an instant. But give myself to a murderer? No, that was something I could not do.

He said nothing for a moment. His eyes were fixed on mine. He swallowed twice. I thought he wasn't going to answer. Then he said, 'Elizabeth, you are doing what the lawyers call reversing the onus of proof. You are asking me to prove my innocence. That is something I would have great difficulty in doing. The lady who gave me the scarf has long left the hospital. I don't know where she is now not even if she is even at her old address. She left long before you joined us. I can give you her name and you can check it against the hospital records. Then if you wish you can attempt to contact her and verify what I have said. The lipstick, believe it or not, was given to me by a former male patient. I won't tell you his history because to do so would break doctor/patient confidentiality. All I will say is that he came to us after a nervous breakdown. Although he had homosexual leanings he was married but didn't want his wife to know. Covering his homosexuality for years had left him in a terrible state. I spent considerable time with him and managed to convince him that if he told his wife she would understand and his problems would be over. It was the only way. He was amazed when he did so and his wife replied that she had known all about it for years.

She it was who bought him the lipstick. He gave the lipstick to me, saying that he had never used it. Does that settle your doubts?'

His explanation about the lipstick was so fantastic I didn't know what to think. Could he have made it up just there and then? Well, of course he could, but did he? I couldn't check either of his answers without going to the hospital. Even then it would be difficult. Anyway, I had no intention of going to the hospital. Not just yet. I was beginning to tell myself that I had been too suspicious; that I should trust him. He had given me explanations which might reasonably be true. All I had to do was accept them. Why should I deny myself any longer the joy of the two of us becoming one? Why didn't I just let go? Wonderland was within my grasp. He wants you, Elizabeth. He wants you very much. You want him. So what are you waiting for? Let him assuage that ache deep in your psyche that has waited so long for just such a moment as this. Yield, girl, yield. Enter the kingdom ruled by Eros and feel the joy of love to be found only in the arms of another. Your days of loneliness will be at an end. You will have become alive. I was slipping again. That feeling at the bottom of my stomach was too much. I was almost over the line. Then there was Tarsey's worried face again looking into mine as vividly as before. 'Don't, Elizabeth. Don't' she said. 'You must search the house and be fully satisfied that you have nothing to fear, ever. If you don't you might not find yourself in that beautiful kingdom of Eros, you might find yourself in hell and never have peace again.'

His voice broke into my thoughts, 'Elizabeth, I need badly to go to the bathroom. Will you please release me so I can go there?'

Now, I had a problem. How was I to take him to the bathroom without running the risk of his making me his hostage again? I made up my mind in a second. This was something that had to be done.

'Certainly I will take you to the bathroom, Caspar but I will not release you. I will do the same as you did with me. You will have one hand only free. I will hold the cord behind you and I will have the knife, this knife,' and I held up to him the large knife I had found in the kitchen. 'If you make the least attempt to be free I will plunge it into your neck. Don't doubt me. I will not be your hostage again. I will kill you rather than let that happen.'

He smiled. 'I will not try to escape, Elizabeth. I promise. I know how dangerous a woman with a knife can be.'

He was as good as his word. I took him to the bathroom and back without incident. When he was back, safely secured in the bed, I told him that I was going to search his room and asked if he wanted to tell me anything before I did so. There was just that slight hesitation again before he said boldly, 'Search as much as you wish, my dear. If you find anything you feel I should explain please tell me. I will be happy to put your mind at rest.'

It was an ambiguous statement. He hadn't said I would find nothing. I was sure he was hedging. It seemed to me that there was something I might find and he was setting the ground for an explanation that would allow him to get off the hook.

CHAPTER THIRTY ONE

I put my clothes on again and went to his room. I wondered where to begin. I was not a detective, I knew nothing about how to conduct a thorough, totally revealing search, so what was I to do? My mind went back to the camera on that tripod and I thought I would start with having a look at it. I detached it from the tripod and sat on the side of the bed to examine it. It had several buttons but only two interested me: the review for the video and the stills. I pressed the review for the stills. I received a shock such as I never had before. I don't think even realising that I had been kidnapped hit me with such force. I felt as if I had been kicked in the heart by a mule. I'm sure my heart stopped for an instant. Any wonder. There in the frame looking back at me was me. I was lying on the bed tied hand and foot completely naked. I was flat on my back. I wasn't exactly looking back at myself for my eyes were closed. This photograph had obviously been taken whilst I was asleep. There were several others of me in different poses. I was to some extent relieved that none of the poses was obscene but they showed a me I had never seen before. Never in all my life, except in the mirror, had I seen myself as I now saw myself. Here I was, completely naked, for him to show to any other person he so wished. I was mortified. Even though I was alone I felt myself blushing. How could he do such a thing to me? Why had he done it? When had he done it? Either he had photographed me when he had first kidnapped me and made me unconscious, or when he had injected me or else when he had drugged me. He must have put something in my food or drink. Some, if not all of those beautiful meals which he had so readily provided, and I could not see in the dark, had most likely been laced with a drug that had anaesthetised me. No wonder I sometimes awakened mad with thirst. Had he only photographed me? A chill ran through me. What else had he done to me? I had a panic attack in which I imagined all kinds of things. Then I took a deep breath and regained control. He hadn't done anything else to me. If he had I would have known. He had not gone that far. The simple truth was that he was a pervert as well as being mad. Maybe he was part of some ring that dealt in such material. I was repelled and revolted. Deep inside in some strange way I had hoped to find nothing. Nothing like this. I had hoped to be able to convince myself that he really was in love with me and wanted me for what I was not for what he was. Just for the joy of being taken in his arms and truly loved I was almost prepared to accept that the silk scarf and the lipstick had come into his possession as he had said; now that was all swept away with the discovery of these photographs. No man would do that to the person the loved. He was not for me. He wasn't just a pervert. He was cruel. I sat on the bed and wept. Wept for myself and what I had never known. Maybe never would know. I searched no further. I had learned more than I wanted to know. Well, I would do as he had suggested. I would show him the photographs and see if he could explain and set my mind at rest.

Clutching the camera, I returned to where he lay. He was lying on his side looking at the door. He watched me intently as I entered. I saw him look at my hand holding the camera. He smiled but said nothing. He obviously knew what I had discovered but was waiting to hear what I had to say. He really was the coolest person I had ever met.

I came up beside him and said, 'How do you explain these?' I held the camera before his eyes and clicked though the several photographs. When I had finished I said, 'Well?'

'There you go again, Elizabeth, thinking the worst of me. You are so unfair.'

I couldn't believe it. It was all my fault.

'Look at those photographs closely, Elizabeth, and tell me what you see?'

I was infuriated. He had not the least apology. He had invaded my space and he was blaming me. 'I have looked at them and what I see is the work of a pervert,' I retorted. 'No one with any decency would do this to any lady let alone one you profess to love. You are simply despicable.'

'You haven't heard my explanation, yet you condemn me before you do. Do you want to hear it or is it simply that you gave found me guilty already?'

I was so taken aback I almost apologised to him. It was as if I had done something wrong. What explanation could he have? Wasn't I the person who had been offended by his behaviour? Wasn't he the person who had been caught out having done something reprehensible? Yet, there he lay with an expectant look on his face waiting for me to explain.

I looked back at him trying not to let him subdue me. I squared my shoulders and said, 'All right, then, explain.'

'Thank you,' he said, in a quiet, gentle voice. 'I didn't think you would damn me without giving me a fair go.' I wondered what was coming.

'Look at those photographs, Elizabeth, and tell me what you see.'

'I see me, lying where you are now lying, stark naked in a variety of poses. Tell me, is that how a gentleman expresses his love for a lady.'

'Is that all you see?'

'Isn't that enough?

'Are any of those poses inelegant?'

'That has nothing to do with the matter.'

'That has everything to do with it. Will I tell you what I see?'

'I don't think what you see will take the hurt out of what you have done.'

He didn't respond to that. He just looked into my face with what I can only describe as a dreamy other worldly look and said with a voice charged with emotion, a voice I had never heard him use before, 'Elizabeth, when I look at those photographs I see the most beautiful female form I have ever seen. A completely flawless form with which nothing I have ever experienced could compare. This is every man's dream of what the woman of his desire should look like. Not only me but no red-blooded man could look at that form and not be sent into a state of euphoria beyond bliss. And the strange thing is, Elizabeth, you are not aware of it. Not aware that you are simply perfection in the flesh. I have never seen anyone like you. If any of those old masters had had you for a model you would be famous throughout the world to the end of time. Neither Mona Lisa nor Venus de Milo could compare. My great regret is that you keep rejecting me. I want you so desperately, so desperately, I would do anything, anything, to win your love. Can't you see that? I know I committed a great wrong in kidnapping you. I ask your forgiveness for that. I know that I also did you a great wrong in taking those photographs when you were asleep. Again I ask your forgiveness but, you know, you would never have given me permission to do so. I took those photographs with the intention of showing them to you when you were in a suitable frame of mind. I would have explained to you why I took them and asked you what you thought of them. Then if you were not happy with them I would have destroyed them. Believe me, that is the truth. The trouble is you keep getting ahead of me. First you free yourself. The back of my head and my bruises know about that. Then you find the photographs. Next you condemn me without hearing my side. I am tired of this battle of wills. You are too good for me. I can do no more. You are just that tiny, tiny little bit beyond my reach. Go to the police. Tell them what I have done to you. I will agree to everything you say about me and gladly go to gaol if that is what you want. What I ask in return, because I know I will never have your love, is that you allow me to keep the photographs. Now, I have nothing more to say.'

What could I say to that? He was telling me something I had never known before. I knew I wasn't ugly but I didn't know I could have such an effect on any man. His words sent me into paroxysms of delight. Here was a man who really wanted me. I couldn't believe it. Yet, he had spoken with such sincerity that I had no doubt he meant what he said. My spirits soared. My suspicions had no basis. He had kidnapped me because he loved me. He had photographed me because he loved me. I could give myself to him, unreservedly. And I so wanted him. I bent over him and said, 'Oh, Caspar! I believe you. I am so sorry for my suspicions. Please forgive me.'

'I forgive you and ask that you forgive me.'

'I forgive you with all my heart,' I said

I would have loosed his bonds there and then, torn off my clothes, again, joined him on the bed and cared not about anything else other than losing myself in his arms except that there, at the bottom of the bed, was that Sally Adams-sized skeleton gaping at me. It pulled me up short. It seemed to say, 'What about me? Are you in such a hurry to give yourself to this man that you are prepared to accept his word alone? Are you so naïve that you accept the unsupported word of a kidnapper? He did kidnap you, didn't he? Where is all that training and experience you have from the mental hospital? Did you accept everything your patients told you? Just a short time ago you thought the good doctor was not so good; that he was mad, that he was evil, that he was Satan himself. Now, you seem to have forgotten all that. Is your lust so great that you will accept anything he says on his word alone just so you can leap into bed with him? So he says he loves you. Good! Tell him that you accept his love but also tell him you are going make one last check at the hospital about me. Ask him if he has any objection. See how he responds to that. If you find that what he has told you is true then you can allow him to take you in his arms and change your world for ever. Satisfy yourself on that then you can satisfy your lust, if that is what you want? If you want peace of mind before you step over the threshold and through the door that will shut behind you never to be reopened make that call. Then you will have no regrets. No reservations. You have been here several days, taking another few minutes to find out about me may save you a lifetime of guilt.'

A skeleton accusing me of lust! Was that what my longing was? Just sheer animal lust. No, it wasn't lust. It couldn't be lust. I was never that kind of person. Could that be how my new, natural, free, me appeared? Could my inner feeling be so easily read? Did lust show on my face? We used to say in the hospital that we could often see on the face what was in the mind. No, I was not lustful. I knew what I was and I would prove the skeleton wrong, I would make that call.

'I am going to untie you, Caspar,' I said. 'But before I do I am going to check with the hospital that you did borrow that skeleton as an aid to your lectures. I'll do that now on your mobile phone which is in your other bedroom. I will also explain your non attendance by advising that you have had an accident but assure them you will be fit enough to return to work within the next few days. Please excuse me whilst I make the call.'

He gave me the most beautiful smile that set my heart trembling again as he said, 'You don't have to untie me, Elizabeth, I am happy that you have forgiven me and that I will soon be able to take you in my arms and love you as I have wanted to do since the first time I saw you. Before you make that call would you please take me to the bathroom, I am again in desperate need.'

The phone call could wait. That smile and his demeanour convinced me that the phone call was only a formality. Of course I would take him to the bathroom so that he could wait in comfort whilst I made the call. I helped him from the bed and, with the cord in one hand and the knife in the other, led him from the room.

He spent some time in the toilet whilst I waited impatiently outside. Then, when he was finished, I took him to the bathroom where he washed and dried his hands. As we walked back to the bed he said, 'Now you can make that call, Elizabeth. Please don't delay. I can't wait to hold you.' We were then at the side of the bed. What he said made me even more sure that I had been mistaken in my assessment of him - he wasn't a murderer. No, he couldn't be a murderer. He was a decent man, just madly in love with me. My nerves tingled all through me. My knees trembled. I relaxed my vigilance for just a fraction of a second and in that fraction of a second Caspar acted like lightning. Before I knew what had happened he had pulled the cord with overwhelming force out of my hand, swung me round, threw me on to the bed and fell on top of me. He lay across the arm that held the knife, I could do nothing. The next thing I knew his hand was on my throat and squeezing. I struggled with all my might. He would kill me now after he had raped me. I knew he would. My struggles were in vain. I was no match for such a powerfully fit person. What a fool I was to have thought that I could control him. I fell into the blackness. My dream of everlasting love was over.

CHAPTER THIRTY TWO

My recurring dream was back. I was skiing down an almost vertical mountain slope. I was going faster and faster. I had lost both my alpine poles. I had nothing to stop me. Then I was flying over the edge of a precipice and was falling, falling, falling. I awoke with a start. It took me a moment to realise where I was and what had happened. I was on the bed, totally naked, tied hand and foot again and it was very, very dark. I was terribly afraid. Oh, God! He had me again and he was going to rape me. I couldn't help myself; I cried out in terror. Then, out of the blackness came the most soothing, gentle voice I had ever heard. It could only be his.

'Have you had that dream again, Elizabeth? It's all right. You have no need to be afraid. I am here. You have to learn to trust me. I would never hurt you. When you and I are lovers that dream will go and will never return. I assure you that is truly the case. All it illustrates is the great yearning within you that has not yet been assuaged. On several occasions you have almost broken down that last barrier but then you freeze when it comes to taking that last step. You know I have not violated you in the way you most fear and I never will. You must be positive and leap over that barrier without the least hesitation. You must stop finding reasons for holding back. I am a psychiatrist, Elizabeth, I know. I want you to take that step yourself of your own free will. I know you want to. To show you that I mean what I say I am going to set you free from your bonds. Then we will both be free, in every way. I am going to put on the light so that your fear of the dark will be gone. You can then decide what you want to do. You can stay with me or leave me. I will not attempt to hold you. Before I do so I would like to have the mobile phone so that I can make that call to the hospital and tell them that I have had an accident but will be returning to work in a few days. I will also tell them this address. That is something I have never told anyone before. I will not try to hide anymore. If you wish I will give you the phone to make any call you wish. I am sorry that I have had to use force on you again. This time it was to free myself, not to kidnap you. You see, I now know you love me. All I wanted to do was prove to you that I wanted you above all else. I couldn't do that whilst I was bound. Do you understand that?'

Was I hearing correctly? He was going to free me. He loved me above all else. What more did I need. Surely the skeleton and Tarsey would be satisfied with that. If they weren't, I was. I had wasted enough time. I told him where the mobile phone was, he bent forward, kissed me gently on the lips and left the room.

He was back within seconds with the mobile phone in his hand. He switched on the light. I could see that he was still naked. He sat down beside me on the bed, dialled a number, put the phone to his ear and spoke to someone at the other end. I heard him tell who he was and give the address he was speaking from. He said he was indisposed because of a domestic accident, nothing to worry about and that he would be back to work as soon as possible. He apologised for any inconvenience then finished the call and put down the phone.

He looked at me and said, 'Well, there you are, Elizabeth. I've done it. Now I am going to cut your bonds. You will be free physically and spiritually. Your new life is just about to begin.' He took the knife cut away my bonds and set me free. He picked up the phone again and held it to me. 'There you are,' he said. 'You can now make any call you like. Ring the hospital and ask them about the skeleton. I know that they will confirm what I have already told you. I have nothing to fear. And neither have you.'

For a few seconds I just lay there wondering if I wasn't dreaming. Was this nightmare really at an end? I looked at the phone in his outstretched hand and his eyes looking into mine. Then I shook my head. I had no need to make any call. I believed what he said.

'No, Caspar, there is no need for any call. I should have trusted you before. All I want now is for you to take me in your arms and show me how much you love me and I will show you how much I regret not leaping over that barrier sooner. I am ready to leap over it now.'

He leaned forward and gave me a kiss so exquisite that I squirmed in his arms. I moved over in the bed to make room for him but he did not come in beside me. Instead, he said, 'I think it proper, my love, before we begin our new life together that I wash away everything that's left of the old you.'

He was a powerful man. I didn't realise when I worked with him in the hospital just how strong he was. He picked me up from the bed as if I were a feather and carried me into the bathroom. He put me down gently in the shower and held me close to him as he turned the taps on full blast. I wrapped my arms around him and luxuriated in the feel of him against me. It was an experience beyond my wildest dreams. He was so masculine, so muscular, that I longed for him then and there. He took the shampoo and massaged it though my hair. Then his gentle, tender, loving hands were all over me, around and down my body massaging as they went. And all the time he throbbed against me. I couldn't contain myself any longer. I cried out in the grip of the most exquisite pain I had ever felt. This was what I had yearned for. He held me so close to him I could hardly breathe. Then, when the tumult within me had stilled, he took a large towel and dried every inch of me sending me into another stratum of delight in the process. During all of this time neither of us spoke. The moment was too precious for speech. To have spoken would have broken the spell. When he had finished he again picked me up and carried me back to the bedroom. He laid me down gently on the bed saying as he did so, 'Now, Elizabeth, this is the moment that, without being consciously aware of it, you have waited for all your life. This is where that recurring dream ends. Let me take you in my arms and make a woman out of you.'

I reached out my arms towards him almost dizzy with longing. He lay on top of me and held me. I wrapped my arms around him. I held him close to me; I wanted him even closer. I could feel his great need for me. My need was just as great. The skeleton could call it lust if it liked, I didn't care what it was called. I would never let him go. Never. He had won my heart. I was his prize. I awarded myself to him. He placed his lips gently on mine. I was ablaze. So was he. He was holding me tightly in his arms. So tightly I thought that he was going to squeeze the life out of me. Then, suddenly, he relaxed. His breath had been coming in gasps of passion, now he didn't seem to be breathing at all and he had stopped kissing me. He wasn't moving. I gripped him tightly and said, 'Caspar, what's wrong? Why have you stopped kissing me? Kiss me harder.' He did not respond. I could no longer feel him hard against me. His arms fell away. I felt afraid. I didn't know what to do. I thought I had done something wrong, that I had offended him in some way. I said, 'Oh, Caspar, kiss me again. Please, kiss me again.' There was again no response. I could no longer feel his heart beating. Why couldn't I feel his heart beating? Then it hit me with earth-shattering force, the reason I couldn't feel his heart beating was because it wasn't. My God! He was in cardiac arrest. My medical training clicked in. I rolled him off me, laid him flat on his back and felt for his pulse. I was right, there was none. I pinched his nose between my finger and thumb, placed my mouth over his and began CPR. I pounded my fist against his chest between breaths. Breath! Breath! Breath! Thump! Thump! Thump! Breath! Breath! Breath! Thump! Thump! Thump! I carried on like that for I don't know how long. It was all in vain. There was no heartbeat and no breathing. It was quite clear to me what had happened; he had had a massive heart attack. His ears and nose were blue. Cyanosed. He was dead. There was nothing I could do. There was nothing anyone could do. My first and only love had died in my arms. Died when the prize was his. I was too devastated to weep. I just lay beside him holding him and kissing him until he began to grow cold. My new world had crashed, crashed before it had begun. What was I to do now?

CHAPTER THIRTY THREE

I got up from the bed put on my clothes and sat down to think. There was no point calling for an ambulance or for the police. What could they do for Caspar, or for me? Absolutely nothing. Call them and I would have to tell them all that had happened. Tell how he had kidnapped me and how I had injured him. Tell how I had fallen in love with him. My story would make the headlines not only in the local newspaper but in all the national newspapers, not to mention the international ones as well. I would be marked for life. I would never outlive the notoriety of it. My new life would be ruined. What would my mother and father think? What would my friends think? Oh, God, help me! Please, tell me what to do. Tarsey where are you now? I need you so badly.

I do not know how long I sat totally bereft. At length I decided I must take control of myself. I could not stay there forever. I had to get away. I had to get back to a normal life. I must act and act quickly. I knew what I had to do to put my life back in order. I would remove all trace of my ever having been there.

First, Caspar. I turned him on his side and brought the bedclothes up around him as if he were asleep. I went to his medical bag and took a pair of rubber gloves from it. Then I took the mobile phone, wiped it clean of my fingerprints and DNA, put it in his hands and pressed his fingers around it. I released it from his hand and placed it on the bedside chest nearest to where he lay. It would look as if the last time he used it had been to call the hospital and tell them of his accident and, more important, where he then was. Then, when he didn't turn up for work, someone would come to see if he were all right and then could begin the business of ascertaining what had happened to him. I set about cleaning the house of everything that might bear a trace of me. I rubbed and scrubbed and cleaned the bedroom, the bathroom, the kitchen and the other rooms where I had been. I left nothing that the forensics could use to find me. I knew Caspar's death would be treated as suspicious not because of that cut on the back of his head, that could easily happen from a fall; but because the bruising I had inflicted on him with the skeleton was at the front of his body, the forensics would ask how it was that he fell forward and injured the back of his head and the front of his body at the same time. That would surely make them ponder. They would go through the house with a fine-tooth comb. I had to leave it as normal as possible. My time as a mental health nurse and the patients we had from the court had taught me much about the police and how they went about their work. I packed everything I didn't want the police to see into plastic bags and put them in his car. I even cleaned out his garbage bin. I took his digital camera and placed that in the car where my suitcases already were. The police would find no photographs of me in the nude. I was all set to go. Now all I had to do was to transport everything to my house, bring the car back and park it in his garage. The best time to do that was when it was dark. As soon as I could I opened the garage and drove to my house in Guildford. I removed everything from the car and put it in my own car. I went back to Caspar's house in Caspar's car. All the time I drove carefully. I didn't want to be stopped by the police for some minor traffic offence and be found driving the car of a person who was later found to have died in suspicious circumstances. I got back to the house safely. All was well. I gave the car a good clean before I parked it in the garage. I was still wearing the rubber gloves so that there would be no traces of me on the steering wheel, handbrake or rear vision mirror, places I knew the police always checked for fingerprints and DNA. I went back into the house and had a last look around. It did not appear that I had missed anything. I left the skeleton at the end of the bed where I had first seen it. It still gaped at me and I still wondered about it. I would make enquiries about it later on. The square of silk and the lipstick I returned to the drawers where I had found them. I bent over and gave Caspar one quick last kiss then straightened quickly before the tear that was trickling down my cheek fell on to his face. That tear could identify me. I left the bedroom and the house, closing the door behind me but not locking it. It would be easier for anyone worrying about Caspar's welfare, who came to the house to see how he was, to gain access if the front door wasn't locked. I walked to the bus station at Kalamunda just in time to catch the bus that would drop me at the bus stop near my street. I slid into a back seat and huddled there until it was time to get out. There was hardly anyone in the bus, certainly no one I knew. It was with relief that I exited at my street and walked home in the dark. I was safe. First thing I did was book a single ticket to Tasmania that same night. I was lucky, I got the last seat on the Red Eye Special leaving at midnight. I arranged a taxi to collect me and drop me at the airport just in time to collect my ticket, pay for it and check-in in time to board. I had a window seat on the plane. I sat down, turned my head to the window, closed my eyes and pretended to sleep. I didn't want any conversation with anyone until I was in Hobart. I didn't sleep, I was too hyped up. Too much had happened to me since Caspar had smashed through my door. In my mind I played and replayed every scene of what had happened throughout the entire journey. Caspar had kidnapped an innocent who thought she knew about life but knew nothing. He had opened her eyes, made a free spirit and, almost, a full woman out of her. A tear trickled down my cheek as I thought how cruel fate had been to snatch from me that fulfilment that I now craved, that I knew was my right to enjoy. I was glad I was facing the window so that my fellow passenger couldn't see that tear. I made no attempt to wipe it away. As soon as the plane landed I cleared quarantine and other landing formalities and phoned Mrs Panic to tell her I was on the way. Then I picked up the hire car the airline had arranged for me and drove to the Blue Wine Cove Motel.

CHAPTER THIRTY FOUR

Mrs Panic was waiting to greet me with outstretched arms. I threw myself into them and wept. She hugged me and said, 'There! There.! Elizabeth. You're home. It's so good to have you here. Roxy and I missed you so much. We waited for you every day and wondered what had happened to you. Roxy thought some hunk might have kidnapped you and carried you off to Shang-ri-la. We did try to get in touch with you. Roxy rang you three times and I, myself, rang you three times as well but you weren't answering your phone. We didn't know what else to do. We didn't know which hospital you worked in. In the end I told Roxy not to worry, that you would come.'

Then Roxy came hurrying out. She, too, hugged and kissed me like the old friend she had become and told me how glad she was to see me. She said they thought something dreadful had happened to me and they were so relieved to hear from me to say I was on the way.

'You poor dear,' said Mrs Panic. 'Come into the dining-room and have something good to eat. That airline food we wouldn't feed to the ducks in Yugoslavia. And you must be worn out after that long journey. You look so tired. Didn't you get any sleep on the plane?'

I said I had had little sleep and I really was very tired.

'Straight to bed with you, after you have eaten. You'll feel much better when you have had a good rest.'

Neither of them said another word. I didn't think I had to say anything. Anyway, there was nothing I could say. Mrs Panic's light-hearted talk about kidnapping almost made me jump out of my skin. She could never have guessed how close to the truth she was. I hoped she didn't notice the involuntary twitch I gave then. With her lovingly holding my right arm and Roxy my left, I was taken into the dining-room where I was treated to a breakfast that only Mrs Panic could have made. It was, indeed, like coming home.

They left me in peace to eat. As soon as I had finished I said I was very, very tired, excused myself and went to the bedroom. I had a long hot shower before slipping between the sheets and falling instantly asleep. I had had no sleep since I awoke the day before in the dark to find that Caspar had again kidnapped me and was again sitting naked beside me. How I wished that he was beside me now. My mind was in turmoil, I dreamed that I was naked again and I was in a maze. I had been in that maze for days and had no hope of ever finding my way out of it. I had to get out or I would surely die there. I felt terribly, terribly alone. I began to walk faster and faster down endless avenues of trees. Next I was running with my breath coming in gasps. Still I could not find the exit. I turned a corner and, there, right in front of me, was Caspar. He was standing beside a swing beckoning to me. I raced towards him and threw myself into his arms. He lifted me up, placed me on the swing and pushed. I went flying upwards towards a great golden full moon. I looked backwards and he was standing below me, laughing. Now I was swinging back towards him. Another push and I was swinging away from him again. I didn't want to be flying away from him I wanted the swing to stop and for him to take me in those powerful arms of his and love me as I had never been loved before. Then, without warning the swing broke and I was falling, falling, falling again. I didn't know what was going to happen to me. This was surely the end of my life. The end of everything I had ever known. No, no, no, it wasn't the end, it was the beginning. Everything was going to be all right for there, below me, was Caspar waiting with his arms outstretched to catch me and hold me. He was naked, too. I could see how much he wanted me. My heart leapt. At last I was out of the maze, the swinging had stopped. I was into a new life where I would know joy like never before. I fell straight into Caspar's arms. He wrapped them around me. I wanted him with a need that only he could assuage. He placed his lips on mine. My whole body quivered at his touch. Then, as I pressed closer to him, I found that he wasn't holding me any more. It was just me holding him. Dear Lord, he was slipping away from me. I tried desperately to hold on to him but it was no good. He had slipped completely out of my grasp. I lunged after him and then I was falling through space again. I awoke with a thud that seemed to jar every bone in my body. For a moment I didn't realise where I was. I felt in the bed for Caspar but he wasn't there. He was gone, gone for ever and ever. I was alone. Dreadfully alone. Fate had cheated me not only in my waking hours but in my dreams. I curled up in the bed and sobbed for what might have been but now I knew never would be.

It was some time before I recovered sufficiently to get up, dress and go into the guest room. Mrs Panic was soon beside me. 'My goodness, Elizabeth,' she said, 'you look awfully pale. Are you feeling all right?' I said that I was fine but had a bit of a headache. Probably all the travelling had knocked me out of rhythm. I had to get away before I was asked too many questions, so I said 'What I need, Mrs Panic, is to see Wineglass Bay again. A couple of hours there will blow away the cobwebs and I'll be on top of the world.'

'Of course you will, my dear,' she said. I took my back pack and was on my way within twenty minutes. At Wineglass Bay I parked the hire car and set off to enjoy what the Aussie's call a 'bonzer' day. The sun was shining with a soft gentleness only to be found in Tasmania; the air was fresh and clear; there was a light breeze blowing, ruffling my hair and lifting my spirits. In spite of Caspar having said so much of my life was over I felt invigorated. A third of my life might have been over, if so, all the more reason why I should enjoy what was left of it. And enjoy it I would. I was still a young woman. I took a deep breath, squared my shoulders and strode out. Life was for living, not for grumbling about. I would throw myself into it and walk my cares away.

It took me nearly an hour to reach the top of the ridge that looks down into the bay. What I saw nearly took my breath away. Wineglass Bay is one of the most beautiful places on earth. Shaped like the wineglass that gave it its name, it is rimmed with white sand that has no equal anywhere on earth. The turquoise water is like liquid silk and the birds calling overhead provided a music that made this a phantom place. As I stood there revelling in the privilege that few people on earth have experienced I wondered how the Freycinet brothers must have felt when they first saw it all those years ago. They must have felt they had been transported to fairyland. They would have been delighted that the national park in which the bay is set bears their name.

I drank in the view until I was sated then scrambled down towards the beach. It took me nearly another hour to reach the silver sand. There wasn't another soul about. I stripped off my clothes and plunged naked into the crystal clear water. I got an awful shock; the water was freezing cold. Ten minutes was all I could take of it. It wasn't so much for swimming in, it was more a tonic for the eye and a tone-up for the spirits. I came out, dried myself and set off walking quickly to warm myself up. Then I climbed half way back up to the ridge, sat down and enjoyed the beautiful sandwiches Mrs Panic had made for me. Looking over the bay I wondered why life couldn't always be like this with beauty all around. Maybe it was? Maybe it was there all the time and I just hadn't been able to see it up to now. My cares were intruding themselves upon me. They were shaken off when down below about a hundred metres from the beach I saw a pod of dolphins. They dipped and dived, played and laughed as if they hadn't a care in the world. They, surely, were glad to be alive. It was all so beautiful that I found the tears trickling down my cheeks again. I seemed to be doing a lot of crying these days. Time to shake myself out of it. I packed up my things, climbed to the top of the ridge, took one last look back at the earthly paradise below, then scrambled down to the road and went to where I had parked the car.

When I got back to the motel, tired and aching from kilometres of hard walking and climbing, I had a beautiful warm shower. It was wonderful. I felt good. I was my own person again. But free though I felt I couldn't stop my mind turning to Caspar lying stiff and stark in that lonely bed of his. I wondered if the hospital had tried to contact him, had been unable to do so and sent someone to the house to check on him. I could imagine the uproar if they had and found him dead. They would have had to report the matter to the police. What would the police do then? Would they turn the house inside out? Surely that was something that would follow naturally in the circumstances: that injury on the back of his head. Would they find something to connect me with him? I thought I had been pretty careful and done my best to ensure that I would not be brought into their enquiries. Then I thought, why should I worry about anything? I had done nothing wrong. Any fault lay with Caspar and he was now out of the loop. All right, I was the last person to see him alive but what of it? I hadn't killed him. At least I didn't think I had. He had died from natural causes: a heart attack. I had to be completely honest with myself, I certainly didn't want him dead, I wanted him very much alive. The stark fact was, however, that he was dead and I was alive. My life was my life, nobody else's. Caspar said he had set me free and seemed very proud of the fact. I was free. I would enjoy my freedom. I went in search of Roxy or Mrs Panic; I was ravenous and wanted something to eat. I found Mrs Panic in the kitchen. She was rolling out the pastry for a pizza. As soon as she saw me her face lighted up. 'My goodness, Elizabeth,' she said 'you do look good. So much better than you did when you arrived. I suppose you would like something to eat?'

I said, 'You must have read my mind, Mrs P. I could eat an elephant.'

'We don't run to elephant steaks in this humble establishment,' she laughed, 'but if you give me a minute till I have finished rolling out this

189

pastry I'll rustle up a sandwich that will keep you running to dinner time. How would ham and cheese or cucumber and tomato grab you?'

I said, 'Very nicely. Thank you. I'll have both.'

She chuckled at that. Her fat friendly face made me feel so much better. We chatted about everything and nothing until she had finished the pizza, then she made the sandwiches and joined me in the dining-room where together we finished a whole plateful. Mrs P enjoyed her food. Little wonder she was plump. Very diplomatically in our chatting she did not raise the reason for my late arrival. I felt I owed her some kind of an explanation but I didn't really know what to say. I was embarrassed about it but I couldn't just say nothing about it. She and Roxy must have discussed my non-appearance. People as close as they were couldn't let something like that pass without some kind of comment. Nobody pays a ten percent deposit then appears nearly two weeks late and not say anything about it. I couldn't tell her the whole truth, I'm sure she would have been horrified if I did, but I wouldn't lie about it. I decided on a potted version.

'Mrs P,' I said, 'I'm sorry I didn't arrive at the time I had arranged for but I ran into a bit of a problem. It took a bit of sorting out and I was not in a position to contact you. I hope you weren't inconvenienced in any way?'

'Not at all,' she said. 'Not at all. Roxy and I just wondered what happened to you. We thought you might be ill but hoped you weren't. I am delighted you are here and hope you can stay the whole month.'

'I'm sorry I can't, Mrs P, duty calls, as always. I have to get back to work as already arranged. A lot of people will be depending on me to be there and I can't let them down. But I will gladly pay for the full month so that you suffer no loss.'

'Indeed you will do nothing of the kind. I wouldn't hear of such a thing. I am only sorry that you weren't here for your full holiday and I hope that your problems have all been sorted out.'

'Oh, yes, they have,' I said, 'as far as possible. I promise I'll be back for the full month next year. I might even be able to coax Mum and Dad to come with me. I'm sure they would both love it here and Dad does need a break from the farm. There is just nowhere on earth like Wineglass Bay.'

'You can say that again,' she said.

Then it was time for her to get back to the kitchen to prepare dinner. She had other guests to attend to as well as me.

I just had time to slip into the township of Coles Bay and buy some postcards and stamps to send off to Mum and Dad, my friends at the hospital and Tarsey before dinner. They must all be wondering why they hadn't heard from me. I scribbled an identical, 'Having a lovely time here in Tassie. Weather beautiful. Scenery out of this world. Glad to be here. Wish you were, too.' Then I hurried to the post office and slipped them in the post box before driving back to the Blue Wine Cove. My life was nearly back to normal.

But my life wasn't back to normal. Would never be normal again. Whilst I waited in my room for Roxy to call me for dinner I nearly cracked up. I switched on the radio for the national news. I wondered if Caspar had been found yet. There was nothing about him on the news. I wasn't sure if that was a good thing or not. I wanted him found and the furore surrounding his death to have abated by the time I returned to Perth. I was unsettled. I knew I would be unsettled until this thing was at an end. How would it end? That's what worried me. The police weren't stupid. If they decided that his death was suspicious, and I couldn't see how they wouldn't, I would surely be on their list of suspects. I would be taken to the police station and questioned. They would find out I had gone to Tassie later than

I had arranged and would want to know why. Where had I been? If I said that I had been ill they would ask why I hadn't called the doctor. Why I hadn't called the hospital? Had I anyone to substantiate what I said? Why hadn't I advised the motel that I was going to be late? If they contacted Mrs Panic and found that I had told her a different story, that I had never mentioned illness to her, they really would be suspicious. There were a hundred and one questions they would want to ask. They would tie me in knots. I would be no match for them. Oh, God! What was I to do? I should have gone to them when I had freed myself. They would think I had murdered Caspar. Now, if I told the true story no one would believe me. I would be charged with murder and go to prison for a long time. Hadn't I cleaned up the scene of my crime? Why did I do that if I were innocent? Maybe I should go to them now and tell the whole story. Would they believe me even then? I was working myself up into a state. I was on the verge of cracking. My heart was pounding, I was shaking. I felt I was going to be sick. Then, with an effort, I took control of myself. I had done nothing wrong. I was letting my imagination run wild. The police could not force me to answer questions. They could ask questions but wasn't the law that although they could ask lots of questions I didn't have to answer? Only one person knew what had happened, that person was me and I did not have to say anything. The police could not force me to speak. I would just refuse to answer. Anyway, this was all speculation. Wasn't no news good news? I must keep calm. I must keep control no matter what. I was on holidays. I had planned to come here to relax and enjoy myself; that's what I would do. Let the police come. I had nothing to be ashamed of. What had happened was that I had been kidnapped and in the process had come to know myself. I had a lot of living to do and live I would. Before I could think anymore, Roxy called me for dinner.

In the days that followed I drove all over Tasmania. I went all round the island. Did a full circle of it. Always in the past when I had been here it was like being in an earthly paradise. There was nowhere else I had ever been that began to compare with it. Here, I always forgot all my cares and always returned to Perth refreshed. Not this time. This time I was not forgetting my cares. I couldn't get Caspar out of my mind. He was lying cold and dead and alone and I was doing nothing about it. It was as if I didn't care. I did care. The trouble was I couldn't do anything. I was trapped. If I went to the police and told them everything, I would be shamed in front of all my friends. If I didn't tell, I had to live with myself. What could I do? That's what I asked myself time and time again. I could I find no peace. I tried to enjoy the scenery, everything so green and beautiful. The air clear, clean and fresh. The people so open and friendly. It should have been idyllic but it wasn't. You see, I was in torment. How can one be free and be in torment? That was the question I continually asked myself. I found no answer because there can be no answer when one has something to hide, No one else could see it. I couldn't see it but I could feel that festering sore gouged deep into my soul. Dear God, would I ever be free from its torment? I was relieved when the time came for me to return to Perth.

I bade goodbye to Mrs Panic and Roxy, hugged them both, smiled a smile that was only lip deep, promised to be back again next year and drove to the airport at Hobart.

CHAPTER THIRTY FIVE

A warm sun greeted me on arrival at Perth airport. I was first off the plane and hurried to the carousel to wait for my luggage to catch up. The quarantine officer didn't seem too happy when I patted her little dog as it sniffed its way past my case. I patted it anyway. I had no fruit or vegetables in my luggage to cause it to sit down and wait whilst its mistress asked me why I had disobeyed the rules and brought something into WA that was strictly forbidden. She at least was one representative of authority I had no cause to fear. I grabbed the first taxi in the rank, the driver stowed my luggage in the boot and I was home in ten minutes. As I closed the door behind me I thought of how Caspar had burst through it and grabbed me by the neck and I was back once more in that fateful night; I just couldn't help wondering if his body had been found yet. To put it out of my head I got out my car and drove to the supermarket at Midland where I stocked up with some fresh bread rolls and enough groceries to last me for a week. Returning home I made myself a cup of Irish Breakfast tea, smothered one of the rolls with honey and tried to think of nothing else but eating until I had demolished it. I turned on the radio but there was no news on it that was of any interest to me. I got my clothes ready for work next day, had a shower and went to bed. I wanted the morning to come quickly so that I could get to work and learn if there was any news on Caspar. I couldn't sleep. I tossed and turned all night and relived every minute of my kidnapping again and again. It was beginning to get light when I slipped into sleep. I awoke with a start to find that I had to rush to get to the hospital to begin my morning shift on time. After my morning shower I looked at myself in the mirror. The person I saw looking back at me didn't impress me. I looked as if I had been dragged through a thorn hedge backwards. It didn't seem that my holiday had done a lot for me. I hoped my colleagues at the hospital didn't think so also. I gulped my breakfast, had a last look in the mirror to see if I could do anything to perk myself up, gave it up as a bad job, got out the car and began to drive down Great Eastern Highway. I was looking inwards so intently that it was only when a third car approaching me flashed its headlights that I became fully aware that two others had already passed me doing the same thing and I was doing seventy km/h in a sixty zone. I managed to slow just in time to pass the police car parked round the curve with an officer standing beside it pointing a radar speed gun directly at me with my speedometer reading ever so slightly over sixty. Phew! That was too close for comfort. I concentrated on my driving until I reached the hospital. It was a relief to drive through the gates and straight into the staff car park.

I caught the lift up to the third floor. I was back. Everyone beamed at me and said how well I looked and how happy they were to have me back. I went to the ward and reported to the supervisor. She said she was delighted to see me back, hoped I had a lovely holiday, then asked if I had heard the news. A nerve jumped in my stomach. I smiled and tried to give myself a blank look. 'What news? I asked. 'Have all the patients been cured and us all made redundant?' 'I wish,' she said. 'Permanent holidays would be nice. Then we could all go and live in Tassie. No, nothing quite so pleasant. Dr Wilderman was found dead in bed. I'm surprised you haven't heard.'

There was nothing pretended about the exclamation I gave. 'Oh, my goodness!' I said. 'I haven't heard. When did this happen?'

'It's been all the rage here. Probably didn't rate a mention in Tassie because it's too local. So many murders nowadays. Not like the old days. Found dead in bed about a week ago. He had phoned in sick saying he had had an accident but was okay and would be back at work in a day or two. When he still didn't come to work some days later the administrator sent Brett Mason to see if he was all right. His front door wasn't locked so after he had knocked and got no reply Brett walked straight in. Dead in bed, he was. Brett as you know is a pretty tough guy. It takes a lot to knock him off balance but even he says he was knocked sideways when he entered the main bedroom and found the doctor dead. Not only did he find him dead but there was a skeleton hanging up at the end of the bed. Can you imagine it, a skeleton in the bedroom? It gave me the creeps when I heard it. One of the orderlies said that maybe the doctor was sleeping with it, that maybe that is how some of these psychiatrists get their kicks. Some of them, he said, are more weird than their patients. I don't know how he could make a joke about something like that. It's in pretty poor taste. Some people have no respect. Of course it was reported to the police immediately. They have been in and out of here every day since questioning all the staff to see if they can get to the bottom of it. You would think one of us had murdered him the way they are going on. One of us murder Dr Wilderman! Did you ever hear such nonsense? Wasn't he the best doctor this hospital ever had, so good at what he did. So kind. So gentle. No wonder we all loved him. Now, we are all wondering what's going to happen next?'

It was on the tip of my tongue to say, 'Hadn't he borrowed a skeleton from the hospital to use in his lectures?' I don't know how I managed to stop myself blurting that out. If I had I really would have put my foot in. The police would surely be interested then to know how I knew that. I put my hand to my mouth as if the whole thing was complete news to me and said, 'I have heard nothing about it. It is a shock. I can't believe it. I'm so sorry for Dr Wilderman. He was, indeed, a lovely man; such a good doctor. Poor man, it must have been awful for him to die alone without anyone to hold his hand.'

'Yes,' she said. 'We will have difficulty finding such a caring doctor to fill his shoes. I wonder when they coroner will release the body for burial. With all the friends he had it will surely be a big funeral.'

'It surely will,' I said.

We chatted all round the subject and then graded on to what I did on holiday before I excused myself saying, 'I suppose we can't stand here talking all day, I'll have to see how my patients have been faring since I've been living it up in Tassie.'

Half way through the morning the administrator rang to say that she would like to see me in her office as soon as possible. Although my heart gave a wobble I managed to keep my voice even as I replied that I would come right away. I advised the supervisor and went to the administrator's office. I wondered what was coming. Had they connected me to Caspar's death? What would I do if they had? I put my hands together and pressed them to stop myself from shaking as I knocked on the administrator's door. She called 'Come' and I entered. She was sitting behind her desk smiling. I relaxed. She wouldn't be smiling if I were in trouble or she knew what I knew. All I had to do was keep my nerve.

'Good morning, Elizabeth. Good to have you back. I hope you have had an enjoyable holiday. I can tell you I could do with a holiday with everything that has been happening here. Please, sit. I'll try not to keep you long. There are two things I would like to talk to you about. The first is Dr Wilderman. I'm sure you have heard about his death? So sad.'

I said, 'Yes I have. It's awful,' as I sat with relief. She didn't know anything. She waited until I was seated comfortably then continued. 'The police have been interviewing members of staff to see if anyone can throw any light on what has happened. Dr Wilderman had some injuries that the police find puzzling and for the moment all they will say is that they are treating his demise as suspicious. They are also baffled by the fact that a skeleton was also found in the bedroom where he died. Examinations are being carried out on it at the moment but they are still ongoing. It all seems so very strange. What was he doing with a skeleton in his bedroom and where did he get it? For my part I don't know what a psychiatrist would be doing with a skeleton. He would hardly be studying it. Psychiatrists are more concerned with the mind than with anatomy. Oh well, I suppose it will all come out in the wash. I'm sorry. Elizabeth, forgive me, I have been thinking aloud. The reason I asked to see you was merely to advise you that the police would like to talk to you. Because you weren't here when the body was discovered they were unable to interview you. Just a formal matter, nothing to worry about. Are you willing to be interviewed and if you are when would be convenient?'

I hardly heard the remainder of what she said after she said that she didn't know why Caspar had a skeleton in his bedroom. If anyone would know that he had borrowed a skeleton from the hospital it would be her. Yet, here she was saying she knew nothing about it. Could it be that Caspar had, after all... No! No! It couldn't be. I wouldn't allow myself to think such thoughts. Didn't want to think that way. Yet the thought persisted. It just wouldn't go away. Wasn't he the cleverest psychiatrist around? So clever, so skilful, that he was able to enter my mind and orientate me in any direction he wished. He was a brilliant actor, too. Had to be, to fool me the way he had. All that smiling as he went about his hospital round and all the time he was sizing me up, making his plans to snatch me from my own home. And he had such nerve. Cutting my bonds and telling me I was free. Looking at me with that look of love as if I were the only woman in the world. Handing me the phone and telling me to go ahead and ring the hospital to enquire about the skeleton, when all the time what he wanted to do was possess me, physically, with my consent. And I fell for it, hook, line and sinker. What a fool I was. He hadn't set me free. By cutting my bonds he had made me more his captive than all the chains in the world could ever have done. How he must have laughed to himself as he told me he would take me to the rainbow far away from cares below; he would set my heart aglow. And I thought that he was being romantic when all he was doing was weaving his spell. Well, he did say that I was his body and soul. He had taken complete control of me and I loved him for it. I had become obsessed by him and the awful thing was that I still wanted him. I still wanted his arms around me to hold me and love me. I must be going mad. Then, another awful thought struck me. What would he have done if I had made that call to the hospital and found that they knew nothing about the skeleton? The answer to that question was too terrible to contemplate. Maybe I was lucky that I was so trusting, that he had gained entrance to my mind so easily. Lucky that I wasn't now also a skeleton and he in search of his next victim to play with and possess. Or was it that I was allowing my imagination to run wild again? Surely he wasn't like that. No one who seemed so gentle and caring with his patients could be that deceptive.

I tore myself away from my thoughts and said, 'The police can interview me any time they like. I would be happy to help in any way I can. I will make myself available any time as long as it doesn't interfere with my work.'

'Oh, don't worry about work, Elizabeth, this is a matter that has to be cleared up as quickly as possible. It is a dark cloud hanging over our hospital. It will put a strain on our staffing position but that comes second place to discovering what happened to Dr Wilderman. Poor man, we are certainly going to miss his wonderful love and care for our guests here. I will do my best to find someone to cover for you, Elizabeth, although I know they won't be you.' She smiled at me. 'Do you mind if I call the police now and find what time suits them?'

When I said I had no objection she telephoned the police and arrangements were made for me to be interviewed at 2 pm that day at Curtin House, the detective headquarters in Perth.

'If you would like a member of staff to be present during the interview I can arrange that,' she said.

'Not at all,' I said. 'I don't see the need. It will be just a formal thing, I'm sure. I don't see how I can help the police but then I'm not a police officer. I am into bedpans and urine bottles, not police investigations.'

She smiled as she said, 'Indeed so. The second thing I wanted to see you about is an application for appointment as a staff nurse from a Theresa Kingston Horrigan who works in a London hospital. She has given your name as a referee. Dr Wilderman was handling her application on which he had given a provisional acceptance pending your return from Tasmania. The doctor's file has been passed to me for completion. What can you tell me about Nurse Horrigan?'

My heart leapt for joy. It was wonderful news. Tarsey's appointment dependent on my say so! Well, Tarsey would not be kept waiting a minute longer than necessary. If I had my way she would have been there that day. I needed badly to see her happy smiling face and hear that fake Jamaican patois that she reverted to so often to cheer us all up, patients and staff alike.

'Tarsey Horrigan!' I exclaimed. 'She was at the London Free Hospital for Nervous Disorders with me before I came here. She is a wonderful nurse, very caring and has a great sense of humour. I have never worked with a better, more dedicated nurse. The worst thing I can say about Tarsey is that I would love to be working with her again.'

'I am so glad to have your approval, Elizabeth. As you know we are desperately short of nurses. I shall recommend to the board that she be appointed as soon as possible. Again, Elizabeth, I am so glad to have you back from your holidays. If only we had this dreadful business relating to Dr Wilderman cleared up we would be well on the way to getting things back to normal here. Thank you for coming to see me so promptly and for your help with Nurse Horrigan's application.' She rose and extended her hand to indicate that the interview was over. I said it was always a pleasure to help and returned to the ward.

CHAPTER THIRTY SIX

At 2 pm I was at Curtin House explaining to the police officer behind the counter why I had come. He checked on a computer on the desk in front of him and said, 'Yes, Nurse Bradley, we have been expecting you. Take a seat and I'll let Detective Neumann know you are here.'

I had barely sat down when a tall, dark, handsome man of about thirty, dressed in civilian clothes but wearing no jacket, came forward and said, 'I'm senior detective Adam Neumann, Nurse Bradley, thank you for coming in.' He extended his hand and grasped the one I held out in response in a firm dry handshake. He smiled and said, 'Let's go somewhere more private where we can talk in comfort. This shouldn't take too long, there are just one or two points we need to clear up.'

He led the way down a short corridor to a small room furnished with only a table and three chairs. He pulled out one of the chairs for me to sit on and when I was comfortable took one of the chairs opposite.

'Before we begin, can I get you a cup of tea or a coffee or a soft drink?' he asked.

I declined any refreshment saying I was anxious to get home as I had only recently returned from my holidays and had a lot of household chores to attend to.

'I understand,' he said. 'Let's begin. You can call me Adam. Do you mind if I call you Elizabeth, or would you prefer Ms or Nurse Bradley?'

'Elizabeth will be fine,' I said.

'I would like to record our conversation. Have you any objection?'

I didn't like the idea but didn't see how I could object without making him suspicious. Under the table my knees were trembling. I had difficulty controlling them. I smiled and said, 'I have no objection, Adam. Taping our conversation will, I'm sure, speed things up.'

He pressed a button under the table and a small device popped up in its centre. He looked at me and said, 'Now we are all ready to go.'

He asked my name and my address, how long I had lived there and my telephone number. How long I had been a nurse. How long I had worked at the hospital and a host of other questions that I had no difficulty in answering. I began to think this is going to be a breeze when he asked how long I had known Dr Wilderman and what kind of terms we were on. My knees began to tremble again. I pressed them together, smiled and said that I had known him as a doctor at the hospital and that I supposed that I was on the same terms with him as any other nurse at the hospital in our usual doctor/nurse relationship. He nodded at that as if that was what he expected. I began to relax a little though a pulse in my neck was beginning to beat a little faster. I hoped he didn't notice.

His next question jarred me.

'Were you here when he died?'

It was the brevity of the question that caught me unawares. He was looking directly into my face as he spoke. He hadn't looked at me so directly when he asked the other questions. It was a simple straightforward question that should have caused me no problem but I could not stop my breath coming that little faster. I tried to look relaxed as I said, 'That is a question I don't think I can answer, Adam, you see I have been on holiday in Tasmania and I don't know when Dr Wilderman died. I only heard he had been found dead when I returned to work at the hospital.'

'Oh, yes, I forgot that. I'm sorry. We had been awaiting your return from your holidays. Now, we know when you got back from Tassie but what I would like to know is when you went there?'

That direct look into my face again. My heart was racing. He was getting too close for comfort. I'm sure he knew the answer to the question before he asked it. What do I do now? Should I decline to answer further questions the way I had already told myself I could? How would I do that? Just decline outright and say I did not wish to answer any more questions or should I be more diplomatic and say I wasn't feeling too well and ask to be excused. Then, once I was excused refuse to come back. They couldn't force me and I didn't have to answer any questions. I didn't think they had any evidence to connect me to Caspar's death. But I was damned no matter what I did. If I refused to answer further questions, no matter why, they would know I had something to hide. If I carried on I would surely walk myself into a corner. All this went through my mind like lightning. I decided that I would carry on. I might still be able to extricate myself from the maze I was getting into.

I looked directly back at him and said, with my heart pounding, 'I went later than I had arranged. You see I was all set to go when I caught some bug or other that really knocked the stuffing out of me. It took me over a week to recover. I was in bed most of the time. When I did get back on my feet I took another couple of days just to make sure I was okay to travel. You see I had already paid a ten percent deposit for my accommodation which I didn't want to lose. The outward half of my return ticket was lost when I didn't show. I didn't want to lose it all. So I just paid the outward half again and went.'

'Didn't you go to a doctor at all?'

'I didn't need to. I am a nurse. I knew what was wrong with me. I knew that, like all flu's, it would run its course and I would be over it in up to ten days. That, of course, was what happened.'

'So you didn't call your doctor, Elizabeth. Tell me, then, did you call the hospital and advise that you were ill so that you could have your annual leave converted to sick leave and so save the days you were ill from being a complete loss?'

'No, I didn't.'

'Why didn't you do that? Wouldn't that have been the prudent thing to do? Save yourself some annual leave for when you were well enough to enjoy it, say, maybe, next year?'

'Adam, I thought you wanted to talk to me to see if I could tell you anything about Dr Wilderman that might help your enquiries about his death. I didn't think I was coming here to answer questions about my personal life. If you have no more questions to ask me on that I would like to be excused, I have lots of things that have piled up since I've been away.'

I knew I was being foolish but Adam's questions were becoming too pointed, too close to the truth for me to allow him to continue. He was very clever. Very good at his job. Very handsome, too, I thought. How such a frivolous thought entered my mind at such a critical moment I don't know. I only know that it was there. I also knew that I had to stop him before he asked any other questions that I couldn't answer without it being clear that I had something to hide.

He smiled and said, 'I'm sorry, Elizabeth, I did not mean to offend you or be personal or invade your privacy but, you know, these are the kind of questions that are asked in a case like this. What we are dealing with is the death of an, apparently, highly respected doctor which might or might not be murder. Usually, in these cases we ask all kinds of questions of people we think might be able to assist us in coming to a positive conclusion about how and exactly when such a person died. People who worked closely with him are generally able to help us build up a background picture of the person. We have no idea what we are working with here. We are working completely in the dark. I can tell you now, Elizabeth, this is not a straightforward case. There is more to it than meets the eye. We have one or two pointers, what you might call clues, that are causing us to wonder about the doctor's personal life. We'll know more about that very soon when our scenes of crime people have followed up certain leads. In the meantime I would ask that you answer my questions so I can cross your name off the list of people we think might know more about the doctor than they wish to become public knowledge. I can tell you now, anything that you care to tell us about Dr Wilderman will be treated with the utmost confidentiality. It will not be for public consumption. I want you to understand that.'

I understood all right. He had me in the frame. I had a cold feeling in my stomach. The thing was he was so nice. So gentlemanly. He was looking at me expecting me to speak but I was having difficulty speaking. I just didn't know what to do.

He saw my hesitation and said, 'I suppose this is all a bit much for you, Elizabeth, and I don't want you to feel under any kind of pressure. I will only ask you one more question and then we will leave it there for the moment. If necessary I can see you another day. If that is all right?'

I just nodded.

'This is really two questions in one,' he said. 'For the record, Elizabeth, can you tell me the day and date you went to Tassie and the day and date you got back?'

There wasn't much else I could do except tell him. I didn't know why he needed me to tell him; that was something he could have obtained from the airport. Then he was shaking hands with me and saying, 'It may be necessary to talk to you again, Elizabeth, and if it is, I'll let you know. Thank you for coming in.'

He walked me to the door and I hurried away. I just wanted to be out of there. I was so afraid of what was coming. I could see a black future looming and I didn't see how I could dodge it. I didn't go back to the hospital. I went straight home, made myself a cup of tea, sat down at the dining-room table, put my head on my arms and wept. I don't know how long I sat there. What I do know is that I sat there immobile for hours. I tried to think myself out of the mess that Caspar had got me into since he had burst his way into my life. Only a short time ago I had been revelling in the new found freedom that he had given me. Now it seemed that I was on the verge of losing that freedom and ending up in prison for years for a crime I didn't commit. When I came out of prison I would be an old woman. Certainly my best years would be past. Not much hope of that fulfilment I so much yearned for. How I hated Caspar now. He had made me aware of myself, promised me boundless happiness in the future that would be mine, then had gone when I most wanted him. In the middle of my hate for him I wanted him so desperately that I would have damned myself into eternity just to be in his bed again with him on top of me holding me in his arms and pressing himself into me. But that could never be. All that was left for me now was to live my life, the rest of my life, as an old maid. The thought struck me then that Caspar had proved one thing: the Stockholm Syndrome wasn't a myth. Wasn't I living proof of that? And that was a proof that would never be published. I couldn't write to The Lancet or Nature and tell the world all about it. What a comfort that was? Right then I hated not just Caspar but myself and the whole world. I went to bed and curled up into myself. I wanted to dream that all my troubles were over, that I had found a man who would love me with passion that would equal mine and that we would live happily ever after. I would even have settled for my recurring dream. I didn't dream at all. I lay awake the whole night tossing and turning. When morning finally came I almost did what I had never done before and called in sick. But I couldn't do that. My place was at the hospital and even though I felt like a wrung out rag I presented myself on the ward for the morning shift.

Things went along very quietly in what usually passed for normal for three days. All that time I couldn't get Adam Neumann out of my mind. Every minute of the day I expected him to call me to Curtin House or arrive at the hospital in a police car to tell me that I was under arrest for the murder of Dr Wilderman. When the third day dawned and he still hadn't appeared I began to think I was off the hook. Maybe the police had decided that I had told the truth and that there was nothing more they could gain from questioning me further. Maybe I had outsmarted them. That would be too good to be true but it was possible. The police didn't know everything. They were just human like the rest of us. When I wasn't thinking of the police and Caspar I thought of Tarsey. How I longed for her to arrive from London. How I longed to get my old life back and have my good friend there beside me. I needed a friend, someone whom I could trust, laugh with and share confidences. I had never been bored in my life but to be bored now would be wonderful. I began to feel just a teeny weeny bit relaxed. My relaxation was too premature. I had just come from the exercise area after walking there with one of our involuntary police patients when the charge nurse came to tell me there was a telephone call for me. My heart hit the floor. I just knew this was it. I was right, Adam Neumann was at the other end of the phone.

'Hi, Elizabeth,' he said, so cheerily and friendly that I thought everything was going to be all right. What he said next banished any thought of a happy ending. 'I would like you to come in and see me as soon as you can. What time do you finish your duty?'

I said, 'I'll be free about five. Is everything all right?'

He didn't answer that. I knew then that everything wasn't all right. He just said, 'Oh, there's just one or two little points to clear up. I'm hoping it won't take too long. Could you be here about six?'

'Yes, I'll be there,' I said.

'See you then,' he said and broke off the call

I was in a turmoil for the rest of the day. I wondered if I should contact a lawyer and get some legal advice. How would that help? If I arrived at Curtin House with a lawyer in tow the police would surely know I had something to hide. Anyway, if they were going to arrest me they would have come to the hospital and taken me away in handcuffs in a police car. Surely the police don't just allow murder suspects to walk into the police station. Don't they come after them and make a big thing out of affecting an arrest. No, I'd go to Curtin House and try to be brave. If things got to the point where I needed a lawyer I would say so. Oh, why hadn't I gone to the police when I had turned the tables on Caspar instead of trying to be smart? What a fool I was.

Six o'clock on the dot I was at Curtin House. Adam and a female detective were waiting for me. The first thing he said was, 'Elizabeth, let me introduce detective Caitlyn Stillwell to you. She will be sitting in on the interview. You may call her Caitlyn.'

I shook hands with Caitlyn. Adam led the way to the same room we were in before and when we were all seated he went straight to the point and said, 'Elizabeth, last time you were here I asked you some questions which you answered quite voluntarily. In answer to one of my questions you told me the day and date you went to Tasmania and the day and date you got back. You agree with that?'

'Yes,' I answered.

'You also said you had been ill from the time you left hospital to go on annual leave and that you had been at home all of that time. Correct?'

'Yes.'

'You never left home?'

'No.'

I noticed that Caitlyn was making notes in a pad in front of her.

'You never left the house at all during that period?'

'No. I told you, I was ill.'

'Indeed you did tell me that. Now tell me this, Elizabeth. How is it that you used no gas or electricity during that time and made no phone calls?'

I had never thought of that. Of course I hadn't used any gas or electricity or made a phone call. I wasn't there.

'I told you, I was ill.'

'Yes, you did. But you couldn't have been so ill that you didn't eat or make yourself a cup of tea during that time. What about the two days when you were recovering before you went to Tassie? How could you be so very ill one minute and then completely better the next? Sufficient to make an eight hour journey not to mention the waiting time at the airport?'

'How are you able to say that? How do you know that?'

'It's very simple, Elizabeth, we checked with the various utilities. I have all the relevant data here.'

It was then that he produced several papers and said. 'The power people supplied us with these. They each support what I say. Here, too, is a very precise record from the water board. Not a drop of water used during that time. Not a single drop. Not a cup of tea or coffee made, not a drink of water, the toilet not flushed, the shower not used. On top of that, Elizabeth, Mrs Panic at the Blue Wine Cove Motel where you stayed in Tassie, a lady who thinks the world of you, told us, in answer to our enquiries, that you never mentioned to her that you were ill. She said that she and one of her employees rang you at least six times at your home address and received no response. We know the telephone is beside your bed. So you didn't eat, drink, use the bathroom, use the telephone, switch on the light, or use your stove during this time? Is that, really, what you want us to believe, Elizabeth?'

'I don't want you to believe anything. That's what I have told you.'

'Oh, yes, Elizabeth, that is exactly what you have told us but is it what happened? If it is, would you be so kind as to elaborate so that we, Caitlyn and I, can get our heads around it. I confess we have both tossed this around between us and it just doesn't gel, Elizabeth. Would you like to reconsider your position and tell us what really happened?'

'No, I wouldn't and I don't want to answer any more questions. I want to leave right now.' I stood up.

In my mind then I damned Caspar. My anger towards him was back more black than ever. He had done this to me. I was no longer sorry that he was dead. He was just a callous murderer. He deserved to die. The pity was that he hadn't stood in the dock for all those who adored him to see what he was really like.

Adam stayed sitting and said, 'I think you'd better sit down, Elizabeth, I haven't quite finished.'

My heart quailed, my knees were trembling again and I could not hide the shakes. I knew then that I was not going to get out of this by lying. I stood defiant for a moment then the stuffing went out of me. I sat.

Adam then looked at me directly with those dark eyes of his and said, 'I'm sorry to say this, Elizabeth, but I don't think that you are being completely frank with us. I believe that you are hiding something. Something vital to our enquiries in this matter. Let me put it to you as kindly as I can and say, please, Elizabeth, tell us what happened in those days when you say you were ill and we have reason to believe you weren't?'

'I wish to answer no more questions. I wish to see a lawyer.'

'It is your right not to answer any of my questions and you certainly may have a lawyer but before we get to that stage let me tell you where we are at with our investigations surrounding Dr Wilderman's demise. I am going to tell you something that the general public does not know. I had hoped that you would be more forthcoming, it would certainly be in your best interests if you were, without us having to drag everything out of you. I am well aware that police stations are scary places for those people who have no experience of them but they are less scary if you tell the truth. Please treat everything that I now tell you with the utmost confidentiality. It must not go out of this room.'

I could hardly breathe. I wondered what was coming. I was almost petrified with fright. I never felt more like fainting in my whole life. If only Tarsey were here. Oh, Tarsey, where are you! Please come quickly wherever you are!

Adam continued with his eyes never leaving mine. Caitlyn, too, was staring directly into my face. I was the rabbit in the headlights.

'The forensics have gone through Dr Wilderman's premises with a fine-tooth comb. What we found you will no doubt find interesting, that is, if you don't know already. We found a skeleton in the bedroom where he died. That skeleton was what remained of Sally Adams who used to w…' I cried out 'No! No! No!' as my hands went to my mouth, involuntarily. He stopped and waited until I recovered. 'You all right?' he asked. I couldn't speak, just nodded. He continued, 'Young, lovely, innocent Sally Adams who used to work in your hospital and went missing on her way home from work. I'm sure you remember her. DNA has established beyond doubt that that skeleton is Sally's. We also found a silk scarf which her mother has positively identified as Sally's. A lipstick found there has also been identified through DNA. It belonged to Mavis Addison who also disappeared without trace on the way home from work about eighteen months ago. We have as yet to find any other trace of Mavis. It is our belief that she and Sally Adams were both murdered by Dr Wilderman. What we don't know is if Dr Wilderman was working alone or had an accomplice. You weren't in Perth when the serial killers, the Burnies, were active. They worked together picking up girls and murdering them. But I'm sure you now see where this enquiry is leading. Does what I have just said cause you to change what you have already told me?'

He waited on my reply.

I was thunderstruck. I could see now what he was implying. I was the willing partner to Caspar Wilderman when he murdered Sally Adams and Mavis Addison, very likely after he had raped both of them. What they wanted to know was where, exactly, I fitted in. Had I engaged in some kind of a lesbian involvement with both females after they had been kidnapped? Was I a party to the kidnapping? Had there been some kind of falling out between Caspar and me resulting in my murdering him then heading off to Tassie to cover my tracks? Maybe they thought that not only had I murdered Caspar but that I was also involved in the murders of Sally and Mavis, that I was into murder right up to my neck. Why else would I lie? Me! Involved in rape and murder! The room swung dizzyingly me around. I was in deep trouble. Why hadn't I told the truth at the beginning? Well, I had to tell the truth now. I prayed that it wasn't too late and that they would believe me. Spending the rest of my life in gaol was staring me in the face. I gasped for breath.

Adam said, 'Are you all right, Elizabeth?'

I struggled to get my breath back. It took me several seconds to recover then I said, 'I'm sorry, Adam, I have not told you the truth. I was so ashamed. I just couldn't. I want to tell the truth now.'

'Before you do that, Elizabeth, I must be formal and follow police procedure to the letter. Before you were merely a person assisting us as a witness. That has now changed. Now, you are a suspect and everything you say will have to be recorded. Do you still want a lawyer?'

'No, I don't want a lawyer. I will tell you it all as it happened. I have been an utter fool. I'm sorry I didn't go to the police and seek their help long ago. I tried to be clever but I'm not clever enough.'

He switched on the overhead camera and the tape-recorder and said: 'Elizabeth Bradley, you are not obliged to say anything unless you wish to do so but anything you do say will be recorded and may be given in evidence. Do you understand that?'

'Yes, I do.'

'I believe that there is something you wish to tell me regarding the death of Dr Wilderman? Is that correct?'

'Yes.'

'Would you like me to ask you questions about it, or would you prefer to tell me what it is you know first and then I can clear up any points of ambiguity afterwards?'

'Yes, I would prefer to tell the whole story from beginning to end, then, after that, you can ask me any questions you wish. I'll be glad to get this all out of my mind. I have been driven almost crazy by it.'

'All right. Please say what it is you wish to say.'

With my head down looking at my hands, which I had clasped together on the table between us, I told the whole story from the moment Caspar had barged through my front door till the moment he had stopped breathing on top of me. I told how I had then tried to revive him and when I couldn't how I cleaned up the house in an effort to remove every trace of my being there. I told him why I had done that. I left nothing out. It was a relief to get it all out in the open. I didn't care about shame. I just didn't want to go to prison for something I hadn't done. When I had finished I said, 'That is the whole story, Adam. Now, I am ready to answer any questions you wish to ask. I'm sorry that I have not told the truth before, I hate lying but I was so ashamed of it all.'

He was very kind. He smiled and said, 'Elizabeth, you appear to have had a terrible time. I regret having had to put you through all this but that is the way police work is and you didn't leave me much option. I am but a simple cop; sometimes I don't enjoy what I have to do but do it I must. I can't think of any questions I need to ask at the moment. I will have to go through your statement and make more enquiries. Police work at times is all enquiries. There is one thing I would like you to do before we finish for the day. Believe me, it is very necessary. Have you any objection to accompanying Caitlyn and me to Dr Wilderman's house where you can show us how you were tied on the bed and how you tossed him to free yourself. If we could do that now, we could have these enquiries all wrapped up that much sooner.'

I said I had no objection and we went to the house. Entering into the bedroom again sent my pulse racing. So much had happened there. I could hardly believe that it had happened to me. I pointed out where and how I had been tied on the bed and how I had tied Caspar in the same position. I showed how I had gone down on one knee and thrown him over my shoulder and how he had hit the bed post with back of his head and where I had cleaned up the blood. We went all through the house. I even showed the camera tripod and said I was sorry that I had destroyed the camera. Adam said he understood. I answered every question he asked me without hesitation. When we had finished he ran me home. I invited Caitlyn and him in for a coffee. I didn't know what else to do. They declined saying there was much to do and they had to get back to Curtin House. I asked him what was going to happen to me.

'That's a question I can't answer at the moment, Elizabeth. There is still a lot of work to do in this matter. This I promise you, I won't keep you in suspense a moment longer than necessary. Now, are you all right?'

I said I was. 'Good,' he said. A shake of the hand and he and Caitlyn were gone.

He might not have kept me waiting a moment longer than necessary but for every moment of the next week I was in suspense. Every time the phone rang I jumped. Every time the charge nurse came to speak to me my nerves went into spasm. I wondered if I was about to be called to the police station and arrested. I wondered if Adam believed me. He seemed to but I just didn't know. After all, I had lied at the beginning. Lie once and who will believe you afterwards?

A week later I had just got home from the hospital, made myself a cup of tea and sat down to drink it and watch the seven o'clock news on television when there was a knock on the door. I went to answer it. I made sure the safety chain was on. I called, 'Who is it?' 'Adam Neumann, Elizabeth, and Caitlyn,' was the reply. I opened the door with my heart banging against my ribs again. Was I for the high jump?

He and Caitlyn were both smiling at me. My heart eased a little. 'Hello, Elizabeth.' He said, 'Caitlyn and I bring good news. We didn't want to go to the hospital because we didn't want the people there wondering why we needed to see you so often. People become curious very easily, you know. May we come in?'

'You certainly may,' I said.

When they were in and seated Adam said, 'Sorry for keeping you so long, Elizabeth, it may have seemed a long time to you but since we last saw you things, for us, have been more than hectic. Forensics have done a lot of work. A lot of experimenting in light of what you have told us. You see, we knew what caused Dr Wilderman's death. It was a clear case of heart failure but the way he was lying in bed, so neatly tucked in, just didn't gel. We knew that someone else just had to be involved. After a heart attack he couldn't have done that for himself. Also, it was clear that an effort had been made to wipe the house clean. What we couldn't work out was how he came by his injuries; they were contradictory to a simple fall. You might have thought you cleaned up all the blood from the bed post and the floor but you didn't. Blood is very hard to wipe away completely. The blood traces that remained told the forensics a lot. What you said enabled them to work out how he fell. It was entirely consistent with the throw you described. The bruising on his body, under ultra violet light, matched up exactly with the circular weight at the bottom of Sally Adam's skeleton. You really gave it to him there, Elizabeth. Sally would have been proud of you. There was, also, bruising on his chest that accorded with your applying physical force there to try to restart his heart. I am happy to tell you that your story agrees totally with all the evidence. In any case there are no other witnesses to gainsay what you told us. You will be happy to know that the injuries you imposed on Dr Wilderman in no way contributed to his death. There is only one matter that bothered my superiors; the fact that you destroyed evidence that might have been vital to our enquiries. The matter was put before the DPP, that's the Director of Public Prosecutions. He is of the view that you have suffered enough. In fact, he says you should have had a medal for what you have been through and what you did. In any case he says it would not be in the public interest to prosecute. The police are happy that they have got their man. We can now close our books on the case. I am happy to tell you, Elizabeth, that so far as you are concerned this matter is now at an end. You are free of all blame. I shouldn't say this and I will deny it if I am ever asked about it by anyone in authority, but I think that Dr Wilderman's dying when he did was the best thing that could have happened, for a whole lot of reasons. It saved the great expense that would have been involved in his trial for murder. Also, it may have saved your life and the lives of God knows how many other innocents. When he had finished with you it is very likely that he would have murdered you, too. It seems to me that he was a brilliant psychiatrist who could just about read peoples' minds as clearly as I can read a newspaper. Professional thinking is that he was very good at conditioning people. He knew exactly what you thought and how to make you think what he wanted you to think. In setting you free and handing the phone to you to make that call to the hospital about the skeleton, you might now think that he was taking a great risk. Maybe he was? Maybe he took no risk at all? What he did was take things to the edge. He appears to have been good at that. What would have happened if you had made that call, do you think? My experience tells me that before you had had a reply to your query he would have cut the connection and killed you on the spot as he surely did Sally Adams and Mavis Addison. You came that close, Elizabeth. So very, very close. Somebody 'Up There' must like you. You were very, very lucky. What I can see from this case, Elizabeth, is that you are a very trusting person. Perhaps too trusting. I would have thought that in your job you would recognise just how dangerous some people can be. One good thing comes out of this case; the parents of Sally Adams and Mavis Addison will have closure at last. Pity the poor police officer who has to tell them their daughters will never come home again. So far as you are concerned this matter is all behind you. Your privacy has been maintained totally throughout our investigations. Your name will not be mentioned in any way in relation to this case. None of the people at the hospital need know, not even your closest friends, unless you, yourself, wish to tell them, of course. Incidentally, I would think you could make a fortune by selling your story to the media, if you wanted to. But that's another matter. All I have to say now, Elizabeth, is you are free. Strangely enough, it is a freedom a murderer has given you. That's one for the record book. Go and enjoy your life. Life is for living. Go for it!'

I could hardly take it all in. If I hadn't been sitting I would have fallen down. It was all over. It took me a minute to gather my wits. I tried to speak whilst Adam and Caitlyn just sat there smiling at me but no words would come. Suddenly, I was overwhelmed and was sobbing my heart out. My black anger was gone. I no longer hated Caspar or wanted to see him in the dock. I am not a good hater. I just wanted to live my life to the full to enjoy that which I had never known. Caitlyn came to me, took me in her arms and held me. 'It's all right, Elizabeth,' she said. 'It really is all over.' I hugged her back. Then Adam came and hugged me, too. It was then that it really hit me, my nightmare was over. I was in a man's arms again. A man who was hugging me. A young vibrant man. I pressed close to him. Very close. He pressed back. Ahhh! The joy of that pressing back. I wondered what he would be like lying close to me in bed. Very close. Both of us with our clothes off. Would he press hard against me then? I quivered at the thought. I'm sure he felt that quiver. I would like to find out if his touch then would thrill me like that time I had touched Caspar and been thrilled into ecstasy. Imagine thinking such a thing at such a time but I couldn't help it, the thought was there. And with the thought was that all-consuming ache deep within me that would not be denied. Adam would assuage that ache. I knew he would. Then he was pulling away from me, his eyes never leaving my face. I wanted him to pull me back into his arms again and kiss and kiss me and kiss me into oblivion. I didn't care what Caitlyn would think, or what anybody else would think, but he was more discrete than that. With his back towards Caitlyn and still looking into my eyes he said, 'Keep well, Elizabeth.' Then as he turned to leave he stopped, turned back towards me again and pulled out his wallet. He extracted a card from it as if the thought had just struck him and said, as he handed it to me, 'You've had a harrowing time, Elizabeth. You've stood up to it very well. These things are not easily handled on your own. If my experience is anything to go on you might need a shoulder to cry on. They call it counselling, which I'm sure, with your background you know very well. If you need support for a little while, just till you are over this don't hesitate to give us a ring. Caitlyn and I will be here before you can say Adam Neumann.' And he laughed that easy masculine laugh of his. Caitlyn smiled at me. Then they were both gone and I was alone in a lonely house.

I looked at the card. There was only his name on it, no Caitlyn, and as well as his office number there was his mobile number. I could ring him direct without anyone else having to know. My spirits soared. I would give it a couple of days just in case he decided to ring me. Then, if he didn't, I would ring him and invite him round, alone, for a coffee.

The wonderful, wonderful thought of it.

I was a free woman. I knew what I wanted. I wanted Adam Neumann. What a wonderful name! He would become my new man. The first man to know me. I trembled at the delicious thought. I would become this latter day Adam's Eve. I would hold out my apple to him. That apple that had never been picked. He would take me in his arms again. This time I would respond with a passion such as he had never known. There would be no one else there. Nothing between us. Just the two of us. I have that overpowering feeling deep in my stomach again. I can't wait. I am already squirming at the thought of it. I ache to live. And it is a beautiful ache.

The end

ABOUT THE AUTHOR

Ken Moore is an Anglo-Irish Australian. Born in Ireland, he wanted to see the world from as many different angles as possible. He farmed mushrooms, joined the navy, drove double decker buses, became a detective, police inspector, school teacher, public prosecutor, barrister-at-law, registrar of the Supreme Court in two different jurisdictions and a stipendiary magistrate. He lived and worked in nine different countries. Now he writes stories.

You may contact the author at KenMooreBooks@outlook.com

Printed in Great Britain
by Amazon.co.uk, Ltd.,
Marston Gate.